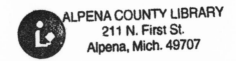

CUTTER'S RUN

THE BRADY COYNE NOVELS

Close to the Bone
The Seventh Enemy
The Snake Eater
Tight Lines
The Spotted Cats
Client Privilege
Dead Winter
A Void in Hearts
The Vulgar Boatman
Dead Meat
The Marine Corpse
Follow the Sharks
The Dutch Blue Error
Death at Charity's Point

NONFICTION

A Fly-Fishing Life
The Elements of Mystery Fiction
Sportsman's Legacy
Home Water
Opening Day and Other Neuroses
Those Hours Spent Outdoors

OTHER FICTION

Thicker Than Water (with Linda Barlow)

CUTTER'S RUN

A Brady Coyne Novel

WILLIAM G. TAPPLY

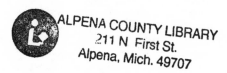

St. Martin's Press
New York

Design by Nancy Resnick

Library of Congress Cataloging-in-Publication Data
Tapply, William G.
    Cutter's run : a Brady Coyne novel / by William G.
  Tapply.—1st ed.
      p.   cm.
  ISBN 0-312-18561-8
  1. Coyne, Brady (Fictitious character)—Fiction.
  2. Boston (Mass.)—Fiction.   I. Title.
PS3570.A568C88   1998
813'.54—dc21   98-5331
                                     CIP

First Edition: July 1998

10 9 8 7 6 5 4 3 2 1

For Marshall Dickman

Solver of mysteries entomological, piscatorial,
psychological, Sherlockian, and literary;
angler and friend, and certainly not
your typical fictional character.

ACKNOWLEDGMENTS

I am indebted to Vicki Stiefel (my virtual spouse, for her incredibly perceptive, helpful, and candid editorial criticism, not to mention her love and support), Keith Kahla (an editor who actually edits), Keith Wegener (my hunting and fishing partner and my main man in Maine), Dr. Charles Damitz (for his technical help on veterinary medicine), and Jed Mattes (my good shepherd), who were all wonderfully generous with their time and expertise, and without whose faith, interest, and insights this story would undoubtedly be a mess.

CUTTER'S RUN

ONE

———————————————

I'd picked up my *Globe* at Leon's store and was bumping over a Maine dirt road on a Saturday morning in late August, taking the long way back to Alex's house, when I spotted the woman shuffling along up ahead of me. Her head was bent forward and her shoulders were humped over, and she moved painfully slowly. She wore high-top canvas sneakers and a loose-fitting brown dress that hung to her ankles. Sweat made a dark patch between her shoulder blades, and her long black hair was tied loosely back with a pink ribbon.

When I pulled up beside her, I saw that she was hugging a yellow dog against her chest. I stopped and leaned over to the open window on the passenger side of my secondhand Jeep Wrangler. "Can I give you a lift?" I said.

When she turned and lifted her head to look at me, I saw that she had skin the color of dark Maine maple syrup and cheekbones like Lena Horne. I admit I was a bit startled. Stereotypic thinking, maybe. But I didn't recall ever before seeing an African-American of any description in the western Maine countryside, never mind one who was quite beautiful.

She gazed straight into my eyes. Hers were the color of hot fudge, wide-set and slightly uptilted, with tiny crinkles at the corners. She had a narrow aristocratic nose and a wide mouth. She was, I guessed, around forty.

After a moment of taking my measure, she nodded. "My dog's sick," she said softly. "Thank you." In her voice I heard the hills of western Carolina, or maybe Tennessee, not the sandy back roads of Maine.

I yanked up the emergency brake, got out of the Jeep, and went around to hold the door for her. I braced her elbow and helped her climb in, closed the door, then went around and got behind the wheel.

She was bowing over the dog on her lap, whispering to it. It was about the size of a springer spaniel, a mongrel with a long pointy nose and floppy ears. It lay limply on her lap, panting rapidly with its tongue lolling out and its eyes half closed.

I reached over, patted its head, then touched its nose, which felt dry and hot. I've been told that a healthy dog's nose should be cool and moist, although that may be a myth.

"His name's Jack," said the woman. "He's just a puppy."

Jack lifted his head and gave my hand a halfhearted lick, then let it fall back onto the woman's lap. "How long has he been sick?" I said.

She looked up at me. "He started vomiting last night. And he voided right where he lay. He can hardly stand up."

"You were headed for the vet?"

"Yes, sir."

"That's about three miles from here."

"Yes, sir. I know. I have to get him there."

I put the Jeep in gear and started up. It was only about seven-thirty on that Saturday morning, but already the oppressive late-summer heat had begun to gather in the piney woods, and the dust that hung over the roadway had smeared on her sweaty forehead. Her pink ribbon had come loose so that her hair hung in damp ringlets around her shoulders.

"Awfully hot morning to walk," I said.

"I don't have a car. Ride my bike, usually. I couldn't carry Jack on the bike."

"I'm Brady Coyne," I said.

"Charlotte," she said. "Charlotte Gillespie."

"I haven't seen you around."

"I try to keep to myself." She dipped her head and murmured something to Jack. Then she looked up at me and gave me a quick smile. "What about you, Mr. Coyne?"

"Me?"

"I haven't seen you around, either."

"Oh, I'm staying a few miles back down the road," I said. "Actually, my lady friend—Alexandria Shaw—maybe you know her?—it's her place. I come up to visit on weekends. Been doing it for about a year now."

"Oh, yes. Alexandria Shaw. Of course." When I glanced over, she was again bent over the dog in her lap, stroking his head and whispering to him.

Charlotte Gillespie showed no inclination to engage in further conversation, and I didn't push it. We emerged from the woods and passed Leonard Potter's dairy farm. A few dozen Holsteins grazed in the lumpy field behind Potter's aluminum-roofed barn. I stopped at the crossroads, where the Garrison post office shared space in the old Victorian that served as town hall, then turned right onto the two-lane blacktop, Route 160, the only numbered state highway that led into and out of Garrison. We passed Hadley's Feed and Grain, MaryLou's Grill, and then, across the street from the cemetery, the white clapboard Congregational church, whose pastor, a middle-aged woman named Gretchen Carroll, lived alone in the farmhouse next door. She was also Garrison's only notary public and, if you believed the rumors and cared about such things, the town's only lesbian.

Then we were in the country again. The road wound past farmland long abandoned and now thick with second-growth hardwood, past Perch Pond, where the local kids fished and swam and worried about snapping turtles biting their privates, and past Mason's lumberyard, where the aroma of fresh-cut pine sweetened the air.

At the top of the hill, I pulled into a parking area beside a rambling one-story building. The sign in front said "Garrison Veterinary Hospital and Kennels." When I got out and slammed the car door, it set off a chorus of barks, howls, and growls from out back.

I opened the door for Charlotte. Jack lay limp in her arms. "Let me carry him," I said.

She smiled quickly and shook her head. "No," she said. "Thank you."

So I steadied her elbow as she climbed out, then helped her up the steps onto the porch, held the door for her, and followed her inside.

A gray-haired woman was seated at a desk behind the counter. Her back was to us, and she was working at a computer. "Excuse me," I said to her. "Is the vet available?"

She swiveled around in her chair. She wore half-glasses down toward the tip of her nose, and she ducked her chin to look up at us over them. "I'm the vet," she said. She was probably around sixty, and when she pushed back her chair and stood up, I saw that she was tall and lanky and rawboned. "Dr. Spear," she said. "Laura Spear." She came to the counter, and when she saw Jack cradled in Charlotte's arms, she murmured, "Oh, dear."

She opened a hinged door in the counter. "Bring him on in," she said to Charlotte.

Charlotte lugged Jack through the office area, and they disappeared through a doorway. Neither woman looked back at me, so I went out on the porch for a cigarette.

I'd smoked two of them before Charlotte came out. She was not carrying Jack. I arched my eyebrows at her, and she shrugged. "He's very sick," she said.

"Did she say—?"

"She wasn't sure what it was." I saw that her eyes looked smudged, and I figured she'd been crying. "She gave him a shot, and that seemed to perk him up a little. She wants to keep him. I guess she can take care of him better than me." She gave a soft, wry laugh. "I guess I haven't done a very good job of it."

"Animals get sick," I said stupidly.

She smiled quickly and nodded. I told her I'd drive her home. She said she could walk, she was in no hurry. I told her that I was just killing time while Alex worked, so she shrugged and got into the Jeep.

4

I headed back to where I had seen her beside the road. Charlotte stared out the side window, and I didn't try to make conversation. As we approached the place where I'd picked her up, she said, "There's a road on the left about half a mile up ahead. I can get off there."

It was another dirt road, this one narrower than the one we were on. As I turned in, I said, "I'll take you all the way. It's too hot to walk."

"It's a bad road," she said.

"I've got four-wheel drive. That's why I got this old thing. For bad roads. I love to drive bad roads."

She shrugged, which I took for an affirmative, so I kept going.

Her road climbed a steep hill, then fell sharply on the other side, and halfway down I had to edge around a jumble of large boulders along the side. At the bottom of the hill, a narrow wooden bridge with no rails spanned a little brook that ran through a rocky stream-bed. An ancient stone wall paralleled both sides of the roadway. Alders and scrubby pines overhung the edges, and it was deeply rutted and potholed.

Navigating it on a bicycle would be a challenge.

"You can pull in here," Charlotte said after we had climbed half-way up the hill beyond the brook.

A pair of ruts disappeared through a break in the stone wall into the pine woods. When I turned in and stopped, I noticed that a big slab of plywood had been nailed onto a tree trunk. On it someone had painted in big black capital letters the words NO TRESPASSING. NO HUNTING. NO SHOOTING.

I also noticed that someone had spray-painted a big ugly red swastika over those words.

"I just want privacy, Mr. Coyne," Charlotte said. "That's why I live here. It doesn't seem like too much to ask."

"Do you know who—?"

"That swastika?" She shrugged. "You can't get away from them. I know exactly what they want. But it's not going to work. They don't scare me." She opened the door and slipped out of the car. She started down the rutted road into the woods, then stopped, turned, hesitated, and came back to the car. She put her hands on the rag top and bent to my window. "I forget my manners," she said. "You were very kind. Thank you."

"I'm glad I got the chance to meet you," I said. "I hope Jack gets better."

She reached in and touched my arm, smiled quickly, then stepped back. She narrowed her eyes and opened her mouth as if she wanted to say something. Then she shook her head. She lifted her hand. "Good-bye," she said. Then she turned and trudged down the roadway.

As I watched, an orange cat popped out of the bushes. Charlotte bent to it and scooped it into her arms. Then a black cat with a white blaze on its chest appeared, and then a tiger cat, and then another orange one, and as she disappeared into the woods, more cats joined the parade behind her.

TWO

Fifteen minutes later, I pulled into Alex's peastone driveway. The yard had been neglected when she'd moved in a year earlier, but now geraniums spilled out of window boxes and the boxwood shrubs were trimmed and the lawn was green. Alex spent mornings at her computer and afternoons puttering around the yard. "Decompressing," she called it. She had a pretty view from up there on her hilltop. Out back facing west, a meadow sloped down to a brook, then rose to a hillside planted in corn. On a clear day you could sometimes see the round-topped purple-and-green New Hampshire hills humping up on the horizon.

I took my newspaper inside, careful not to let the door slam, and poured a mug of coffee. Alex had set up her office at one end of the open downstairs, partitioning it off with chest-high bookcases. There she worked at her big flat-topped desk with her computer, her files, her telephone and fax machine, and her tape recorders.

I heard the soft buzz of voices coming from behind the partition and guessed she was listening to tapes of her interviews.

Alex's publisher had given her a nice advance for her book, which was to be an elaboration of a series she'd written for the *Boston Globe*. She was calling it *The Legacy of Abuse*. Her thesis, as I understood it, was that spouse abuse was symbiotic, that abusers and victims sought each other out, that both abusers and their victims tended to come from abusive families, and that abusive parents provided models for their children: Boys tended to emulate their abusive fathers, and girls sought out boys who behaved just like their daddies, the way their mothers had.

It wasn't, she said, a particularly original idea. Sociologists and psychologists had explored it thoroughly. But Alex's publisher believed that her powerful case studies would "popularize" it, and that her book would be a big seller.

She'd been working on it for almost a year. She'd moved to Garrison the previous Labor Day. The *Globe* had given her a two-year leave of absence, and she figured she could live that long on her advance, so two years was the deadline she'd set for herself to finish her book.

She'd given up her apartment on Marlborough Street in Boston's Back Bay, and she'd given up our nightly sleepovers at my place overlooking the harbor. For almost a year I'd been driving up to Garrison, Maine, on Friday afternoons.

"Brady? That you?"

I peered over the bookcases. She was staring at her computer monitor through her big round glasses.

"I'm back," I said.

"Cool," she mumbled, still peering at the screen. "Have fun?"

I smiled. "I'll tell you all about it when you're done."

"Absolutely. Right."

Alex had the remarkable ability to write and talk at the same time, a talent she'd picked up in the *Globe* newsroom. But her conversations didn't always make much sense, and afterward she never remembered a thing we'd said to each other.

I took my coffee and newspaper out onto the deck that spanned the back of the house, sat in a rocking chair, and admired my woodpile. In the fall, we'd had three cords of hardwood dumped in the back. Got them cheap because they were green logs twelve feet long. It took me all winter with the chain saw to cut them into sixteen-inch woodstove lengths, and when I finished that, I'd begun splitting and stacking them. Now I was about half done.

Splitting and stacking wood was engrossing and rewarding work. I imagined that my shoulders and back had grown bulky and knotty with new muscles from the repeated, rhythmic lifting of the heavy splitting maul. I liked studying the grain on a chunk of cordwood, deciding where to hit it, then dropping the maul precisely there with just enough force to send the two halves flying. And I enjoyed stacking it, adjusting the split pieces of wood so they fit together, and watching my woodpile grow. It was like building a sturdy old New England stone wall that would withstand a hundred winters of frost heaves without toppling. It was good, healthy, old-fashioned Robert Frost New England work, a welcome relief from writing separation agreements and probating wills.

Splitting and stacking firewood was hypnotic and relaxing. It demanded my full attention on one level while allowing my mind to wander on another, and I didn't mind the backache that always followed. It gave me an excuse to drink a beer, take a hot leisurely shower, and afterward sprawl naked on the bed while Alex straddled me and gave me a long, languid backrub that usually ended with both of us under the sheets.

I would split no wood today. It was too damn hot. I sat on the deck on the shaded back side of the house, rocking and sipping my coffee and reading my *Globe* back to front. About the time I had turned to page two, I felt Alex's hand on my neck.

I reached up and steered her face down to mine.

She kissed my cheek. "Hi, babe," she said.

"Done for the day?"

"I've got a little transcribing I want to finish up." She plopped into the rocker beside me and put her heels on the deck rail. Her legs were smooth and tanned and shapely. She was wearing gray gym shorts and a dark blue sleeveless T-shirt. Her work clothes. Alex claimed that the best thing about holing up in a house in Maine to write a book was that she didn't have to wear panty hose or bras or high heels or makeup.

"Thought I'd take a coffee break," she said.

I lit a cigarette and offered her one.

She waved it away with the back of her hand. "How was your morning?" she said.

"I took a sick dog to the vet. Met a friend of yours."

"Oh?"

9

"The lady with the sick dog. Charlotte Gillespie."

Alex shrugged. "I don't know her."

"Well, she seemed to know you."

"Hey," she said. "I'm a famous journalist."

"And soon you will be a famous author," I said.

"Yeah, maybe."

"She's an African-American woman," I said. "Forty, maybe. Very attractive."

She shrugged. "I haven't met any African-American women up here. Attractive, eh?"

"Yes. She reminded me of Lena Horne. She keeps a lot of pets, and she's got a No Trespassing sign by the woods road that leads to her house." I hesitated. "Somebody spray-painted a swastika on it."

"Huh?" said Alex. "A swastika?"

"Yes. A big hateful red one."

"Jesus," she murmured. "What a world."

Alex and I slept in the next morning. I made Canadian bacon and French toast for breakfast, which we drowned in real Maine maple syrup and ate on the deck. We lingered there sipping coffee, smoking, and watching a little flock of early-migrating warblers. We admired the way the slanting morning sunlight painted the countryside in vivid colors, and it was after nine by the time I climbed into my Jeep to fetch my Sunday *Globe* at Leon's.

I remembered Jack, Charlotte's dog, and decided to swing around to the animal hospital. When I went in, Dr. Spear was talking to a teenaged girl and a man in overalls who I assumed was the girl's father. A shrouded birdcage sat on the counter.

Dr. Spear glanced at me, lifted her chin in greeting, then turned back to her conversation.

A minute or two later, the girl picked up the birdcage and they left. Dr. Spear took off her glasses, rubbed her eyes, put her elbows on the countertop, and shook her head.

"The dog?" I said.

She nodded. "He died. He only lasted a few hours after she

brought him in. Didn't surprise me. He was in bad shape. There was nothing I could do."

I let out a long breath. "That's a damn shame," I said. "Charlotte will be devastated. She really seemed to love that dog."

Dr. Spear shrugged. "Of course she did."

"What was it? Distemper or something?"

She leaned toward me. "Mr.—I don't know your name."

"Coyne. Brady Coyne."

She nodded. "Mr. Coyne, I'm not sure what killed that dog. She told me he was fine the day before she brought him in. He got sick and died within twenty-four hours. I've been doing this for over thirty years, and I don't know as I've ever seen an animal disease that works like that."

"So . . . ?"

"Poison," she said. "That dog got into some kind of poison."

I remembered the swastika on Charlotte's No Trespassing sign. "Or someone poisoned him," I said.

She nodded. "That's certainly possible."

"Jesus," I mumbled. "Who'd do something like that?"

"Oh, you'd be surprised," said Dr. Spear.

"It was a rhetorical question," I said. "I assume you'll report it."

"To whom? Report what? That I think the dog swallowed something poisonous, or maybe somebody fed it to him? Where do we go with that?"

"I don't know. What about running some toxicology tests on the animal?"

"I'd like to," said Dr. Spear. "If it was poison, it's not anything I've ever seen before." She shook her head. "I'd have to do an autopsy, and I'd need the owner's permission—if she can pay for it. I can't autopsy dead animals unless the owners give their okay, even when we don't know why they died. Pet owners can be pretty sensitive about things like that. What we normally do, Mr. Coyne, is, we offer to cremate the animals. Many people prefer to take the body back and bury it themselves."

"What does Charlotte say?"

Dr. Spear shrugged. "I don't know how to get hold of her. She

11

left no address or phone number. I tried looking her up, but she's not listed. I don't even know where to send the bill."

"I'd like to know what killed him," I said.

"Oh, so would I. If somebody did poison the poor creature, you can bet I'd like to string him up."

"Me, too," I said. "I'd be willing to pay for the autopsy."

"I'd still need her permission." She pinched the bridge of her nose and let out a long breath. "When you see Ms. Gillespie, you might ask her."

"I'm not sure I will see her," I said. "I don't really know her. I just saw her carrying that dog, so I gave her a ride."

"Well," she said, "I can't keep the dog forever. If she doesn't tell me what to do, I'll have to incinerate it."

"I'll drop by her place," I said. "Try to get an answer for you."

"That would be a big help, Mr. Coyne."

"Look," I said. "I'd like to take care of the bill."

She smiled, and I realized it was the first time I'd seen her smile. "That's very nice of you."

I handed her my Visa card and signed the stub after she'd run it through her machine. Eighty-five dollars.

"A lot of people bring in sick animals and never come back for them," she said.

"And never pay their bills."

She shrugged.

"I'll talk to her," I said.

I picked up my paper at Leon's store, then drove over the dirt roads that led to the plywood sign with the evil spray-painted swastika.

I left my Jeep under the sign and began walking down the narrow rutted roadway where I had seen the cats come out of the woods and trail behind Charlotte. It followed a curving stone wall, crossed a dried-up streambed, climbed uphill through a stand of second-growth poplar and alder mixed with juniper and old apple, and ended about a mile into the woods at a rolling meadow on a knoll.

Charlotte's house sat with its back to the dark pine woods, facing across the meadow to the south. It looked as if it had originally been a hunter's shack—a simple square, shingled cabin with a door in the middle flanked by two small windows with an aluminum stovepipe sticking out of the roof. Flat-roofed ells had been added onto each end. No electric or telephone wires led into it.

It was a pretty spot, with a long view across the sloping meadow to the hills in the distance. A stream snaked its way through the valley. A good place for somebody who liked the outdoors and wanted a heavy dose of solitude.

Charlotte was doing her best to make a home out of it. The door was barn red, recently painted, and a variety of annual flowers—petunias, marigolds, impatiens, and several that I didn't recognize—were blooming along the fieldstone path leading up to it. A mud-spattered mountain bike—the kind with knobby tires and about a hundred gears—leaned against the side of the house next to the door.

I walked up the path and knocked on the door. I waited a minute, then knocked again and called, "Charlotte? It's Brady Coyne."

A moment later I heard a voice behind me. "Mr. Coyne," she said softly. "Hello."

I turned. She was wearing overalls over a gray T-shirt, work boots, and cotton gloves. Her hair was tucked up under a wide-brimmed straw hat. "I was out back tending my vegetable garden," she said. She tucked a stray strand of hair up under her hat and started to smile, then stopped herself. "Is it about Jack?"

I nodded.

She tugged off her gloves. "He died, didn't he?"

"I'm afraid so, yes."

She took off her hat, dropped her gloves into it, and shook out her hair. "He wasn't even two years old," she said. "I made sure he had all his shots."

"The vet," I said, "Dr. Spear, she thinks it might've been poison."

Charlotte looked at me. "Poison," she said softly. "Oh, dear." She shook her head, then went to the steps that led up to her front door and sat down. I sat beside her.

"I'm sorry," I said.

She leaned forward with her elbows on her knees and her chin in her hands. "You're very kind to come by, Mr. Coyne," she whispered. "He was the cutest little dog. Who'd want to poison a sweet little dog like Jack?"

"He might've just gotten into something."

"Like what?"

I shrugged. "Antifreeze. Rat poison. Mushrooms. Maybe somebody put out something for coyotes."

"He liked to wander through the woods," she said, "but he never went far." She turned to me and smiled. "Jack had some spaniel in him. He loved to hunt. Chased chipmunks and sparrows. I used to worry about porcupines. The day he got sick, in fact, he went for a long romp, came back all wet and muddy and bedraggled. Trying to catch ducks, probably." She smiled at the memory, then shook her head. "I don't keep anything poisonous, Mr. Coyne. I took very good care of him."

"Dr. Spear mentioned running some toxicology tests," I said gently.

"Why?"

"Well, to determine exactly what caused it. She said it was very unusual. Not like any poisoning death she'd ever seen."

"Sure," she said, "but I mean, what good would that do?"

"If someone poisoned Jack—"

"On purpose, you mean?"

I shrugged.

"I know what you're thinking," she said. "You think that swastika . . ."

"Yes. That is what I was thinking."

"Toxicology tests would require an autopsy, wouldn't they?"

I nodded.

She bowed her head. "I don't know, Mr. Coyne. He was . . . I really loved that little dog. Do you understand?"

"Of course."

"The idea of—of cutting him open, and . . ."

"I know," I said.

"I'll have to think about it," she said.

14

"Dr. Spear will keep him until she hears from you."

I continued to sit there with her, and I had the feeling that my presence comforted her a little. After a few minutes she offered me coffee, which I accepted. She went inside, and a few minutes later came back out with a mug in each hand and sat beside me again.

"You've got an awfully pretty spot here," I said.

"It is, isn't it? It's just too bad . . ."

I nodded. "That swastika."

"Well, yes. That. And . . ."

I turned to her. "And what?"

She shook her head. "Nothing I can discuss right now, Mr. Coyne."

"I'm not sure I'd have the courage to stay," I said.

She smiled. "Courage has nothing to do with it. I've got to stay until . . ." She shook her head. "Maybe someday we can talk about it."

But not, I understood, just then. Charlotte had something on her mind, and it wasn't only swastikas or poisoned dogs.

"You can talk to me anytime," I said.

We sat there awhile longer, sipping coffee and gazing across the meadow toward the distant hills. When I'd drained my mug, I stood up. "I'm really sorry to bring you this news."

She stood up and took both of my hands in hers. "You've been awfully kind, Mr. Coyne," she said in that delicious Smoky Mountains accent of hers. "I don't know that many kind people."

I squeezed her hands and headed back to my car. When I reached the edge of the meadow, I turned to look back. Charlotte was standing there in front of her little house with her hand shielding her eyes, watching me.

She waved, and I waved back, then continued on my way.

THREE

T uesday evening I took my portable phone and a glass of Rebel Yell sippin' whiskey and ice cubes out onto my balcony over-looking the harbor and slouched into one of my aluminum lawn chairs. I hadn't spoken to Alex since I kissed her good-bye and drove back to Boston after supper Sunday night. During our Monday-through-Friday separations, we tried to talk on the phone a couple of times, I from my balcony in the city and she from her deck on the hilltop in Garrison. I'd watch the moon come up over the ocean toward the east, while she gazed off to the west, where daylight was fading from the Maine hills.

Alex and I had looked for metaphorical significance in the fact that my view looked to the east, where new days began, while hers faced west, where they ended—but so far we had found none. We decided it might make more sense if it were the other way around.

On this night, the late-August, remarkably smogless sky over the ocean blinked with a million stars, and a half-moon bathed the inner harbor six stories below me in silvery light.

My friends, at least those who liked me enough that they didn't worry about hurting my feelings, told me that they couldn't un-derstand why I didn't find a more elegant home than my cramped two-bedroom rented condo on the waterfront. I could afford a house in the suburbs or a brownstone in Louisburg Square, they

17

said. So why didn't I find something more befitting a successful Boston barrister?

Mostly inertia, I told my friends. I had fallen to earth in this apartment when my marriage to Gloria blew up, and in the decade that followed, I'd found no compelling reason to leave. I wasn't much of a nest-builder, I admitted. I just needed a place to store my fishing gear and a bed to sleep in and an electrical outlet to plug my coffeepot into.

Besides, I never tired of my view of the water, even if the water in Boston Harbor had, until recently, been Number One: the dirtiest in the world. Back during the 1988 campaign, George Bush and Mike Dukakis had tried to blame each other for the harbor's distinguished ranking, which embarrassed both of them. Eventually the feds and the Commonwealth invested millions to clean it up, and the harbor fell out of the Top Ten.

But I still liked it. I liked the mingled aroma of seaweed and dead fish and brine that wafted up to me, and I didn't mind the diesel fumes that sometimes complicated the mix. From my little balcony, I liked to watch the gulls and terns wheel on the breezes and the tankers and sailboats and ferries inch across the chop, and I liked to hear the clang of the bell buoy and the honk of the foghorn on a dark night.

In recent years, the harbor seals had returned, and there had even been good striped bass fishing out among the harbor's islands. I liked looking down on the water and knowing that stripers now thrived in it.

As much as I loved woods, dirt roads, trout streams, and clean air, I wasn't sure I'd ever conquer the inertia that kept me right where I was.

Alex had pretty much stopped mentioning it, but I knew she still couldn't understand why I wouldn't sell my Boston law practice, clean out my apartment, and move into the rented post-and-beam house in Garrison with her. We could buy it and settle down there. She was a writer. All she needed was a place to plug in her computer and a telephone.

And they needed lawyers up there, she'd hinted more than once. I could make a living just doing real-estate law. Or I could set up a private practice like the one I'd had in Boston for the past twenty years. There were no lawyers in Garrison. Anybody who wanted to make a will or get divorced had to hire what they called a "city shyster" from Portland, an hour's drive to the east. If I was there, they'd call me.

I'd thought about it. I told myself that I couldn't abandon my clients, most of whom were elderly and dependent and uncomfortable with change. They trusted me. It would be unfair to desert them. I told myself that I didn't want to move too far from the house in Wellesley, where I'd half-raised my two boys, where Gloria, my ex-wife, still lived, and where Billy and Joey, now pretty much grown and off on their own, crashed whenever they were around. I told myself that if I moved to Maine, I'd miss my view of the harbor at night.

And when I was being entirely candid with myself, I admitted that I just wasn't sure I wanted to live with Alex full-time.

I was sure I loved her, and I knew I missed her when we weren't together. But I *liked* missing her. I liked seeing her again after being apart for several days, and I liked almost forgetting—and then rediscovering—the way her eyes looked when she smiled in the dark and the way the skin at the base of her spine felt when I stroked it with my fingertips.

I hadn't tried to explain this to Alex. But sometimes I saw the hurt in her eyes, and I knew that she understood.

I lit a cigarette, took a sip of Rebel Yell, placed the glass down beside me, and poked out her number on the phone.

It rang four times. Then her recorded voice said, "Hi. It's Alex. Either I'm not home just now or else I'm working. Leave your name and number and I promise I'll get back to you."

I glanced at my watch. It was a little after nine. Usually Alex was sitting on her deck around nine listening to the night birds and sipping a beer, with her phone beside her, hoping I'd call. If I waited until ten to call her, as often as not I found her already in bed, and her languid, husky voice made it easy to visualize her tousled auburn hair and the man-sized T-shirt she always wore to bed riding up over her hips, and the moonlight spilling over her through the skylight in her bedroom ceiling.

 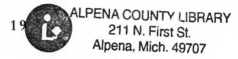

"It's me, honey," I said to her machine. "Calling around nine. I'll try again."

Where the hell was she?

In the shower, maybe. Or maybe she was in the yard and hadn't brought her phone with her. Maybe she was at her desk polishing prose and letting her answering machine earn its keep.

I finished my cigarette, flipped it over the railing, and watched it spark down to what used to be the dirtiest water in the world.

At nine-thirty I called again, and again her machine answered. This time I left no message.

I tried again at eleven, and again after my shower, and once more around midnight before turning off the light beside my bed.

"Hi. It's Alex. Either I'm not home, or . . ."

I lay there staring up at the dark ceiling. I thought of the lecherous men who hung around the potbellied stove at Leon's store telling dirty stories, with too much time on their hands and perpetually angry wives back in their trailers. I thought of morons who painted swastikas on No Trespassing signs—and maybe poisoned women's dogs. I thought of Charlotte Gillespie up there in the woods at the end of a long tote road, alone and mourning her dead puppy.

Okay, I also thought of the handsome young architects and dentists and securities salesmen who were buying and renovating old farmhouses in Garrison. Alex was beautiful and single and living alone.

Shit.

It took me a while to fall asleep. I hoped the phone would wake me up. But it didn't.

The next day at my office I started to pick up the phone to call Alex several times. But I didn't. I was afraid I'd get her machine.

I waited until nine-thirty that evening, and I didn't bother fixing a glass of Rebel Yell or taking the phone out onto the balcony. I lit a cigarette at my kitchen table, took a deep breath, and poked out her number.

She answered on the second ring. "Hi, sweetie," she said.

20

"You knew it was me."

"Sure. Who else'd call?"

"I don't know. There's David, there, that architect, and what's-his-name, the new dentist, and—"

"Hey," she said. "What's this all about?"

"Nothing. I'm just kidding."

"You don't sound like you're kidding."

"Where were you?" I said.

"What?"

"Last night. I kept trying to call. I was worried about you. Somebody up there goes around painting swastikas outside ladies' homes and poisoning their dogs, and—"

"I was at a fucking dinner party," she said, and I heard the anger in her voice. "But I do appreciate your checking up on me, and I apologize for not clearing it with you beforehand."

"I didn't mean—"

"Oh, yes, you did. You want me right here where you can keep tabs on me. It's all right for you to do what you want, and I don't ask you to account for your every minute. But if I decide to go to a party, and you're down there so you can't go with me, protect me, keep an eye on me, I'm supposed to clear it with you, assure you that there's not going to be some architect or dentist there hitting on me."

"I was worried," I said.

"Worried," she repeated.

"Well, maybe a little jealous, too. But mostly worried."

"I can take care of myself, Brady. I've done it all my life. Believe it or not, I managed to survive all those years before I had you to watch over me. I survived rather well, actually."

"Yes. You did."

"I know everybody up here," she said. "It's a helluva lot safer than living on Marlborough Street."

"I guess it is."

"Jesus Christ," she mumbled.

"I've been doing a lot of thinking about Charlotte Gillespie," I said.

"Me, too," she said. I heard her blow out a breath. "It is kind of scary. I guess I can see why you'd worry."

"Well, to tell you the truth, I was maybe a little jealous, too." I took a sip of Rebel Yell. "Tell me about your party."

"You remember Noah Hollingsworth?"

"The apple guy?"

"Yes. I ran into him at Leon's on Monday and he said he was having a few people over for a barbecue on Tuesday. So I went. And, okay, David the architect was there, and yes, Brady, the man is sort of an asshole. But Noah is a lovely old man and he's really into his apples. His orchard has been in his family for several generations. He dragged me into a corner and told me all about Northern Spies and Baldwins and Granny Smiths, and he gave me a recipe for apple butter. I met his daughter, who's a successful businesswoman in Portland. Susannah's her name. And Paul something, her boyfriend." She paused. "Susannah is really nice. Smart. Pretty, too. If you lived up here and I lived down there, I guess maybe I'd be jealous, too."

"Did I say I was jealous?"

"You did. It's okay. I'm sorta glad you were jealous."

"It was not pleasant, feeling jealous and worried at the same time."

"It's good for you."

"But you're not jealous when I'm down here all week, with all my beautiful clients coming on to me?"

She laughed. "Your clients are senior citizens, Brady."

"Not all of them."

"Okay," she said. "If it'll make you feel better, I will hereafter make a point of being jealous. Anyway, I really liked Noah. He's got this Yankee pragmatism, and you feel like he can see right into your brain."

"He dragged you into a corner, huh?"

"Oh, yes. He told me all about grafting apple trees. It was very erotic."

"I can imagine," I said. "Did you mention Charlotte Gillespie and her dog and that swastika?"

"Sure. I told everybody how you had given her and her poor

22

dog a ride to the vet's and how the dog died and you paid the bill, and how you took it upon yourself to break the news to her. I made you the hero of the whole thing. I wanted everyone to know that I had a hero. They were impressed. Noah and Susannah and Paul want to meet you."

"I don't care about meeting anybody," I said. "I'm content to be your hero. You can worship me properly when I get there Friday."

"Oh, I will," she said softly.

"Be careful, okay?"

"Please don't worry, Brady."

"Someone in that town is painting swastikas and poisoning single women's dogs," I said. "I guess I'll worry."

Four

❯❯————————————————❮❮

Since Alex had moved to Maine, I'd told Julie, my long-suffering secretary, to make no Friday-afternoon appointments for Brady L. Coyne, Attorney-at-Law. Occasionally I had an unavoidable Friday-afternoon court appearance, but judges tend to recess early on Fridays, especially during the summer, so they can head for their places in Chatham or Boothbay or Winnipesaukee or the Vineyard. So I usually managed to beat the traffic out of the city and pull up in front of Alex's place in Garrison by five or six in the afternoon.

She liked to make our Friday-afternoon reunions special. She'd change into a dress and dab perfume behind her ears. When I got there she'd be sitting on the front steps reading a novel, and she'd jump up, run to the car, lean in the window, and give me a big wet kiss on the mouth before I could even climb out.

And when I did get out of the car, she'd clamp her arms around my neck and press herself against me. Then she'd grab my hand, lead me out back to the deck, and instruct me to sit there and relax. She'd disappear inside and emerge a few minutes later with beers in frosted mugs, a bowl of crackers, and a wedge of extra-sharp Maine cheddar on a platter. We'd sit there smoking and munching and sipping beer and telling amusing stories about what had happened to us during the week, and when she got up to get more beer,

I'd follow her inside. Generally we ended up having our second round in the bedroom.

On this particular Friday afternoon, I had an appointment with Franny Halloran at the BMW dealership in Lynnfield. My old Beemer had close to two hundred thousand miles on her. Commuting from Boston to Garrison, Maine, every weekend piled them on fast. It was time for a new car.

When I started driving BMWs nearly twenty years ago, they didn't symbolize anything. They were just well-made, responsive automobiles that tolerated considerable abuse and were fun to drive. Then someone decided they were status symbols. Anyone who drove one had to be a yuppie.

I'm not quite sure what a yuppie really is. But I'm pretty sure it's not anything I aspire to become.

I'd thought about switching to a Volvo or a Saab or even a Ford, just because I hate facile labels and status symbols. But people can make every car into a symbol of something, even the banged-up old Wrangler I got for exploring the old woods roads around Garrison. So I said the hell with it and decided to get myself another Beemer.

I'd ordered a dark green sedan with a sunroof, a CD player, and top-of-the-line speakers. Franny had called on Wednesday to say it had come in. All the paperwork would be done by Friday afternoon, in time for me to pick it up on my way to Maine.

I hadn't told Alex about it. It would be a fun little surprise for her. When I got there, maybe we'd take a spin through the countryside. I knew she'd love listening to a Beethoven CD and having the breeze from the open sunroof blow through her hair.

I called her from the office a little after noontime. "I might be a little late," I said.

"What's the matter?"

"Nothing," I said. "I've just got a bunch of stuff to clean up here at the office, that's all."

She was quiet for a moment. Then she said, "Well, okay." Another pause. "Are you all right, Brady?"

"Sure. A little hassled, that's all."

"Well, take your time. Don't get a speeding ticket."

I got to the BMW place around three, but it turned out that there'd been some confusion with the insurance company and they hadn't run the papers over to the Registry yet. Franny was full of apologies and said I could come back on Monday.

I decided to wait. I wanted that car.

So I didn't get started to Maine until after five, and then I hit the Friday-afternoon rush-hour traffic heading north on Route 95. It took twenty minutes to creep through the tollbooth at Hampton, and it was after eight by the time I pulled into Alex's driveway.

She was not waiting on the front steps, nor did she come bounding out of the house when I slammed the door of my shiny new BMW.

I found her in a rocking chair on the deck out back. She was wearing jeans and a sweatshirt—not a dress—and she was holding an empty beer bottle on her lap.

I leaned down and kissed her forehead. "Hey, babe," I said.

"Hi," she mumbled without looking up.

"You wouldn't believe the traffic," I said. "The Hampton tollbooth was—"

"Don't," she said.

"Don't what?"

"Just don't."

"Were you worried," I said, "or were you jealous? Or maybe both?"

"That's not fair," she said.

"I'm sorry. You're right."

"I had a dress on," she said softly. "The one with the scoop neck you like. I even put on lipstick, for Christ's sake. And perfume on my throat and—and inside my thighs, and . . ."

"Listen," I said. "I've got—"

"After a while," she said quickly, "I said, Fuck him, and I washed my throat and legs and wiped off the lipstick and put my jeans back on. And then I sat out here sucking on a beer bottle and wondering if you were coming at all. And I'm thinking, He just doesn't give a shit, and at the same time I'm also thinking, Oh, God, he smashed into a bridge abutment on Route 95."

27

I took her hand. "Come on," I said. "I've got something to show you."

She allowed me to help her up from the chair. I kept hold of her hand and led her down off the deck and around to the front of the house, where my sleek forest-green BMW sat.

I put my arm around her shoulder. "How about that?" I said.

She hesitated for a minute. Then she said, "It's nice, Brady."

"Nice? Hell, it's got a CD player, Bose speakers, sunroof . . ."

I stopped. Alex had slipped away from my arm and was standing there, staring off into the woods.

"Don't you like it?" I said.

"Sure. It's fine."

I sighed. "What's the matter?"

She turned to face me. "Has it got four-wheel drive?"

"Well, no."

"How is it on ice, in the snow?"

"Terrible. You know how Beemers are. Remember the trouble I had getting up your driveway last winter . . . ?"

"Exactly."

Then I got it. A BMW was not a Maine car. A man who'd buy a new BMW did not care whether he could make it over poorly plowed winter roads and up icy driveways. A man who lived in Boston and bought a new BMW was not fully committed to a relationship with a woman who lived in Garrison, Maine.

It wasn't the car. It was the thought—or the lack of thought—behind it.

"I'll be here every weekend," I said to Alex.

"Let's hope for a mild winter."

"Look—"

"Don't worry about it, Brady."

"You're reading way too much into this," I said.

"Am I?"

"Yes," I said. But I realized that, in a way, Alex was right. When I'd decided to turn in my old Beemer for a new one, I had never once thought about driving to Maine in the winter. That was probably more significant than I was willing to admit.

We stood there in uncomfortable silence for a few minutes. Then Alex said, "How about a beer?"

"Sure."

We went back to the deck. Alex sat in one of the rockers and I fetched two bottles of Pete's Wicked from the refrigerator.

I handed one to her and sat beside her. "Look," I said. "About the car."

"I really don't want to talk about it."

"Okay," I said.

So we watched the night birds swoop against the sky and sipped our beers. "I meant to tell you," said Alex after a few minutes. "I invited Noah Hollingsworth and Susannah and Paul over for supper tomorrow night."

"Yeah, okay."

"You'll like them," she said. "They're eager to meet you."

"Me," I said. "Your hero."

She reached over and touched my arm. "You are." She sighed in the darkness. "I just wish . . ."

"What do you wish, honey?"

"I guess I wish I were your heroine."

"You are."

"Sure I am." She laughed quickly. "I bought T-bones," she said. "Feel like grilling them?"

"Absolutely," I said with what was supposed to sound like cheerful enthusiasm. "I'm starved."

I was standing guard by the charcoal grill a half hour later when Alex came out onto the deck. She handed me an envelope. "This came in the mail yesterday."

It was addressed to me, handwritten in green ink. A fountain pen, it looked like. Elegant penmanship. Mr. Brady Coyne, c/o Alexandria Shaw, Garrison, Maine, postmarked Garrison, no return address on the envelope.

I opened it and took out a folded sheet of expensive stationery that matched the envelope. The writing was in the same green ink. "Dear Mr. Coyne," it read. "Thank you so much for all your kindnesses. I have decided to have those tests done on Jack. I'd like to

talk with you as soon as possible." It was signed, "Sincerely, Charlotte Gillespie."

I showed it to Alex.

"Sounds important," she said.

I nodded.

"What's she want to talk about?"

"I don't know. When I visited her, she hinted that something
was on her mind. She said she wasn't ready to talk about it. I guess
now she is."

"Didn't you say she refused to okay an autopsy on her dog?"

"She didn't exactly refuse," I said. "But she was reluctant. I guess
she changed her mind."

"Or something changed her mind for her."

"Swastikas," I said.

FIVE

———————————————————

Leon's store sold gasoline and diesel fuel from the three pumps out front and just about everything else inside, from beer to panty hose to *Penthouse* magazines to night crawlers. In the back, four stuffed chairs bracketed an old-fashioned potbellied stove, and most mornings you'd find a few locals sitting around it drinking coffee and gossiping.

Leon's was, literally, an old-time Maine mom-and-pop store. Leon and Pauline Staples, a pair of Garrison natives straight out of a Grant Wood painting, had inherited the place from Leon's father back in the sixties and had been running it ever since. They opened at six every morning and closed at eight at night—except during deer season, when they opened for coffee and doughnuts and .30/ 30 cartridges at four-thirty.

It was a little after nine on Saturday morning when I pulled up beside Leon's ancient silver-colored four-wheel-drive Dodge van in the gravel parking area out front. I got out of my Wrangler, climbed the three wooden steps to the porch, and went in. The bell over the door jangled when I pushed it open. The boys at the wood-stove in the back glanced up at me, then resumed their conversation. I took a skinny Saturday *Globe* from the rack and brought it to the cash register. Leon was sitting on a stool behind the counter eating a doughnut.

"Mornin', Mr. Coyne," he said.

"How's it going, Leon?"

He shrugged. "Same as always," he said. "Nothin' much changes, don't you know." Leon Staples had a weathered, ageless face and a shock of unruly black hair, with pale penetrating eyes and shaggy black eyebrows. He was a big, lanky man, with sloping shoulders and strong, gnarly hands. He looked to be somewhere in his early fifties, although I could've been off by ten years on either side.

I leaned across the counter to him. "Leon," I said quietly, "do you know anything about somebody around here who likes to paint swastikas on other people's property?"

He blinked and jerked his head back. "Swastikas?"

"You know, the Nazi—"

"Hell's bells, I know what a swastika is. I had two uncles got killed at Normandy." He shook his head. "Swastikas," he mumbled. "Why you askin' about swastikas?"

"Someone spray-painted one on the No Trespassing sign at the end of Charlotte Gillespie's roadway."

"She ain't a Jew, is she?"

"I don't know," I said. "Would that make a difference?"

"Not to me, for Christ's sake," he said. "That ain't why I asked." He shrugged. "Goddam ignorant kids, more'n likely. Never seen a colored person before. Or maybe it's just their way of sayin' they're pissed off she posted her property."

"Her dog was poisoned," I said.

"Poisoned, huh?" Leon shook his head. "You mean it got into something."

"Maybe."

"You think that swastika, and her dog . . ."

"I don't know, Leon. What do you think? You know everything that goes on in this town."

"Well, I don't know nothin' about swastikas or poisoned dogs, Mr. Coyne. But I tell you what. I'll keep my ears open. Let you know if I hear anything. We don't need no goddam swastikas in this town. And anyone who'd poison a dog . . ."

———

32

After I left Leon's store, I swung by the Garrison Veterinary Hospital and Kennels. I found the waiting room empty. I stood there for a minute or two before I noticed a bell on the counter, the kind that summons a bellboy at an old hotel. I tapped it with my forefinger, and a moment later Dr. Spear emerged from the back room, drying her hands on a towel. When she saw me, she smiled and said, "Oh, hello, Mr. Coyne." She tossed the towel onto a chair and leaned her elbows on the counter. "To answer your question, yes, the dog's all taken care of."

"Have you got the results yet?"

She frowned. "Pardon?"

"From the autopsy."

She shook her head. "There was no autopsy."

"I don't understand."

"Ms. Gillespie took back her puppy."

"Oh," I said. Charlotte's note had indicated she wanted the autopsy done. "What did Charlotte say when she picked him up?" I said.

"Oh, she didn't come for him. Not Ms. Gillespie herself. She sent somebody for him."

"Really," I said.

Dr. Spear arched her eyebrows. "You seem surprised."

I told her about the note Charlotte had sent me.

"Well," said the vet, "I guess she changed her mind. Her dog, I'm sure, received a nice burial."

"This person who picked up Jack," I said. "Did you get a name?"

Dr. Spear cocked her head. "Now why would you ask me that?"

I shrugged. "I guess I just thought Charlotte didn't have any friends, that's all. Living out there in the woods like that, no phone or anything. Seemed like she just wanted to be alone."

She nodded. "He didn't give us a name, Mr. Coyne, and we didn't ask. He knew the dog's name and Ms. Gillespie's name, and who else would want a dead dog?" She frowned. "Is there a problem?"

I shook my head and smiled. "No, I'm sure there's no problem. But it was a man? What did he look like, do you remember?"

"I never saw him. We were really busy. I was working on an

animal in one of the examining rooms, and one of the girls came back, said someone was asking for the pup. I told her I wanted to speak to Ms. Gillespie, ask her to wait for a minute. I was hoping I might talk her into okaying the tests. But my girl said it wasn't her, it was some man, and he was in a hurry. That seemed reasonable to me, so I had her take the pup out the rear entrance. Don't like to bring dead animals out through the waiting area, you know."

"Maybe when you see that girl, you can ask her if she remembers the man."

She nodded. "Sure can. I hope I haven't done something wrong."

"I don't know," I said.

It was a cool Saturday morning near the end of August. On the ride over to Charlotte's, I noticed that the swamp maples had begun to show flashes of crimson, and the smell of autumn was in the air. A long Maine winter was not far behind. I thought of Charlotte up there in her little isolated house with neither telephone nor electricity, snowbound and alone.

Well, I thought, she had at least one friend—whoever it was who'd fetched her dead pet for her.

I left my Wrangler under the No Trespassing sign with the red swastika and tromped up the long rocky roadway.

Her little house looked exactly the same as it had a week earlier. Flowers bloomed gaily along the path, the mountain bike leaned against the wall, and the long view stretched across the valley to the hills. Some autumn colors had begun to show down in the valley.

Except this time, for some reason, it felt desolate up there. Those preliminary hints of fall, probably. Autumn always feels a little like death to me.

I went up to the house, knocked, called Charlotte's name, knocked again. I heard only silence from inside, and she did not come around the corner tugging off her gardening gloves. After a few minutes, I went to one of the windows. I tiptoed up, cupped my hands around my eyes, and peered inside. It was dark and shadowy. It felt deserted.

I didn't like that feeling.

I went around back. Her vegetable garden was large and lush and well tended. Fat ripe tomatoes hung heavily from the vines, and there were peppers and cucumbers and squashes ready to be picked. Nasturtiums and marigolds grew in colorful clusters among the vegetables.

Charlotte was not there.

I called to her again, and listened to my voice echo from the hills.

She's gone for a walk, I thought. Maybe she went blueberry picking. Or she took off for the day with her friend.

But that swastika and that poisoned dog wouldn't go away.

I was tempted to try her front door. But I didn't. I told myself I was overreacting. She was okay. She just didn't happen to be home.

I took a business card from my wallet and a pen from my shirt pocket. I wrote: "Ms. Gillespie: I got your message. I'll try again. Please call me." I wrote down Alex's phone number and slid the card halfway under the front door.

Then I got the hell out of there.

When I rounded the bend at the end of the roadway where my Jeep was parked, I stopped. I blinked, took a couple of quick steps closer, and looked again.

Somebody had spray-painted a big red swastika on the hood of my Jeep.

I sprinted to the end of the driveway. I looked up and down. A thin layer of road dust hung in the air off to the right, and in the distance I heard the diminishing throb of an engine with an exhaust system that needed repair.

I stood there for a minute, then went back to the Jeep. I touched my finger to the red paint. It was still tacky.

SIX

There are, of course, no local police in little Maine villages like Garrison. There's a county sheriff's office and there are the state police. It was a little before noontime when I got back to Alex's house. She was behind her bookcase partitions tapping away at her computer. I found the cordless phone, took it out onto the deck, and called the sheriff's department in Alfred, the York County seat.

I gave my name and address and told the woman who answered that somebody had spray-painted a swastika on the hood of my car, and it wasn't the only swastika I'd seen in Garrison.

"Was anybody hurt?" she said.

"What?"

"Do we need to dispatch an emergency vehicle?"

"No. Everybody's fine."

"Just property damage, then."

"Sure, but—"

"Estimated cost?"

"I don't know," I said. "Whatever it costs to repaint the hood of my car." I gritted my teeth. "Look. The point is, these are swastikas they're making."

"Yes, you said that."

"So it's not just property damage."

"I'll pass on your report to the sheriff, sir."

"Then what?"

"Well," she said, pronouncing it "way-all," "I'd expect the sheriff might send one of the deputies over to talk to you, but I cain't speak for him."

When I hung up, Alex was standing beside me. "What was that all about?" she said.

I told her.

"A swastika on your car?"

I nodded.

She covered her mouth. I saw that she was stifling a smile. "What?" I said. "What's funny?"

"Sorry," she said. "It's really not funny. I was just thinking they got the wrong car."

"You're right," I said. "It's not funny."

"So what's going to happen?" she said.

"Probably nothing. I guess I should've mentioned the poisoned dog, too. And the fact that Charlotte seems to be missing. They've got more to worry about than kids vandalizing private property."

"You really think she's missing?"

"I don't know," I said. "It felt that way."

Alex nodded. "Swastikas aren't just vandalism."

"Of course not. But that's most likely how they'll look at it." I shrugged. "Leon thinks it's kids."

Alex frowned. "You don't believe that."

"It's not my car I'm thinking about," I said.

"I know. It's Charlotte and her dog, too. And that other swastika."

"Yes. All those things taken together . . ."

"Well," she said, "you did all you could do. You called the authorities."

"I don't think that's all I can do," I said.

Alex rolled her eyes. "My hero, the sleuth."

After lunch, Alex announced that we had to get the place cleaned up. Noah Hollingsworth and his daughter and her boyfriend were coming for dinner. She gave me the choice of vacuuming or scrubbing.

I chose the vacuum and ran it around the house while Alex cleaned sinks and toilets. By the time I finished, a little of the edge had worn off my concern for Charlotte and my anger at the swastika vandal.

I tucked the vacuum cleaner into the back of the hall closet and went out onto the deck. Alex joined me a few minutes later. She plopped into the rocking chair beside me, thrust out her bottom lip, and blew a wisp of hair off her forehead. "Remind me not to invite people over again," she said.

"I will if you'll consult me ahead of time instead of presenting me with a *fait accompli.*"

"Want a beer?"

I pushed myself to my feet. "I'll get it."

"That's what I meant," she said.

I brought back two bottles of Samuel Adams lager and resumed my place in my rocker. We rocked and sipped and shared a cigarette and admired my woodpile. After a while, Alex said, "I'm sorry."

"What for?"

"For asking them over tonight. It seemed like the thing to do at the time, and I guess I was mildly surprised when they accepted." She reached over and took my hand. "I like our evenings alone, especially now that we've really got only one a week."

"We've got two. Friday and Saturday."

"Friday doesn't really count. Especially when you don't get here before nine."

I glanced sideways at her, hoping I wouldn't see that look on her face that meant: "I'm still upset about the car."

She had her head tilted up to the sun and her eyes closed. She looked relaxed and peaceful and beautiful.

"I usually get here before that," I said quietly.

"Yes, but then we have to get reacquainted. Fridays are exciting. Saturdays are for relaxing."

I gave her hand a squeeze. "Don't worry about it. I'd like to meet Noah. Get some tips on grafting apple trees."

"All you think about is sex," she said.

Alex and I showered together. She soaped my entire body, and when it was my turn, I stood behind her and did an especially thorough job on her breasts. She pressed her butt against the front of me and tilted her head back against my shoulder. I moved the soap in slow circles down over her belly.

"Let's not . . ." she whispered.

"Mmm," I murmured. "I know. Save it for later."

"Is that okay?"

"It'll be hard."

She giggled.

While we were toweling each other, Alex snapped her fingers. "Damn," she said. "I meant to have you pick up some coffee at Leon's this morning. We're almost out."

"We absolutely must not run out of coffee," I said. "I'll run down there now. I'll take the Wrangler and show off my new swastika."

Leon was perched on his stool behind the counter when I got there. His glasses had slipped down to the end of his nose, and he was hunched over a ledger, frowning and chewing on the eraser end of a pencil. He didn't look up when the bell over the door chimed.

I found a can of Maxwell House on a shelf and took it to the counter. Leon looked up. "Mr. Coyne," he said, jerking his chin in greeting. "Twice in the same day." He stuck the pencil over his ear and used his forefinger to push his glasses up onto the bridge of his nose. "You ain't interested in investing in a country store, are you?"

I smiled. "I don't think so, Leon."

"I'll throw in the woman that goes with it for free."

"It's tempting," I said.

He grinned. "Like hell it is. Tell you what I'll do. I'll pay you to take the both of 'em off my hands. How's that?"

"Sounds like a deal, all right." I gave him a five-dollar bill for the coffee.

Leon made change and put the coffee in a paper bag. "Did a little inquirin' about that swastika."

"And?"

He shook his head. "And nothin'. Couple of the boys noticed Miz Gillespie's sign, but nobody's seen any other swastikas around. Someone don't like havin' colored folks in town, is how they see it. They all figure it was probably someone else's kid doin' it."

"If it was kids," I said, "I doubt it was just one of them. This is the sort of thing people do in gangs. They feed off each other."

"Yup-suh," said Leon. "That sounds about right to me."

"I went out to see Charlotte this morning."

He grinned. "Well, did you, now?"

"Leon, for Christ's sake," I said. "Don't you start passing around lies about me and Charlotte Gillespie, you hear me?"

"I'm not much for tellin' lies," he said. "I just listen to everyone else tell 'em. I got a pretty good ear for what's a lie and what ain't."

"I don't doubt it," I said. "Anyway, she wasn't there. Her bike was leaning against the side of her house, but no one was home."

He shrugged.

"It was a bit worrisome," I said, "what with swastikas and her dog being poisoned and all."

"So she was out hunting mushrooms, gatherin' firewood . . ."

"You're probably right," I said. "Point is, I parked down at the end of her roadway, and when I got back to my car—well, take a look." I pointed out the window to where my Jeep was parked beside his van.

Leon craned his neck to look outside, then muttered, "Jesus H. Christ." He turned to peer at me. "This ain't that kind of a town, Mr. Coyne. I'm damn sorry. What're you going to do?"

"I called the sheriff's office. I don't know what else I can do." I leaned toward him. "Whoever painted that swastika," I said, "was driving a car with a bad muffler."

He smiled. "That'd describe the majority of vehicles in Garrison."

I was helping Alex slice tomatoes for the salad when we heard a car door slam out front. I glanced at my watch. "What time did you tell them?"

41

"Six," she said.

"Six on the button." I smiled. "The difference between the country mouse and the city mouse. If someone on Beacon Hill told you to appear at six, and you actually arrived at six, you'd find them in the bathtub."

"Around here," she said, "people say what they mean. It's refreshing. Get the door, will you?"

I opened the door and stepped outside. A black Lexus was parked behind my shiny new BMW, and Noah Hollingsworth was climbing out of the passenger door. He was a tall, skinny, stooped-over guy with short bristly gray hair in a white seersucker suit and a plaid shirt with no necktie.

A woman—his daughter, Susannah, I assumed—was holding his arm, helping him. She was wearing a green short-sleeved blouse and white slacks and sandals. She wore her blond hair pulled tight to her head and snugged into a ponytail. She was nearly as tall as Noah.

A compactly built young guy—her boyfriend, Paul, apparently—slid out of the driver's side. He oozed vigor and fitness, from his tanned face to his white, even teeth to his broad shoulders and narrow hips. He had short, neatly barbered brown hair and a pleasant but forgettable face. He was wearing a blue Oxford shirt with the sleeves buttoned at his wrists and pleated chino pants. He looked to be in his late twenties. I pegged Susannah a little older, mid-thirties, maybe.

I waved to them. "Hi. Welcome."

I went down to meet them as they came up the path. Noah let go of his daughter's arm and held his hand out. "Evenin', Mr. Coyne," he said. "Good to see you again."

"Brady, please," I said, trying to remember when I'd met him. All I could come up with was one time when I'd passed him going into Leon's as I was coming out. I was the stranger in town. The locals would all know about me, even if I hadn't formally met them. I gripped his big bony hand. "How've you been?"

"Oh, just fine," he said. "I'm fine."

I turned to Susannah. "I'm Brady Coyne."

She had a long narrow nose, a wide mouth, and pale gray eyes, almost silver, which sparkled when she smiled, transforming her face. Without the smile, she looked severe. With the smile, she was almost beautiful. "Hello, Brady," she said. "I'm Susannah Hollingsworth. This old goat's chauffeur and chaperon. And this"—she turned to Paul—"is my friend Paul Forten."

I shook hands with Paul. His grip was firm. "We've been hearing a lot about you, Mr. Coyne," he said with a grin. "Alex couldn't stop talking about you the other night."

"Yeah," I said. "I'm her hero, all right. And you'd better call me Brady, or you'll make me feel like an ancient hero."

"That your Beemer over there?" he said, jerking his head in the direction of my car.

"Brand new yesterday, actually," I said. "CD player, Bose speakers."

"Awesome," he said.

"That Lexus of yours ain't bad."

He shrugged. "Boys and their toys, right?"

I smiled, then turned to Noah and Susannah. "Well, it's great to finally meet you all. Alex is inside."

I ushered them in. Alex came to meet them, wiping her hands on a towel. She accepted a kiss on the cheek from Noah, another from Paul, and a hug from Susannah. I mentioned drinks, and Noah wondered if I could make him a martini. I told him we had no vermouth, and he chuckled. "I don't need vermouth, and it wouldn't bother me if you left out the olive and served it in a jelly glass."

"Straight gin, then," I said. "In a jelly glass. Susannah?"

"Beer, if you have it."

"That we do. Paul?"

"A beer would be great."

I made drinks for all of us, then went out to get the charcoal started. Noah and Paul sat at the kitchen table, keeping Alex company, and Susannah followed me out onto the deck. She sat in a rocker and lit a cigarette.

"The best way to rock," I said, "is with your heels propped up on the rail."

"Oh, I know." She smiled. "I try not to be too unladylike on the first date." She hitched her chair closer to the rail and put up her feet. "Ah, yes. That's more like it. Glad I wore pants. It would be awkward with a dress."

"That never bothers Alex," I said. "But she's not very ladylike sometimes."

"I'm glad."

I poked at the coals in the grill, verifying that they had begun to glow, then took the rocker beside her. "Alex says you're an important executive."

She laughed. "Not that important."

"What do you do?"

"I make deals. Pretty boring, really."

"What kind of deals?"

She brushed a mosquito away from her face with the back of her hand. "My business card calls me a marketing consultant, for lack of a better term. My clients are small firms that don't have their own marketing departments. They retain me to find jobs, prepare bids, and work out contracts for them. Public-sector stuff mostly."

"Government work, huh?"

She nodded. "Say you own an engineering firm in Bangor. You hire me, I snoop around the state legislature, Capitol Hill in D.C., hear some talk about building a bypass on the Maine Turnpike. I call you, tell you about it, and if you want it, I help you get the job. Then you pay me a lot of money." She smiled. "I'm a freelance facilitator, you might say. I help people get what they want, that's all. And you? You're a lawyer, right?"

"Yes. I help people, too."

"What kind of law?"

"Some of this, some of that. Estate, divorce, tax, contract. A bit of litigation now and then. I have a one-lawyer practice, just a few clients. Most of them keep me on retainer for whatever comes up. As much as anything, I'm an adviser, I guess you'd say."

"You and I would make a good team," she said. "My clients can always use legal advice. I work with lawyers a lot."

"Alex wants me to bag my Boston practice, hang out a shingle up here."

She smiled. "You'd be busy enough. But you'd probably have to, um, adjust your expectations."

I laughed. "I'd go broke, you mean."

"It's all relative," she said. "You know, my father could use a lawyer like you."

"Unfortunately," I said, "there are very few people who can't use a lawyer these days. Does he have a problem?"

"Maybe." She turned and tilted her head toward me. "He needs advice, and he won't listen to me. He's only sixty-three, but he's talking about selling everything and retiring to North Carolina."

At that point Paul slid open the glass doors. "Excuse me," he said, "but Alex wants to know how the coals are coming along."

I went over and took a look. "Tell her I'll throw the fish on in about ten minutes."

Paul relayed my message, then came outside. He put his hand on Susannah's shoulder. She reached up, patted his hand, then shrugged. He removed his hand and sat up on the railing, facing us.

"You mentioned Noah's retiring," I said to Susannah. "Is there a problem?"

"Oh, the retirement part is fine," she said. "It'd be good for him. He's worked hard all his life. Barely keeps his head above water with the orchard. He had a little stroke last year, and that's slowed him down a lot. Sure, he ought to retire. But he's got no head for business. He'd take the first offer that came along. He owns nearly seven hundred acres up here. Been in the family for four generations. I keep telling him to be patient. Property values in this part of Maine are going to triple or quadruple in the next ten years." She smiled. "People think old Mainers like my father are shrewd, but—"

"Noah's hardly shrewd," said Paul. "He's just tight with a dollar." He leaned toward me. "Keeps his money in the bank, if you can believe it. His idea of a sound investment is putting new tires on a broken-down tractor."

Susannah shot Paul a look that, if I wasn't mistaken, meant: "I can say things like that about my father, but you can't."

45

Paul glanced at me, gave a little shrug, and rolled his eyes.

"Well," I said to Susannah, "of course I'll talk to him, if he wants."

I went inside, fetched the salmon steaks from the refrigerator, and brushed them with olive oil. Then I brought them out and slapped them onto the grill. "Do you folks know Charlotte Gillespie?" I said.

Paul shrugged. "I live in Portland. I don't really know anybody here in Garrison except for Susannah and Noah."

"Never met her," said Susannah. "Alex mentioned that you'd given her and her sick dog a ride to the vet's last weekend. She's the woman renting the cabin off County Road, right?"

I nodded.

"That's Arnold Hood's property," she said. "Right across the river from ours."

"How long has she been living there, do you know?"

"She moved in sometime last spring, I think." Susannah hugged herself. "I wouldn't want to live there."

"I've been up there," I said. "It's a pretty spot."

"Perfect for a couple, I guess," she said. She glanced at Paul, who was gazing off into the dark woods. "Plenty of privacy, that's for sure. Too isolated for my taste."

Susannah, I understood, did not consider herself to be part of a couple.

Over dinner, Noah, Susannah, and Paul insisted I tell them all about driving Charlotte to the vet with her sick dog, and about seeing the swastika on her No Trespassing sign. I told them that the dog had died, apparently poisoned, and that somebody had fetched the body for Charlotte. I announced that I'd become the proud owner of my own brand-new swastika on my old Wrangler.

Noah, who had declined the wine in favor of another glass of gin, said he was sorry about my car, but it didn't surprise him. "These damn kids," he said. "They see something on TV, the next thing you know . . ."

"Suppose it's not kids?" I said.

"Nobody around here'd do that," said Noah.

Susannah was shaking her head. "That's not true," she said quietly. "There's a lot of anger and frustration these days. Nobody feels secure. People with twenty-five years in the company get fired, just like that, no reason. Up here, a lot of people barely scrape by."

"Sure," said Paul. "It's like Germany in the thirties. Everybody's scared and frustrated. They're looking for somebody to blame. They'll listen to anyone who'll give them easy answers to complicated questions. These neo-Nazi groups are springing up everywhere."

"I wouldn't go that far," said Susannah.

"Well," I said, "someone around here is making swastikas, and Charlotte's dog was probably poisoned, and she might be missing, and I don't like it."

"Kids," said Noah. "Kids've always done things like that. Hell, when I was a kid . . ."

They left promptly at nine. Noah shook my hand heartily and invited me to visit his orchard. Susannah and I exchanged chaste kisses. Paul shook my hand with both of his. Susannah led Noah out to Paul's Lexus. He leaned heavily on her, and it was obvious we'd given him too much gin. Alex and I stood at the doorway, waving to them as they got into the car and pulled away.

After the headlights disappeared, Alex pulled my face down to hers and gave me a long deep kiss. When she pulled back, she exhaled loudly. "Whew!" she said. "That was nice."

"The visit?"

"The kiss, dummy."

"Yes," I said. "The kiss was very nice. Might I infer that I am forgiven for buying myself a new car?"

"You don't get off that easy, buster."

"That's what I was afraid of."

She hugged me. "So are you ready?"

"Ready for what?"

"To clear the table and load the dishwasher, what else?"

"What else, indeed," I said.

SEVEN

The next morning when I went for my paper, Leon's wife, Pauline, was behind the counter. She was a big-hipped pear-shaped woman with short iron-gray hair, steely blue eyes, and a perpetually sour disposition. She took my money for the fat Sunday *Globe* with an impatient nod.

"Where's Leon this morning?" I said.

"Sleepin' it off, like usual on a Sunday mornin'."

"Well, say hello for me." I turned to leave.

"Mr. Coyne," said Pauline.

I stopped. "Yes?"

"I see you got a decoration on your four-wheel out there." The trace of a smirk showed at the corners of her mouth.

"Yes," I said. "I've got to get it repainted. Who can do that around here?"

She shrugged. "If it was Leon, he'd slap a coat of house paint on it, call it better'n new. That's how he does most things. Half-assed. I hear that colored lady got one of them decorations, too."

"That's right. I'd like to know who's doing it."

"Could be anyone," she said. "Too bad about your car, but she oughta know better."

"Oh, really?" I said. "Better than what?"

49

She shrugged. "I guess you know what I'm talkin' about, Mr. Coyne."

I felt the anger rise in my throat, but I bit my tongue and got the hell out of there before I said something that might make life unpleasant for Alex. There's satisfaction sometimes in finding clever ways to tell people that they're ignorant and bigoted and hateful. But saying clever things to ignorant, bigoted, hateful people, I have found, is generally a waste of time.

I was reading the sports page out on Alex's deck when I heard a car pull into the driveway. I got up and walked around to the front just as a man in khaki pants and a matching shirt was climbing out of a dark green Ford Explorer with a county sheriff logo on the side panel and a light bar on the roof.

He saw me and nodded. "You Mr. Coyne?"

"Yes. You're a sheriff's deputy?"

He came over to me, removed his sunglasses, and held out his hand. "Name's Dickman," he said. "Actually, I'm the sheriff himself." He was, I guessed, somewhere in his fifties—short and bald with an open, sun-baked face, burly shoulders, and barrel chest.

I shook his hand. "I guess I didn't expect to see you."

"You're the man with the swastika?"

I nodded.

"Swastikas interest me," he said. He looked around, spotted my Wrangler parked between Alex's Volkswagen and my new BMW, and went over to look at it.

I followed him. "Your dispatcher seemed mainly interested in having me put a dollar value on the property damage."

"She's not a Jew," he said. He looked up at me. "What can you tell me about it?"

I told him about the swastika on Charlotte Gillespie's No Trespassing sign and how her dog had been poisoned. "I went up to see her yesterday," I said. "She was missing."

"Missing?"

I shrugged. "She wasn't there. She uses a bike to get around. It was there, but she wasn't."

" 'Missing' is a strong word, Mr. Coyne."

"It just felt—I don't know. Like something was wrong."

"I never mistrust feelings," said the sheriff. "Unfortunately, you can't take feelings to court. Tell me about your swastika."

I told him how I had come to be the proud owner of my own red swastika when I parked my Jeep at the end of Charlotte's roadway, and about the local consensus that it was the work of ignorant kids.

"Kids, maybe," he said. "If so, I'd sure like to know who put 'em up to it." He cocked his head and peered at me. "What about you? Got any enemies around here?"

"Not that I know of. I only come up on weekends. My, um— my friend—lives here."

"That'd be Miss Shaw," he said. "Your friend."

I shrugged. "We don't exactly know how to refer to each other."

"Virtual spouse?"

"Yes, that's good." I smiled. "Anyway, I don't think I've been up here enough to make any enemies. Certainly not long enough to make friends."

He pressed his lips together and shook his head. "These country people don't care much for weekenders, Mr. Coyne. They make friends slowly, anyhow. But," he said with a nod, "they make enemies quick enough. You sure you haven't offended somebody?"

"I probably have. It's something I do easily. But I suspect Charlotte Gillespie is more likely to have an enemy than me."

"How so?"

"Well, for one thing she's African-American."

Dickman's mouth tightened. "There are some who would consider that ample justification for painting swastikas and poisoning dogs. Could be enough to drive a person right out of town."

I nodded. "I thought of that. She might've just decided she'd had enough. Although I think she's got a lot of backbone. She didn't seem like the kind of woman who'd run away from anything."

"Everybody's got their limit," said the sheriff. He reached into his hip pocket, withdrew his wallet, and took out a business card. "I tell you what," he said. "If you hear anything about swastikas, or if you get anything new on Ms. Gillespie, or if you want to share a name with me, give me a call direct." He handed me the card. It read: "Marshall Dickman, High Sheriff, York County, Maine." There was an address in Alfred and two phone numbers on the bottom.

I put the card into my shirt pocket. "She sent me a note last week. Said she needed to see me. I'm a lawyer."

"What's she need a lawyer for?"

"She didn't tell me that. But when I talked with her earlier, I got the feeling that she had something on her mind."

"A feeling," he said.

"I know," I said. "You can't take feelings to court. The vet wanted to do an autopsy on her dog. At first Charlotte said no. Then on the note she sent me, she said she'd decided to do it. Then she sent somebody to pick up the dog's body." I shrugged. "Seems like more than feelings to me."

"You think something happened to her."

"Yes," I said. "Yes, I do."

He ran the palm of his hand over his bald head and gazed out toward the meadow behind the house. "I was a cop in Philadelphia," he said. "Nineteen years on those streets. When I got the chance to come up here, I jumped at it. Went to the university in Orono. Always hoped I could come back. But you know what, Mr. Coyne?"

I shook my head.

"People're the same everywhere," he said. "You can't get away from it. Stupidity, greed, hatred, bigotry." He shrugged. "It's prettier up here, anyhow. And most of the time, the air smells better." He shook his head. "Swastikas. I don't like that smell." He lifted his hand in a quick wave, turned, and climbed into his truck. "If you hear anything," he said through the window, "you let me know. About swastikas, about poisoned dogs, about Ms. Gillespie."

"And you'll do the same?" I said.

He nodded. "Sure."

I watched him drive away, then went inside. I bent over Alex's partition and said, "The sheriff was here."

"Mm," she murmured. Her glasses were perched down at the

52

tip of her nose, and she held her head tilted slightly back so she could peer at her computer monitor through them. "That's interesting." She bent forward suddenly and hit a couple of keys. "Nice," she mumbled.

"I'll tell you about it later," I said.

"That's great."

I left her with her non sequiturs. Her powers of concentration were awesome when she was writing, and I doubted if anything I'd said had penetrated all the way to her brain.

I found one of her yellow pads and wrote: "Went to see Charlotte. Hope the work's going well. Be back for lunch." I signed it "Your virtual spouse," added a few X's and O's, and left it on the kitchen table. Then I went outside, climbed into my Wrangler, and headed for Charlotte's place.

As I bumped over the dirt roads, I couldn't avoid noticing the big red swastika on the hood in front of me. The Wrangler was ten years old, with assorted rust spots, dings, and scratches. I'd bought it from a kid in Limerick who was off to the Marines. The new Beemer was my Massachusetts lawyer car, and the Wrangler was my Maine wood-splitter car. It was in good mechanical condition, but the kid had driven it hard, and it showed. It wasn't worth repainting. On the other hand, I did not like driving a Nazi advertisement. Maybe Leon had the right idea. Slap on a coat of house paint and call it done.

I pulled onto Charlotte's old rutted woods road and decided to keep going at least far enough to hide my Jeep from anyone passing by. It already had enough decorations. I slipped it into four-wheel drive and inched my way a hundred yards or so down the curving slope until I came to the dried-up boulder-strewn streambed. I parked there and walked the rest of the way in.

I hoped I'd see smoke curling up from the stovepipe and Charlotte in the yard weeding her flower garden or holding a cat in her arms or sipping coffee on her front steps.

But it looked the same as it had the previous day. It felt the same, too. Desolate. Abandoned. Her mountain bike leaned against the side of the little house in precisely the same place. No smoke curled from the chimney, and Charlotte was not in the yard.

I went to the front door and knocked loudly. There was no answer, no sound from within.

No sign of life whatsoever.

"Charlotte," I called, loud enough to be heard from inside or from the woods out back. "It's Brady Coyne. Are you there?"

I turned away from the front door, lit a cigarette, and scanned the meadow. I saw nothing. I went to a window and looked inside. The tall pines behind the house left it in morning shade. By holding my hands around my eyes, I could make out the shapes and shadows of furniture. I was looking into her living room, which held a sofa, several bookcases, a woodstove, and a couple of big rocking chairs. A braided rug sat in the middle, and no cat or dog was curled up on it.

I didn't know Charlotte's habits, of course. Perhaps she was one of those compulsive walkers who was never home and who I always seemed to come upon striding along back roads when I was out exploring in my Wrangler. And maybe her cats lived in the woods, and Jack had been her only house pet.

But I didn't like it.

I peeked around the side of the house to her vegetable garden, but she wasn't there. Then I went back to the door and knocked again, with no expectation that it would be answered. While I waited, I glanced down and saw the corner of a piece of paper sticking out from the crack under the door. I bent and pulled it out.

It was my business card with the note I had written to her the previous day, exactly where I had left it.

Okay, maybe she just hadn't noticed it. Of maybe she was away for the weekend. Maybe the swastika and Jack's sudden death had spooked her, and she'd decided to go stay with a sister somewhere.

There were plenty of explanations for Charlotte Gillespie's absence.

But she'd sent a note asking to see me. If she had wanted to talk to me, as her note had said, then why wasn't she here? Why hadn't she called or written another note, either telling me where I could find her or else letting me know that she no longer wanted to talk to me?

I didn't like it at all.

I walked slowly all the way around the little house. By peering into the windows, I saw that the ell on the right side held a pair of bunk beds and the one on the left was a kitchen. There was a hand pump beside the sink, a gas stove, and a small refrigerator. Steep narrow stairs at the back of the middle room climbed up into what I assumed was a loft or maybe just an attic, which had a tiny square window on each end. There was a back door off the kitchen. A well-worn path led from it into the woods, where I could make out the shape of an unpainted plywood-sided outhouse.

A big propane tank on the outside of the kitchen end provided fuel. But no electrical or telephone wires came into the house.

No electricity and no plumbing and no telephone. Spartan living. I wondered where Charlotte Gillespie had lived before she moved to this place, and why she had come here. I wondered if she had chosen to live here because it was where she wanted to be, or if she'd been trying to escape from the place she had been.

It struck me as lived-in but abandoned.

The more I thought about it, and the longer I spent peering into her dark, empty little house, the more ominous it felt.

I circled the house twice. When I again stood by her front door, I shaded my eyes and scanned the meadow. It was knee-high in grass and weeds, punctuated here and there by big boulders and juniper bushes. It sloped away down to the stream, which glinted through the trees and brush that lined it and marked its course through the valley. Beyond the riverbed the ground rose again to Noah Hollingsworth's orchard.

Where was Charlotte?

I wandered out back and followed the path into the woods where I had seen the outhouse. It was shielded from the main house by a clump of scrubby pines, and when I turned the corner and saw it clearly, I stopped.

A large red swastika had been painted on the outhouse door.

EIGHT

I clenched my fists against a sudden surge of emotion—a strong dose of anger, mingled with sadness and profound apprehension.

I wanted to hit somebody.

I wanted to cry.

I took a deep breath. It was one thing to paint a hate symbol on the sign at the end of the roadway. It was quite another thing to come into Charlotte's yard with a can of spray paint and leave what was clearly a message on the outhouse, less than fifty feet from the house itself.

This was purely evil.

I went up to the outhouse and touched the bright red paint on the door. It was dry. Perhaps it had been there the previous day when I was there. For all I knew, the painter had just finished his work when I arrived, and he'd doubled back while I was looking around calling for Charlotte, and when he—or she—spotted my Jeep, he'd decided to practice his artwork.

I've spent plenty of time in outhouses. You don't visit remote fishing camps in Maine and Canada without accepting—and even welcoming—outdoor plumbing. I'd done enough camping to appreciate the comfort of an outhouse when compared to hanging onto a tree and squatting in the woods.

Some outhouses are decidedly utilitarian. The holes cut into the bench are rough and misshapen, and you sit on them gingerly lest you fall in or get splinters. An old Sears Roebuck catalog serves double duty as reading matter and toilet paper. Other outhouses are comparatively elegant, with actual toilet seats nailed onto the benches, a roll of real toilet paper hanging in front of you, a bucket of lime on the floor, and a few old magazines in a rack within reach of the seat. After you finish, you toss a scoop of lime down the hole. The lime is supposed to keep the odor under control.

I was never able to determine that the lime did much good. Regardless of how comfortable—or painful—an outhouse might be to one's bottom, they all smelled the same. No one I have ever met actually enjoys the distinctive odor of the inside of an outhouse.

It wasn't the anticipated aroma, however, that made me hesitate to open the door to Charlotte Gillespie's outhouse. It was the omen that had been spray-painted on it, and what that swastika made me fear I might find inside.

It opened with a creak. It smelled as I'd expected. And I saw instantly that it was empty.

It was a two-holer with store-bought seats nailed to a slab of thick plywood that hinged against the back wall so that the whole bench could be raised. A nearly full roll of real toilet paper sat between the two holes, and a month-old copy of *Yankee* magazine lay on the floor. At the top of the back wall was a rectangular screened opening for light and ventilation. The light was dim, and the ventilation was ineffective.

I clamped my mouth shut, lifted the hinged wooden bench, and looked down into the pit. In the dim light, I could see that it held nothing except what one would expect to see in an outhouse pit, and I let the bench slam down.

I felt vaguely foolish, half expecting to find a body in the outhouse. But I'd had to look. I stepped outside, took a deep breath of clean air, turned, and followed the path around to the front of the house.

I tried the knob on the front door. It turned and the door opened inward. I stood there for a moment with the door half open. Yesterday I'd felt that I shouldn't go inside. But that was before I knew about the swastika on the outhouse door.

I stepped inside.

Except for the hum of a motor—the propane-powered refrigerator—it was dead quiet inside.

I cleared my throat. "Charlotte?"

I expected no answer, and when none came, I called louder. "Charlotte? Are you in there?"

I closed the door behind me. I admitted to myself that I was still looking for a dead body.

There were no bodies downstairs, so I climbed the steep wooden stairs into the loft, which turned out to be an open attic that Charlotte had converted into her sleeping quarters. A box spring and mattress lay directly on the plywood floor. The bed was neatly made, with crisp sheets, a plaid blanket, and two pillows at the head. A low dresser crouched beside it. There was a rack where a few dresses and shirts hung on metal hangers. A wind-up alarm clock, a flashlight, a kerosene lamp, a stack of books, and a battery-powered radio sat on the floor beside the bed. The clock, I noticed, had stopped at nine-fifty. Whether it was A.M. or P.M., and what day, of course, I couldn't determine.

I picked up the flashlight and shone it on the books. They included novels by Alice Walker and Tolstoy, worn old Modern Library editions of Plato's *Republic, The Federalist Papers,* and Machiavelli's *The Prince,* a thick Thoreau anthology, and several volumes, mostly by unfamiliar authors, on animal rights and nature and environmental politics.

You can learn a lot about a person from the books she keeps beside her bed.

I swept the flashlight around the dim recesses of the attic. There were several cardboard boxes and a few piles of folded clothes, but no bodies. I poked through the drawers in the dresser, feeling vaguely voyeuristic and perverted, and found only socks, underwear, and sweaters.

I went back downstairs and looked around again. The small bedroom on one end was pretty much taken up by the two sets of bunk beds, all of which had bare mattresses. A tiny dust-coated desk was jammed in between them under the window. A narrow straight-backed wooden chair was wedged into the kneehole of the desk. I sat in the chair and pulled open the drawers. They were all completely empty.

On the table in the kitchen was a glass, a bare plate, a dog-eared paperback novel, and a pewter candle holder. The candle had burned all the way down, leaving a hard puddle of orange wax that had spilled onto the tabletop. The glass was about one-third full of milk. I sniffed it. It had gone sour.

I picked up the novel. *My Antonia*. Willa Cather. I'd read it in high school, and remembered only that I'd found it tedious.

I opened it to Charlotte's place about halfway through, which was marked by a bookmark. She had stopped reading in the middle of a scene. Her bookmark was an old business card. Harrington, Keith & Co., Certified Public Accountants, with a phone number and address in Portland, Maine. The card was old and smudged and wrinkled, as if Charlotte had been using it for a bookmark for years.

I slipped it into my pocket.

A couple of bowls sat on the floor next to the refrigerator. One contained a few nuggets of dry dog food. Poor Jack would never eat from it again. The other dish, which I assumed was for water, was empty. The refrigerator held half a loaf of bread, an unopened package of hot dogs, two cans of Diet Coke, a jar of mustard, four eggs, a stick of margarine, a container of cottage cheese, and a half-empty carton of milk.

I opened the cabinets, which held a few cans of soup and baked beans and dog food. The kitchen drawers yielded stainless-steel flatware, woven potholders, and a few cooking implements.

I went into the living room. Worn sofa, a couple of rocking chairs, braided rug on the floor, and a wood-burning stove built into the fireplace, with a few chunks of cordwood stacked beside it. A mounted rack of antlers hung over the mantel. A bookcase held some old novels, several *Reader's Digest* condensed books, a few old copies of *Field & Stream* and *Sports Afield*, and an ancient set of the *World Book Encyclopedia*. Not the sort of literature that a Willa Cather fan would likely read. I figured this stuff had come with the place.

A kerosene lamp sat on an end table. I picked it up, held it beside my ear, and shook it. It was empty.

I sat on one of the rocking chairs. I didn't know what I was looking for or, indeed, whether it made any sense to look at all. This was not my home, and I had no business being here.

There was no evidence of a break-in, no sign of a struggle, nothing to suggest what—if anything—had happened to Charlotte . . . except for that burned-down candle, the unfinished glass of sour milk, *My Antonia* marked at a place where one would not normally stop reading, and the empty kerosene lamp. It was as if she'd been sitting at the table in the evening, sipping her milk and reading by candlelight, with the lamp burning in the other room, when she was interrupted. As if she'd marked her place, gotten up, and never returned. As if someone had come for her and taken her away and done her harm.

Maybe the explanation was simpler and less malign. Maybe I just wanted to invent a story to explain why Charlotte wasn't there. I sat there, rocking and thinking about it. But nothing else occurred to me.

After a few minutes, I went outside and took one more turn around the house. But I saw nothing new. So I headed back for my car. I had to talk to the sheriff.

Just as I came within sight of my Wrangler, I spotted a large animal standing in the roadway. A moose, was my first thought. Alex and I had seen moose several times while driving the back roads.

Then I saw that it wasn't a moose. It was a horse. And then I saw Susannah Hollingsworth leaning against the side of my Wrangler. She was wearing jeans and sneakers without socks and a man's blue cotton shirt with the sleeves rolled up past her elbows and the tails knotted over her belly. Her blond hair was pulled back into a tight ponytail, and big silver hoops hung from her ears.

She held up her hand, and I waved. When I was close enough to speak without shouting, I said, "I thought your horse was a moose."

"His name is Arlo," she said. "We do worry about Arlo during hunting season. A lot of out-of-staters carrying thirty-ought-sixes don't know the difference between a horse and a moose. Some of them," she added with a shrug, "don't care."

"I know the difference," I said.

She smiled and patted the side of my car, inviting me to lean beside her.

I accepted and lit a cigarette.

"So what are you doing here?" she said.

"I was going to ask you the same question."

"I came to see the swastika," she said. "It's hateful, isn't it?"

I nodded. "There's another one on her outhouse."

She touched my arm. "No," she whispered.

"Yes." I told Susannah how I'd searched the outhouse and the cabin, looking for a dead body. I told her about the burned-out candle, the paperback book, and the glass of sour milk.

She peered into my eyes. "Do you think . . . ?"

I nodded. "It feels bad."

"What're you going to do?"

"Call the sheriff. I talked to him this morning. He said he was interested in swastikas."

Susannah pushed herself away from the car. "Let's go for a ride."

"Where?"

"I want you to show me that swastika. We'll take Arlo. He can hold both of us."

"I really want to get home and call the sheriff," I said. "I'm very concerned about Charlotte."

"Me, too," she said. "Maybe I'll notice something you missed. Come on. It'll only take a couple minutes."

I nodded. "Okay. Maybe you can tell me I'm crazy to be worried about her."

Arlo had no saddle. Susannah slithered up on his back. I handed the reins up to her and then took her hand and managed to scramble awkwardly up behind her.

"Hold on," she said over her shoulder.

There was nothing except Susannah Hollingsworth to hold on to. I placed my hands tentatively on her hips.

"If you don't want to fall off and break your neck," she said, "you'd better put your arms around me."

I realized she was right. I was a long way from the ground up there on Arlo's back. So I circled Susannah's waist with my arms and hitched myself forward until I was pressing against her back. I could smell her hair in my face. Violets.

She laughed. "Don't be afraid of me. I can't bite from this position. Relax and hold tight. Arlo's a good old horse, but it's a bumpy ride."

Arlo picked his way back up the sloping rutted road that I had just walked down. Every time he took a step, I bounced. I noticed that Susannah seemed to roll her butt in synchrony with Arlo. I couldn't quite find Arlo's rhythm. So I embraced Susannah from behind and concentrated on not getting bumped off.

"What did the sheriff say?" she said over her shoulder.

"Nothing, really. Just that he considers painting swastikas on other people's property more than vandalism. I had the feeling that he wouldn't blow it off."

We came to the clearing and circled behind the house. Susannah reined in Arlo by the outhouse, gazed at the swastika on the door for a moment, muttered, "Jesus," then turned Arlo back toward the meadow, where we stopped. I let my hands slip down so they rested lightly on her hips, and we sat there that way up on Arlo's back, looking across the meadow toward the hillside beyond.

"You went into the house?" she said.

"Yes." I summarized what I'd seen.

"I don't think I want to go in there," she said. She breathed out a long sigh. "What a world." She pointed across the meadow. "That's our orchard, over there."

Even from that distance I could see that the trees were heavy with red fruit. They had been planted in perfect lines, so that the orchard made a patchwork-quilt pattern on the hillside.

"The river's down there," she said, indicating the valley between the meadow where we sat on Arlo's back and the orchard on the hillside beyond. "It's the boundary between this property and ours."

"That must be the same stream that passes under some of the back roads around here," I said. "I've often wondered if it held trout. I'm interested in moving water."

"When I was growing up," she said, "the boys used to catch trout from it. I don't know about now. I'm not much for fishing. Let's take a look."

Before I could tell her that I just wanted to go home and call the sheriff, she clucked to Arlo, who began to canter down the sloping meadow toward the stream. I had no choice but to hold tight. As we approached the line of alders and poplar trees that marked the streambed, I could see that it looked more like a pond. It had flooded the valley, so that some of the poplars stood knee-deep in water. They still held their leaves, which had begun to turn into their autumn yellow. A forest of gnawed-off stumps rimmed the flooded area.

"Beavers," I said.

Susannah nodded. "A hundred years ago it was dammed. There was a tannery over there, on our side of the river, and the water turned some machinery for them. A family named Cutter ran the tannery. My great-grandfather bought the property from Cutter after the tannery went out of business. He planted the orchard. Around here they call the stream Cutter's Run. The dam blew out a long time ago. This is definitely beavers."

New beaver ponds, I knew, made prime trout water. I made a note to explore it sometime.

We gazed at the water for a few minutes. Then Susannah leaned back against me. "Want to head back?" she said.

"Yes. I'm anxious to get hold of the sheriff. Anyway, Alex is expecting me for lunch."

"Will you tell her about me?"

"What about you?"

She chuckled. "That I followed you here, took you for a ride, made you hug me?"

"Did you?"

"What?"

"Did you follow me?"

"Of course not. I was just kidding."

"I'll tell Alex, yes. Any reason I shouldn't?"

She patted my hand where it held her hip. "None whatsoever."

When we got back to my Wrangler, I slid off Arlo's back and held my hand up to Susannah. "Thanks for the ride."

She gave my hand a quick squeeze. "Let's do it again. There's a lot of country around here you can see best from horseback."

"Sure. I'd like that." I scratched Arlo's muzzle and told him he was a fine animal. I started to get into my Jeep, then stopped. "How can I find Mr. Hood, do you know?"

"I know how you can find him," she said. "Getting him to talk to you might be another story."

"He's not friendly?"

She smiled. "Hoodie don't take kindly to strangers askin' questions." Susannah's Down East twang sounded perfect. "If you want," she said, "I could introduce you. He likes me."

"I bet he does."

She laughed. "I've known him since I was a baby." She shrugged. "I'll let you draw your own conclusions. How about if I drop by this afternoon, take you over there?"

"That'd be great. Thank you."

"Bring Alex."

"I'd intended to," I said.

NINE

It was a few minutes before one in the afternoon when I got back. The muffled click of typing from Alex's office told me she was still working.

I took the cordless phone onto the deck and called Sheriff Dickman's office. He was off-duty. I asked to have him call me. "Please tell him it's important," I said. Then I tried his home number. His answering machine picked up. "It's Brady Coyne," I told the machine. "I really think something has happened to Charlotte Gillespie. Please give me a call."

A few minutes later Alex came into the kitchen, where I was bent over peering into the refrigerator. She patted my butt. "Hungry?"

"Yep." I found a big plastic bag that held the remnants from the salad we'd served to Susannah and Noah. I turned and held it up. "How's this?"

"Perfect." She tiptoed up and kissed my chin. "Did you see Charlotte?"

I shook my head. "Let's dump this into bowls. I'll tell you about it."

Which I did while we ate at the kitchen table. When I told Alex about the swastika on the outhouse door, she put down her fork, dabbed at her mouth with her napkin, and muttered, "God!" And she sat there, her eyes peering intently into mine, as I recounted my search of the house.

Then I remembered the business card she'd been using as a bookmark. I took it out of my shirt pocket and showed it to her.

She shrugged. "You think this means something?"

"I don't know."

When I told her about meeting Susannah and our ride on Arlo the horse, she smiled. "And you're the one who's jealous when I go to a party without you."

"She's coming by later on to take us to meet Arnold Hood," I said. "He's Charlotte Gillespie's landlord. I'm hoping he might shed some light on the situation."

"Us?"

"If you'd like to come."

"Sure," said Alex. "I've heard Arnold Hood is quite the character. I'd like to meet him."

We took coffee out onto the deck and lit cigarettes. "Oh," said Alex. "I forgot to tell you. Noah called. He wants you to call him."

"What's he want?"

She shrugged. "He didn't choose to confide in me. He sounded a bit anxious, though."

I stubbed out my cigarette and picked up my coffee mug. "I'll do it right now, lest I forget."

Alex remained on the deck while I went inside. I found Noah's number in the skinny local directory and dialed it.

Susannah answered.

"It's Brady," I said.

"Oh, hi. How are you?"

"Aside from a sore backside, I'm fine."

She chuckled. "Did you talk to the sheriff?"

"Left a message," I said. "Your father wanted me to call him. Is he around?"

"Sure. Sorry about your butt. Hang on. I'll get him for you."

I heard her call, "Hey, Daddy. It's Brady Coyne," and a moment later Noah said, "Brady?"

"What's up, Noah?"

"Something I'd like to run by you."

"Shoot."

He dropped his voice. "I'd rather not on the phone. Why don't you and your pretty Alexandria let us return the favor? Come on over, have dinner with us tonight. We'll find a time to talk then."

I opened my mouth to tell him I couldn't do that, that I had a law office back in Boston that was open on Mondays, that this was Sunday, and that on Sundays Alex and I ate an early supper so I could drive back to Boston in the daylight, which, in late August, expired a little after seven o'clock. Alex and I treasured our quiet time alone on Sundays before I had to leave. Saying good-bye for a week was something we liked to do privately.

But then I thought of Charlotte Gillespie and her poisoned puppy and the swastikas. I had to tell Sheriff Dickman about the new one on the outhouse, and about my conviction that something had happened to her. I wanted to see if I could locate a local spray-paint artist, and I was curious to hear what Arnold Hood might tell me and to learn if he could suggest other people to talk to and other places to snoop around.

In the five seconds it took for these thoughts to zing through my brain, I decided I'd call Julie and tell her to cancel my Monday appointments. Julie, of course, wouldn't like it, and she'd try very hard to make me feel guilty. She was very skilled at making me feel guilty, which was one of the reasons I treasured her. Without Julie, I'd probably go broke.

But, I reminded myself, it was my law practice, and if I chose to accrue zero billable hours once in a while, I could do that. That's precisely why I worked in a one-man office.

So I told Noah we'd be there at six.

I hung up and went back onto the deck. "We're having dinner with Noah tonight," I told Alex.

She hunched her shoulders. "Oh, Brady . . ."

I knew what she was thinking. She was thinking that I intended to leave for Boston right after we ate with Noah, and we'd lose our little oasis of quiet time before I left. She was thinking that I didn't care about that time the way she did, or maybe that I'd completely forgotten about it. I put my hand on her shoulder. "I'm not going back tonight, if that's okay with you."

She turned and smiled up at me. "Really?"

I nodded.

"Why?"

"I'm worried about Charlotte," I said. "She wanted to see me. I feel I've got to stick around, see what I can find out."

Alex pulled away from my hand. "Oh. Right."

"I thought you'd be pleased."

"Sure. That's great."

I leaned back against the railing, folded my arms, and looked at her. "Okay. What'd I do now?"

She shook her head and gave me a quick smile. "Nothing, Brady. It's just . . ."

"What? It's just what?"

She blew out a breath. "Sometime it'd be nice if you decided to stay an extra day just because you wanted to have more time with me."

"Ah," I said.

"It's like, on Sundays you can't wait to climb into your fancy new car and drive away from here as fast as you can go. That's how it seems. Am I crazy?"

I stared at her. "No, honey, you're not entirely crazy. There is this tiny little element of sanity in what you're feeling. But it's a helluva lot more complicated than that."

She nodded. "You really are a bachelor through and through, you know that?"

"I love you," I said.

"Yeah, I guess you do. Whatever that means. I should be grateful for that, I guess."

"We've talked about this," I said.

"Yes, we have. And I think we've said about everything there is to say about it, and I really don't want to talk about it anymore."

I shrugged. "Okay. Good."

I went back inside and called Julie at home. She gave me the obligatory hard time about my irresponsibility, my commitments to my clients, and my meager billable hours. I listened and murmured "You're quite right" in the appropriate places, and finally she sighed and agreed to cancel my appointments for the next couple of days.

Alex was loading the dishwasher when I went back into the kitchen. "Done," I said. "I'm taking tomorrow and Tuesday, too."

She turned and wiped her hands on her thighs. "That's fine, Brady," she said. "It'll be nice to have you around."

I pulled her against me. "C'mon, babe. It *will* be nice."

"I guess so," she mumbled into my chest.

I held her there, and after a minute her arms snaked around my back and squeezed, and then she lifted her face. I saw that she'd been crying, and I didn't know what to say, so I began touching my lips to all the wet places on her face, and I eventually worked my way around to her mouth—

—when I heard a car toot its horn from out front. I peered out the window. "Susannah's here," I said.

"That woman's got great timing," muttered Alex.

We went outside and piled into Susannah's Audi. I got in beside Susannah, and Alex climbed in back.

"Where's Paul?" said Alex as Susannah backed out of the driveway.

"Paul lives and works in Portland," said Susannah. "He only comes around to see me." She shrugged. "He'll be there tonight when you guys come for dinner. Daddy invited him, and Paul never turns down an invitation."

I heard the indifference in her voice. Love comes in many complicated guises.

Susannah drove for about fifteen minutes over paved roads before she turned onto a well-used dirt road. I guessed I could find a shorter route to Arnold Hood's place by taking my Wrangler over the lacework of less-traveled back roads.

A mile or so along the dirt road Susannah pulled into the front yard of a square, two-story nondescript farmhouse. Once upon a time it had been painted white, but now the paint was peeling and flaking away, leaving large bare patches on the clapboards. Where the paint remained, trickles of rust stain betrayed the old iron nails that held the place together. A recently washed black Dodge pickup was parked next to the house.

A country-and-western station was turned up to maximum volume on a radio somewhere nearby. An aluminum ladder leaned against the front of the house, and a man was kneeling on the roof tacking down shingles. If he had heard or seen us, he was choosing to ignore us.

"I assume that's Mr. Hood up there on the roof," I said to Susannah.

"That's Hoodie," she said. "He knows we're here. He'll make us scream at him. Then he'll pretend he hadn't seen us, and he'll act annoyed, and he'll probably stay up on the roof with his radio blaring and expect us to carry on a conversation that way, as if he's too busy to be interrupted." She grinned. "Hell, he's been working on this house forever. It's about all he ever does."

"What's his problem?" I said.

Susannah shrugged. "No job, no family, no interests, no money. He inherited a lot of property. He lives off what he can make from letting people cut his woodlot and run milk cows on his pastures and grow corn in his fields. He hasn't got enough ambition to do his own cutting or raise his own cows or grow his own corn." She opened the car door. "Come on. Let's get him down here."

TEN

Susannah went over and stood near the foot of the ladder with her hands on her hips, looking up at Arnold Hood, who continued to bang his hammer on his roof.

"Perverse bastard," she muttered. "He knows we're here." She went around the corner to an open window on the first floor of the house and turned off the radio that sat on the sill. Then she came back and shouted, "Hoodie!"

He looked down, using his hand as a visor, frowning as if he was surprised to see us. He appeared to be somewhere in his forties. He had thick black curly hair and the dark shadow of a few days' growth on his cheeks and chin. He wore metal-rimmed glasses, work boots, and overalls with no shirt underneath, which showed off his thick knotty shoulders and biceps. "I was enjoyin' that tune," he said mildly.

"Git your old ass down here," said Susannah. "I got some folks who want to talk to you."

Hood shrugged, scrabbled over the roof to the ladder, and climbed down. He squinted at us for a moment, then nodded once. "How 'bout some ice tea?" he said, and without waiting for an answer, he turned and disappeared around the corner of the house.

"Lost both parents to cancer less than a year apart," Susannah said. "Never been married. Hoodie's not very comfortable with people, and maybe not the brightest guy on earth, but he's a good soul."

He was back a couple minutes later carrying a blue plastic jug and four glasses. "Sun tea," he said, shaking the jug so we could hear the rattle of ice cubes. "Made it myself."

We went over and sat on the wide front steps that led up to the porch. Arnold Hood poured tea into the glasses. I took a tentative sip. It was faintly bitter and strong, but the mix of herbs was tasty.

"This is our neighbor Alexandria Shaw," said Susannah to Hood, "and this gentleman here is Mr. Brady Coyne from Boston. Miss Shaw is living in the Gartside place."

"I seen her around," he said, speaking to Susannah.

I held my hand to him. "Good to meet you," I said.

His grip was tentative. "You, too," he said. He let go quickly, then turned back to Susannah. "So how come you drug me off my roof?"

"I wanted to ask you about Charlotte Gillespie," I said.

"What's a man from Boston want with her?"

"She's renting your place, isn't she?"

He lifted his glass and took a long swig. When he brought down the glass, he wiped his mouth with the back of his wrist. "Guess she is," he said. "Something wrong with that?"

I shook my head. "Of course not. I was wondering—"

"Paid me six months' rent in advance," he said. "Usually best I do is let a bunch of deer hunters from Portland take it for a couple weeks in November. Otherwise, that old place sits up there, doin' nothing except costin' me taxes. Six months' rent, huh?" He arched his eyebrows as if he expected me to congratulate him on his business acumen.

"Mr. Hood," I said, "do you know where she is?"

"Who?"

"Charlotte. Your tenant."

He frowned. "Course I know where she is. She's livin' in my hunting camp up on the hill there by Cutter's Run."

"She's still living there?"

He looked at Susannah. "What's he gettin' at, anyways?"

"Charlotte Gillespie is a friend of Mr. Coyne's," said Susannah.

74

"He's been trying to see her, but she hasn't been home for the past couple of days."

Hood switched his gaze back to me. "Whaddya want to see her for?"

"I'm worried about her," I said. "Somebody painted a swastika on her outhouse, and—"

"That's my outhouse," he said.

"Yes. You're right. But—"

"Who in hell's painting swastikas on my outhouse?"

"That's what I want to know," I said. "They also painted one on my car."

"That so?" He shrugged. "Well, I'll tell you, Mr. Coyne. I ain't seen Miz Gillespie for some time. She keeps to herself, and I don't go up there to bother her. She said she wanted a place to be alone, and that's just fine with me. I leave her alone. And I sure as hell don't know who's painting no swastikas on my goddam outhouse."

"You said you usually rent the place to deer hunters," I said.

Hood nodded. "Yep. Same bunch every year. Rich boys from Portland." He shrugged. "I guess they ain't gonna git it this year. It's all rented and paid for by Miz Gillespie till New Year's."

"Has anyone else ever rented it from you?"

He shook his head. "Just them boys."

"Is one of them an accountant?"

He cocked his head. "Huh? Accountant? Why'd you think that?"

I shrugged. "I guess I misunderstood something."

"Those boys are scientists. They all work for a place there in Portland. Do some kind of research."

"And no one else has ever stayed up there?" I persisted.

"At the cabin?" Hood shook his head. "Just those Portland fellas, for deer season. Well, actually, one of 'em took the place for a week the past couple of summers." He grinned. "Gittin' away from the old lady, I think. Know what I mean?"

"Shacking up?" I said.

"Believe so," he said solemnly. "I never seen hide nor hair of 'em when they was there, if you follow me."

"What can you tell us about Charlotte?" said Susannah.

75

"What I *can* tell you ain't necessarily what I'm *gonna* tell you, missy," he said. "A person wants their privacy, by Jesus, far as I'm concerned, they're entitled to it, and Arnold Hood ain't gonna be the one to violate it. No, sir."

"I'm afraid something's happened to her," I said. "The cabin doesn't appear to have been lived in for the past several days. There's that swastika, and her puppy was poisoned. You can see how it looks. I was just hoping you'd know whether she's away for a while, or maybe moved out."

"If she moved out, that'd mean she left behind four months' rent," he said thoughtfully. "Nope. I don't think she'd do that. If she just went away for a while, I doubt she'd bother tellin' me."

"How did she come to rent your place?" said Alex.

He turned to her and smiled. "I got a call one day—oh, middle of June sometime. Woman, nice soft voice. She asked if she could rent the place and I told her sure, it was empty. She asked me how much, and I thought about it and said five hundred a month, fig-uring we'd end up at three-fifty, four if I was lucky, but she said five was fine, she'd send me a check and move in the first of July. I mentioned a lease, and she said it wasn't necessary as far as she was concerned, was six months' advance okay?" He shrugged. "Week later I got a check in the mail, and when I was drivin' by sometime the first week in July maybe, I saw she'd stuck up a No Trespassing sign at the end of the road. I never posted it up there. Like I said, I useta rent the place out to deer hunters. But her puttin' up a sign didn't bother me none. Six months' advance rent, I figure the place is hers, and as long as she's there, she can do any damn fool thing she wants."

"Had you advertised it?" said Alex.

"Nope."

"Then how did she know about it?"

Hood rubbed his palm over his stubbly chin. "Dunno," he said after a minute. "I never asked and she never said. Guess she heard about it somewhere. Everyone around here knows about that old place."

"Do you remember her check?" I said. "Was there an address on it, a phone number?"

"Bank check. I remember that. Portland bank, it was. Don't remember which one. I was glad to see a bank check. Knowed that sucker wasn't gonna bounce."

"Portland?"

"Huh?" He frowned, then nodded. "Oh, sure. My deer hunters're from Portland, Miz Gillespie uses a Portland bank. A connection, eh?"

"Portland," said Susannah, "is the closest city to here. I have an office in Portland, too. Most of the banks around here are branches of Portland banks."

I nodded, then turned back to Hood. "So you never met Charlotte before she moved in?"

He shrugged. "Nope." He cocked his head at me for a moment, then nodded. "Oh. You mean, if I knowed she was colored I wouldn't've rented to her. That what you're thinking?"

"No, actually, I—"

He tapped my leg with his fist. "Lemme tell you something," he said. "I got nothin' against colored people. Miz Charlotte Gillespie coulda been green or purple for all I care. Six months in advance was good enough for me, and that's the truth."

"All I meant," I said, "was that I wondered if she mentioned to you why she wanted to live up there, where she was coming from, if she was trying to get away from something."

"Or someone, you mean," he said. "She never said, and I sure'n hell didn't ask. We just talked that once on the phone. Oh, I bumped into her a couple times after she was moved in. Seen her walking that little yellow dog, comin' out of the roadway to the cabin. I'd wave and she'd wave, and once I stopped, told her who I was, asked if everything was okay. She said it was." He shrugged. "Had the feeling she wasn't much for conversation, and I didn't push it none."

"She's an attractive woman," I said.

He nodded. "That she is." He took another sip of his tea. "I know what you're thinkin'," he said quietly. "But I tell you this. If someone took a likin' to her, ended up hurtin' her, it wasn't me."

"I didn't mean that."

He peered into his glass of tea. "Yup, I think you did. It's okay.

No offense. I see you're worried about her, and I appreciate that. I don't know nothin' about where she's at. I mind my own business, and I appreciate it when other folks do the same."

"Have you seen the swastika on her No Trespassing sign?" I said.

He squinted up at me and nodded. "Pretty hard to miss. You're thinking someone's tryin' to scare her off?"

"Yes, I am," I said. "And maybe they've succeeded."

"Well," he said, "all I can tell you is, it ain't me."

"Did she have any visitors?"

He narrowed his eyes. "Look, Mr. Coyne. I been tellin' you, I don't pay Miz Gillespie any mind one way or t'other. I haven't noticed nothing."

"She has a friend," I said. "Her dog got poisoned, and somebody picked up the body from the vet's. Any idea who that might be?"

"Look, I told you—"

"Right," I said quickly. "Sorry." I tilted up my glass, drained it until the half-melted ice cubes clicked against my teeth, then put it down. I stood up and held my hand out to Arnold Hood. "I appreciate your taking the time to talk with us," I said. "Thanks for the tea. It was good to meet you."

He gave my hand a quick shake and nodded.

Alex and Susannah stood also and said good-bye to him. Arnold Hood remained sitting on his steps, his elbows on his knees, holding his iced tea glass in both hands, and as we were walking back to our cars, he called, "Miz Susannah, ain't you going to turn my radio back on?"

"Nope," she called over her shoulder. "I don't care for that music."

"You always was a bitchly woman," he said cheerfully.

ELEVEN

It was about four o'clock when Susannah dropped us off. I retrieved two bottles of beer from the refrigerator and handed one to Alex, who headed out to the deck with it. I checked the answering machine. There was one message. I pressed the button on the machine, heard the tape rewind, and then: "Sheriff Dickman. You called. I'm home. Call me here."

So I found the portable phone, took it into the living room, and tried Sheriff Dickman's home number. This time a woman answered. She said the sheriff was out in the garden, and when I told her I was returning his call, she said she'd fetch him. A moment later, he said, "Dickman. Who's this?"

"It's Brady Coyne, Sheriff. You remember, I—"

"Course I remember. Those damn swastikas. What's up?"

I told him about the new swastika on Charlotte's outhouse and summarized what I'd seen when I searched the cabin. "To tell you the truth, I half expected to find her body," I said. "It looked to me like she left suddenly."

"And you think something happened to her."

"Yes. I do." I told Dickman that I'd just returned from talking with Arnold Hood, from whom Charlotte was renting the cabin, but hadn't learned much from him.

"You've been busy," said the sheriff.

"Well," I said, "I'm worried about her."

"I can appreciate that." There was a pause. Then he said, "I mentioned that poisoned dog to one of my deputies. He said he'd heard about a poisoned animal up in your neck of the woods, mentioned an animal hospital over in Dublin, couple towns west of you. So I called the vet. Interesting story. Seems that someone had brought in their sick dog. A bird dog, purebred English setter that tended to run off and go hunting by itself. The vet couldn't save it. It died fast. He's convinced it was poisoned. Said it was no poison he'd ever seen before."

"Like Charlotte's pup," I said.

"Yes," said the sheriff. "But that's not really the point. The point is, my deputy knew about this vet because we'd been called about a burglary at the hospital. They stole two computers and emptied the cash register." He paused for a moment. "They also stole the dead setter."

"Jesus," I said. "Somebody picked up Charlotte's dog."

"Exactly," he said.

"I assume you haven't caught that burglar," I said.

"No. I'd say we haven't got your normal burglar here, if there is such a thing. We've got someone who's mainly interested in stealing the bodies of poisoned dogs."

"Before they can be autopsied," I said.

"So what do you make of it all, Mr. Coyne?"

"I'm not sure," I said. "Someone's poisoning dogs, then stealing their bodies, and we've got swastikas . . ."

"About Ms. Gillespie, I mean," he said.

"Either she's been frightened off," I said, "or . . ." I let my voice trail away.

"Yes," he said. "Let's hope she's been frightened off. Tell you what. I'll get the word out on Charlotte Gillespie, see if we can track down any of her relatives, maybe figure out where she was living before she moved into that cabin, where she worked, who might be . . . interested in her. Tomorrow I'll come over your way, twist a few arms. I don't like swastikas in my jurisdiction, and I sure as hell don't like women going missing."

"I'd like to be involved," I said.

"Sure," he said. "You already are."

After I disconnected from the sheriff, I went out onto the deck. Alex had her heels up on the railing. Her eyes were closed and her face was tilted up to the afternoon sun.

I touched her shoulder and her eyes blinked open.

"Napping?" I said.

She shook her head. "Thinking."

"Oh-oh."

"Yeah," she said. "Oh-oh. So what's up?"

"I talked to the sheriff."

"What'd he have to say?"

I summarized my conversation with Sheriff Dickman. "He's going to try to find Charlotte. He's definitely concerned."

"Someone's poisoning dogs and then stealing their bodies?"

"That's how it looks."

"And making swastikas," she said.

"I guess so."

"That's sick," she said.

"Given what might've happened to Charlotte," I said, "it's worse than sick." I shook my head. "Anyway, the sheriff thinks I'm a helluva detective."

"He said that?"

"Well, not in so many words."

"What you actually mean," she said, "is, *you* think you're a helluva detective."

"Well? Don't you?"

Alex rolled her eyes. "Of course I do." She pushed herself out of the rocker. "I'm going to grab a shower. We don't want to be late to Noah's."

I reached to her, and she stood there with her arms hanging at her sides, letting me hold her but not holding me back. "Sometimes . . ." she mumbled.

"Sometimes what?" I said.

She stepped away from me. "Nothing. I think too much, I guess. Come on. If you behave yourself, I'll let you give me a shampoo."

"Behave?"

"You know."

81

"Misbehave, you mean."

"Exactly," she said.

An hour later Alex was standing in front of the full-length bedroom mirror, squinting through her glasses, trying to hook hoops into her ears. She was wearing sandals, a pleated white skirt that stopped a few inches short of her knees, and a flowered short-sleeved blouse. I stood behind her and slid my arms under hers and around her belly. "You look gorgeous," I said.

She dropped her arms, reached behind her, and pulled my hips against her butt. "You always say such sweet things right after you get laid," she said. Her hair was still damp and smelled of wild-flowers. I kissed the back of her neck, watching her face in the mirror.

She took off her glasses, closed her eyes, and bowed her head, exposing her neck to me. I nuzzled her and moved my hands up under her blouse.

Her eyes opened. She met my gaze in the mirror for a moment, then straightened up. I let my hands drop. She put her glasses back on and resumed trying to poke her earring into the hole in her left ear.

"This is hard for me," she said, still facing the mirror. "I keep wondering . . ."

Her voice trailed off, and her eyes flickered toward mine in the mirror, then slid away.

"Wondering what?" I said.

She shrugged. "You know. Same old thing."

"If I was here all the time?"

She nodded.

"I can't," I said.

"I know." She hooked on her second earring, turned to face me, gave me a quick smile, and said, "I'm ready. Shall we go?"

I told Alex she looked too pretty to ride in a banged-up old Jeep Wrangler with a swastika on the hood, so we took my new BMW to Noah's place. We put on a Mozart CD and opened the sunroof, and Alex admitted that the car was pretty cool.

She directed me through what seemed like a maze of turns, and after fifteen minutes or so, I pulled into a large peastone parking area in front of a long, low-slung shingled farmstand. I parked between Susannah's Audi and Paul's black Lexus.

The sign on the roof of the farmstand read "Hollingsworth Orchards." Smaller hand-printed signs in the windows said "Old-Time New England Apples," "Homemade Pies and Preserves," "Fresh Cider," "Pick Your Own Apples," and "We Open Labor Day."

The house sat on a short driveway behind the farmstand. It was a classic three-story New England farmhouse—white clapboard, big porch across the entire front, tall windows, and two brick chimneys poking out of the roof. A weathered old barn stood behind the house, and beyond that were several football fields of orchard. Rows of apple trees heavy with fruit marched up the hillside and disappeared over the top.

We got out of the car. "Pretty, isn't it?" said Alex.

I nodded. "Smell the apples?"

"Mmm." She took my hand and gave it a squeeze. "I'm sorry, Brady," she said.

"What for?"

"You know. For never being satisfied. For wanting something, and then getting it and wanting more. It's always been a character flaw of mine."

"It's the only one I've noticed," I said. "I guess I can live with it, since you seem to be able to put up with all of mine."

As we started up the path to the front porch, the door opened and Susannah came out. She was wearing white shorts and a blue-and-white-striped jersey, and her blond hair hung loose around her shoulders. She waved. "Come on in. Daddy's organizing the booze, eager to take your orders."

We went up onto the porch, and Susannah grabbed one of Alex's hands and one of mine and led us inside. Noah was seated at the kitchen table. Paul was at the sink rinsing some dishes. He was wearing an apron.

Noah had assembled his collection of liquor bottles on the counter, and he rubbed his hands and grinned. "We been waiting for you," he said.

I shook his bony farmer's hand, and Alex went over, braced herself on his shoulder, and bent to kiss his leathery cheek.

Paul wiped his hands on a towel and grinned awkwardly, as if he'd been caught shoplifting. I held my hand out to him and he shook it with both of his. He touched the hem of his apron and made a little curtsy. "Guess we know who wears the pants in this family, huh?"

"Hey," I said. "You're a sensitive nineties type of guy."

"Unlike some people we might mention," said Alex.

"Paul," said Susannah, "would you mind getting the ice out of the freezer?"

Paul darted a quick you-know-how-it-is look at me and turned to the refrigerator.

"So," said Noah. "What'll it be?"

Alex and I asked for gin and tonics. Paul fetched beers for himself and Susannah from the refrigerator. Noah made our drinks, then mixed a pitcher of martinis and poured one for himself. He took a large swallow, then turned to me. "Let me show you around," he said.

"Please," I said.

He turned to Alex with his eyebrows raised.

"You gave me your tour last time I was here," she said with a smile. "I admired your collection of trucks, remember?"

Noah nodded. He topped off his martini, grabbed my arm, and said, "Well, come on, then."

I wondered if Paul was joining us, but he had resumed his place by the kitchen sink. So I followed Noah through the sliding glass door onto the back porch. "This is my pissing platform," Noah said. "Since Jessie died, I been sleeping in the room off the kitchen. My bladder wakes me up three or four times a night. It's what happens when you got a worn-out prostate. I like to piss out here under the moon and stars. Reminds me of when I was a boy and too damn scared to go all the way to the outhouse in the dark."

Noah was tall and skinny, stoop-shouldered and gaunt and heronlike, and the image of him urinating off his deck made me smile.

The yard between the deck and the barn was knee-high in milkweed and goldenrod and littered with old farm machinery—one pickup truck on cinder blocks and another sitting on flattened tires, a big flatbed with a cracked windshield, a couple of tractors, and a variety of rusted tillers and harrows and plows. Noah waved his hand at it all. "Jessie was always after me to move this junk into the barn. But I kept telling her that'd mean moving the other junk out of the barn to make room for it. Never got around to it. Wish I had. She always wanted a flower garden out here."

He pointed out to the orchard. "I have to hire people to do my work for me," he said. "Can't do it myself anymore. Hardly ever even get out into the orchards. Keep meaning to saddle up the old horse, but I keep not doin' it. I'm too damn creaky and I get tired pretty easy." He sighed deeply. "I love growing apples, and I love eating them. But since I lost Jessie, I don't have much heart for it." He shrugged.

There were some wicker chairs on the deck. He dropped heavily into one of them. I took the one beside him.

"Susannah mentioned that you were thinking of selling the place," I said.

He waved his hand. "I just say that to put the idea in her head. I ain't going to sell. The way I see it, it ain't mine to sell." He turned to me and touched my arm. "They tell me if I'm lucky I might last another eighteen months. They say only the last month or two will be bad."

I started to speak, but he held up his hand. "You don't need to say anything." He smiled. "When I was a boy, I figured I'd live forever. When I got a little older and came to understand that I was going to die someday, I was afraid of it. But then it got so I was mainly just curious about it." He shook his head. "I'm okay with it. Kind of a relief, actually, knowing. Problem is, Susannah don't know, and I got to tell her."

"I understand," I said. "I'm sorry, Noah."

"My daddy lived to eighty-six," he said. "And Gramps was just a week shy of ninety-one. I always figured . . ." He waved his hand. "It don't matter. But I worry about Susannah." He turned to face me. "I told you I wanted to ask you something, Brady. I need some advice."

"Sure," I said. "Legal problem?"

He shook his head. "Personal."

"Why me?"

He shrugged. "You got nothing at stake. You don't know me well enough to lie to me. Anyways, I can tell you're a truth-teller. You're smart, and I believe I can trust you. I don't know many smart people I can trust. Seems like only the dumb ones are trustworthy, and that's because they're too dumb to know better."

"What about Paul?"

Noah nodded. "Paul's a nice fella. Damn smart, all right. Loves Susannah, I guess, and he sure tries hard with her. I ain't sure how much she loves him, though. She kind of tolerates him, far as I can see." He cocked his head and peered at me. "Anyways, he's just a boy." He waved his hand, dismissing Paul Forten.

"Well," I said, "I don't know how smart I am, but you can trust me."

He nodded, then drained his martini and set the glass down on the deck beside him. He lifted his hand and waved it in the direction of his orchard. "Hollingsworths have had this for almost a hundred years," he said. "My grandfather planted it when he was a young man, and he grew apples until the day he died. My old man kept it going, and now it's been mine for over thirty years. After Susannah, Jessie couldn't have more kids. There's just her. You see?"

"You're worried she'll sell it," I said.

He shook his head. "No, Brady. I'm worried she won't. Or if she does, I'm worried she'll only sell it to someone who'll promise to keep the apples growing, and I know damn well she won't get what the place is worth that way. Susannah's smart, all right, but I worry she won't act smart after I go. I guess she can be a pretty crafty businesswoman. But she's got a sentimental streak in her when it comes to me and this place."

"You've got a will, I assume?"

He nodded, still gazing out at his apple trees. "It'll all be hers, of course. Susannah don't think I'm much of a businessman, and maybe she's right. But I know I could sell some of this land and make out pretty good. I've had some inquiries. I just don't feel like it's mine to sell. Not since I learned . . ." He shrugged. "She's a good daughter, Brady, and after me she's the only Hollingsworth left. She drops by couple times a week to check up on me, clean the house, take care of things I neglect. Stays the night up in her bedroom, makes me breakfast the next morning, then she's off to work again. It's been real nice these past couple weeks, having her around every day. Imagine, a daughter spending her vacation time taking care of her old man. I'll miss her when she goes back to the city."

"Portland?"

He nodded. "That's her home office, and she's got a condo right on the water, though she ain't there that much. Travels all over, making her deals, as she calls it. New York, D.C., the West Coast, Europe, Japan, the Middle East. She sends me postcards. All these pretty places. I never set foot outside of New England in my life." He shook his head. "It's a sign of the times when your kid's been to more places in her short life than you have in your long one."

"Talk to her," I said. "Tell her what's happening. Tell her what you want her to do."

"I guess I know that," he said softly. I noticed that his eyes glittered. "She didn't take it well when Jessie passed. Now me. It'll be hard." He paused. "I wonder if you'd do me a kindness, Brady."

I nodded.

"After I'm gone there'll be . . . business to attend to." He cocked his head and looked at me.

"Susannah will need legal advice," I said. "Of course. I'll do whatever I can."

"It would sure put my mind to rest," he said.

"Don't even think about it," I said. "In the meantime, you'll feel better after you talk to her."

"I suppose I will," he said. "But it ain't me I'm worried about." He reached over and gave my shoulder a squeeze. "Thanks for listening to an old man's ramble." He held up his glass. "I'm empty. That's no good. Let's go get refills."

Susannah grilled chicken breasts for dinner, along with fresh green beans and baked potatoes. Paul tossed the salad and mixed his own special dressing. We shared two bottles of a nice Chardonnay, devoured a warm apple pie, and afterward we sipped brandy on the deck and watched darkness seep into the orchard.

We avoided topics touching on swastikas and business and death. Alex asked a lot of questions about apple-growing, which segued into a discussion of pie and applesauce and cider and a debate over the merits of old New England apples such as Northern Spies and Baldwins versus what Noah called "popsicles" like Delicious and McIntosh.

I mentioned the beaver pond in the valley that separated Noah's property from Arnold Hood's. I said I was thinking of trekking in one morning with my fly rod to see if any brook trout still lived there. Noah said he remembered when the milldam for the old tannery blew out in an April flood. Sometime back in the fifties, he recalled. When he was a kid, the locals used to catch trout out of Cutter's Run, he said. Susannah said that they caught them when she was a kid, too.

Paul sat quietly, smiling at the right times, but he didn't say much. His eyes kept darting to Susannah, and whenever he did, she always seemed to be looking somewhere else. At one point, I caught him glancing at his wristwatch.

We left a little after nine. The three of them stood on the porch, waving as we pulled away. Susannah had her arm around her father's waist, and Paul stood beside her with his hand on the back of her neck.

We drove the back roads in silence, and when I pulled into Alex's driveway and switched off the engine, neither of us made a move to get out.

"Have a nice time?" she said after a minute.

"Sure."

"I worry," she said.

"About what?"

"Oh, it's ungracious of me, I guess. But we've had dinner with them two nights in a row, now. I like them, and it's nice that they like us. But I'm starting to feel like they're latching onto us, you know?"

I nodded. "Yes, I know," I said. I lit a cigarette. Its tip glowed in the darkness inside the car.

"I mean," said Alex, "I'm feeling invaded. I'm not sure I know how to turn them down if they keep wanting to get together. How to say that sometimes we'd just rather be alone."

"Just say it, I guess."

"I have trouble doing that. I don't like to hurt people's feelings."

"Mmm," I murmured.

"So what'd you think?"

"Of what?"

"Paul. Paul and Susannah, I mean. As a couple."

"Paul's all right," I said. "Hell, he washes dishes."

"I didn't sense much chemistry between them," she said.

"I guess not."

After a minute, Alex put her hand on my leg. "What's the matter, Brady?"

I shook my head. "Nothing, hon."

She gave my leg a squeeze. "Come on. What is it?"

I turned to her, touched her cheek, then drew her face against my shoulder. "It's Noah," I said. "He told me he was dying."

I felt Alex stiffen against me. She lifted her head and looked at me. "Oh, Brady," she said.

"He said he's got about eighteen months. He's worried about Susannah."

Alex ducked her head and burrowed her face into my chest. "He's not that old," she mumbled. She tilted up her face, and in the darkness I could see the glitter of tears in her eyes. I touched my knuckle to each cheekbone, and it came away wet. I kissed her eyes.

"I feel like a shit," she said.

"For not wanting to have dinner with them every night?"

"Yes."

I held her against me, and after a while I kissed the top of her head. "Are you done crying?"

"Just about."

"You sure? I don't want to rush you."

She looked up at me. "When was the last time you cried?"

"I don't remember."

She reached up, held my face in both of her hands, and peered into my eyes. "Try it sometime," she said. She kissed me quickly, slipped out of the car, and went into the house without waiting for me.

I sat there pondering the differences between men and women, and a couple of minutes later I heard Alex yell: "Brady! Come here." There was urgency in her voice. Panic, even.

She was standing on the front porch hugging herself. I jumped out of the car and ran to her. She came down the steps, threw her arms around me, and buried her face against my chest. I held her tight against me. She was trembling.

"What's the matter, honey?"

"The machine," she whispered. "The goddam answering machine."

I took her hand and led her back inside. She wedged herself into the corner of the sofa and hugged her knees while I went to the answering machine. I pressed the button. The tape whirred. Then came a muffled man's voice: "You like swastikas, Miss Shaw? How would you like one of your very own?"

That was all.

I replayed the message. The voice sounded hollow, as if the man had whispered through a tube, and I didn't recognize it. He spoke slowly and distinctly, almost if he'd been reading his hateful little message, and I heard no noticeable accent.

I turned to Alex. "You don't recognize him, do you?"

She shook her head.

"What do you think?"

"I think," she said softly, "that if you'd minded your own business, this wouldn't have happened."

I went to the sofa and sat beside her. "I can't just . . ."

"I know, Brady. That's not fair. But . . ."

I put my arm around her, and she laid her head on my shoulder. "It's scary," she murmured.

"I'm sorry, honey," I said.

"I thought this was a nice little town," she said. She twisted her head to look up at me. "You better find the sick son of a bitch. Find him. Okay?"

"Sure," I said. "I'll find him."

TWELVE

A little after Alex slept in my arms, and the next morning when she woke up, she told me she was okay now. She'd received plenty of threats when she wrote investigative stuff for the *Globe*, she said, and nothing had ever happened, and she'd be damned if she'd let some asshole get to her now. People who left threats on answering machines were cowards, she said, and they didn't scare her. "I mean," she said, "poor Noah is dying. I should let some stupid phone message upset me?"

I figured she was trying very hard to be a brave, independent, tough-minded woman, and I admired her for it, even if I didn't share her feelings. I'd pegged Charlotte Gillespie as brave, independent, and tough-minded, and something had happened to her.

But I didn't mention that to Alex.

A little after seven o'clock, we were sipping coffee on the back deck when a car door slammed out front. A moment later a second door slammed. Alex glanced at her watch. "Who could that be? You don't think Noah and Susannah . . . ?"

"No," I said. "They wouldn't come without calling." I stood up. "I'll go see."

Alex glanced down at herself. She was still wearing her nightclothes—my old Property of the Yale University Department of

Athletics T-shirt and absolutely nothing else. "If it's for me," she said, "tell them I'm not presentable."

"You," I said, "are altogether too presentable."

I went back through the house to the front door and stepped out onto the porch. A dust-covered blue Ford pickup was pulled into the driveway and two men were standing beside my Jeep. One was a chunky guy wearing work boots, overalls, and a plaid shirt with the sleeves rolled up past his elbows. Stringy black hair stuck out from under his baseball cap. The other guy wore baggy blue jeans and a soiled white T-shirt. He was a little taller and a lot skinnier, and the stringy hair under his cap was pale yellow and hung down to his shoulders.

As I stood there on the porch, the dark-haired guy said to the other one, "No, sir, by the Jesus." His voice was heavy with anger. "And don't you sass me, boy."

"Well, shit," whined the skinny one. "I don't—"

The first man lifted his arm and balled up his fist, and the blond kid, who I now saw was a teenager, reflexively ducked away.

"Hey, there," I called. "Can I help you?"

They both looked in my direction. Then the dark-haired man grabbed the boy's arm, and the boy shook it off. I went down the steps and they came over and stood in front of me.

"Name's Norm," said the man. His face was creased and sunbaked. "Norman LeClair. This here's Paris. My no-good boy, damn him."

Neither of them offered to shake hands, so I didn't, either.

Norm turned to Paris, who, I saw, wore a hoop in his left ear and a tiny gold cross on a chain in his right. His yellow hair looked pale green where the sun hit it. It obviously had been dyed. A wispy brown mustache and goatee were trying to establish themselves around his small mouth, without much success.

"Well, go ahead, boy," said Norm.

Paris looked at his father with narrowed eyes, then turned to me. "I done it," he mumbled. He looked at Norm again, as if to say, "There. Satisfied?"

"That ain't all," said Norm.

94

Paris shifted his gaze to my feet. "I'll pay for it, sir," he said.

"You mean the swastika on my car?" I said.

"Yeah." Paris glanced quickly at Norm, then met my eyes and said, "I'm sorry. It was stupid."

"Why'd you do it?" I said.

Paris shrugged. "It was just stupid."

"Of course it was stupid. That doesn't answer my question."

"No reason," the boy mumbled.

I waited for him to say more. When he didn't, I turned to Norm and said, "Mind if I talk to him alone?"

Norm waved his hand. "Help yourself."

I touched Paris's arm. "Come over here for a minute."

We walked around to the side of the house. When I figured we were beyond Norm's hearing, I leaned close to Paris and looked straight into his eyes.

He glanced away.

"Look at me, son," I said.

He lifted his eyes, met mine, then let them slide away.

I grabbed his scrawny biceps and squeezed. "I said look at me."

This time his eyes held mine. "I told you I did it," he said, "and I told you I'd pay for it. Ain't that good enough?"

"No." I tightened my grip on his arm. "Do you know what that thing on my car is?"

"It's a swastika."

"Do you know what it symbolizes?"

He frowned. "Huh?"

"Do you know what a swastika means?"

"Sort of. They talked about it in school. It was on a flag or something. I hate history."

"I'm sure you do," I said. I leaned close to him so that our noses were almost touching. "Do you have some reason to hate me?"

He gave a little cynical laugh. "I don't even know you, mister. How can I hate you?" His eyes shifted to the side.

I squeezed his arm harder. "I told you to look at me," I said. "What about Charlotte Gillespie? Do you hate her?"

"Who?"

95

"You know who."

He shrugged. "I don't know anybody with that name."

"Then why'd you paint a swastika on her sign and her outhouse?"

"I told you. It was just—huh? What about an outhouse?"

"You know what I'm talking about."

He shook his head. His eyes held mine. "I admit I did that to your car," he said. "We were driving by and saw that sign, and then we saw that old Wrangler parked there under it. Weezie put me up to it. It was stupid. I was just showin' off." He shrugged. "I'm sorry, mister. I really am."

"Who's Weezie?"

"My girlfriend." He smiled quickly. "My old man—" He jerked his head in the direction of Norman, who was leaning against the side of my Jeep smoking a cigarette. "He thinks I'm queer because I wear earrings." He smiled. "But he's ignorant. Me and Weezie, see . . ." He arched his eyebrows.

"I get the picture," I said quickly.

"We're gonna get married," he said.

"Well, congratulations," I said, without trying to disguise the sarcasm in my voice. "Anyway, you're telling me you did not paint a swastika on that sign or the outhouse?"

"Yes, sir. I don't know nothin' about that." He shrugged. "I told you it was stupid. I was just—you know, showing Weezie what a hot shit I am."

I grabbed Paris's other arm, so that I was holding both of them. My hands went almost all the way around his biceps, and I squeezed them until I brought tears to his eyes. "Listen to me," I said. "I'm sick of your bullshit. I'll give you one minute. Then I'm going to call Sheriff Dickman. I'll press charges against you, and he'll arrest you, I promise. Understand?"

"I don't know what you want me to say."

"I want to know who painted the fucking swastikas on Charlotte Gillespie's property."

"Honest to Christ, mister," he said. "I didn't do it."

"Who, then?"

96

"I don't know. Fuck, man. You're hurting me."

I stared into his eyes for a moment. He held my gaze. If he was lying, he was good at it.

I let go of his arms. He reached up and began to rub them. "Tell you what," I said. "I'll hold off talking to the sheriff for a day or two. Meantime, suppose you check around, see what you can find out about those other swastikas. You get me some answers, I won't press charges. What do you say?"

"Sure. Okay." He gave me a quick smile. "I really am sorry about your car, man. It wasn't personal. I don't even know you."

I nodded. "I want to know if it was personal for whoever did those other ones. Understand?"

He nodded. "I'll see what I can find out. I promise."

"I just want a name," I said. "That's all. We got a deal?"

"I'll pay for your car."

"Bring me a name and you don't have to pay."

"I want to pay. It's my stupid thing, and I should pay."

I nodded. "Okay. I'll get it taken care of and let you know what it costs. But I still want that name."

He held out his hand. "It's a deal."

I took his hand. His grip was firm, and he held my eyes as we shook. "Come on," I said. "Let's talk to your father."

We went over to where Norm was standing. "We've worked it out," I said to him.

He glowered at Paris. "I didn't raise no goddam vandal," he said.

"He's going to take care of it," I said. "Do you have a VCR?"

"Huh?"

"Do you have—"

"Shit, I know what a VCR is. Course we got one. What about it?"

"I want you to rent a movie and sit Paris down and be sure he watches it. I want you to make him pay careful attention. And when it's over, rewind it and make him look at it again. Okay?"

Norman frowned. "You want him to watch a movie?"

"A particular movie," I said. "It's called *Schindler's List*, and it's a very good movie. You might enjoy it yourself."

Norman shrugged. "Whatever you say."

"After you've watched it," I said to Paris, "you come on over here and we'll talk about it."

"I've heard of that movie," he said.

"Yes. It won a lot of awards."

He turned to Norman. "I'm going to pay for the car."

"Damn right you are. *I* sure as hell ain't."

I held out my hand to Norm, who hesitated for a moment, then took it. "Thanks for coming over," I said. "You did the right thing."

"I don't like it," he said. "It ain't the way this boy was brought up, vandalizing someone's property."

"Especially with swastikas," I said.

Norman shrugged. "With whatever." He turned to Paris. "Come on, boy. You got a lot of work to do, you want to earn enough for this man to get his car painted."

They turned, went to the truck, and climbed in. As Norm started it up, Paris leaned out the window. "We got a deal," he said.

I waved and nodded, then watched as Norm backed out and rattled away.

I turned to the house and saw Alex standing on the porch. She had changed into shorts and one of her own T-shirts.

"What was that all about?" she said.

We went inside and I summarized my encounter with Norm and Paris LeClair as I poured myself another mug of coffee.

"Do you believe him?" she said.

"Paris?" I nodded. "Actually, I do. I could be wrong, but I don't think he did the other swastikas."

Alex frowned. "I don't get it, then. Who . . . ?"

"I don't get it, either. Young Paris LeClair did not strike me as an evil kid. He doesn't even know what a swastika is. I have the feeling that whoever painted the outhouse is evil."

She grinned. "*Schindler's List*. Aren't you clever?"

"Probably wasted on him." I shook my head. "Kids always seem to hate history. I know Billy and Joey did. They had teachers who pounded names and dates and battlefields into their brains, made them memorize the Preamble to the Constitution and the seven

98

causes of the Civil War and the twelve main exports of Bolivia, and damned if they could tell you what it feels like to risk your life for something you believe in. Or, for that matter, if they could tell you what it is they do believe in."

She patted my arm. "You should've been a teacher."

"Well, I'm hoping to teach something to young Paris LeClair."

THIRTEEN

꘎————————————꘎

I tried to call Sheriff Dickman to report the vile message on Alex's answering machine. He hadn't come in yet, so I left a message with the dispatcher, who said she expected him to check in soon.

Alex said she intended to put in a long day at her desk. "Find something to keep yourself busy," she said. "Like maybe tracking down the bastard who's leaving me messages."

"Will you be okay?" I said.

"I'll lock the doors and keep my phone and my can of Mace handy. I lived alone in Boston for twelve years, don't forget. I'm not afraid. I'm just mad. Don't worry about me. I can handle myself."

So a little after eight, I drove to Leon's store. I plucked a *Globe* from the rack and took it to the counter. Leon squinted at me as I paid him. "Had any visitors lately?" he said.

I nodded. "Norman Le Clair and his son Paris dropped in on me about an hour ago. Had the feeling you might've had something to do with it."

"I give it some thought," he said. "Remembered young Paris and that wiggly-butt girl of his gigglin' about something when they was in the other day. Something about spray paint." He shrugged.

"QED," I said.

"Sure," said Leon. "Whatever. So I had me a chat with Norm."

"Paris admitted he painted my car," I said, "but he swears he didn't do Charlotte Gillespie's sign or the outhouse."

"You believe him?"

"I'm inclined to. He didn't seem bright enough to be a good liar."

"Oh, he's bright, all right." Leon scowled. "I wouldn't trust that boy, with his yellow hair and them damn fool earrings."

I shrugged. "I could be wrong."

Leon shook his head slowly. "Well, if it ain't that boy, I don't know who it could be. I'll check with Pauline." He rolled his eyes. "That old witch hears everything and don't forget a thing."

"I appreciate your sending Norman and Paris over," I said.

He shrugged. "Just the neighborly thing, Mr. Coyne."

"Oh, that reminds me," I said. "Let me have a can of black spray paint."

"You want Rustoleum or the cheap stuff?"

"What's the difference?"

"Two bucks."

"What do you think?"

"Rustoleum for that Wrangler of yours. If I was you, I'd get me three cans, do the whole thing."

"One can," I said. "That car's not worth three."

After I left Leon's store, I headed over to the animal hospital. A chubby young woman sat behind the low counter talking on the telephone. She wore a white smock, and her curly blond hair was cut short and tight to her scalp. It looked like a helmet.

She had her mouth close to the phone and seemed to be whispering. She glanced at me, lifted a finger, then swiveled around, putting her back to me.

After a couple of minutes, she hung up and turned. "Can I help you?" She wore a plastic nameplate over her left breast. Betsy was her name.

"I'd like to talk to Dr. Spear."

"Laura's with an animal right now. Somethin' I can help you with?"

"Maybe," I said. "Actually, I'm looking for the assistant who returned Charlotte Gillespie's dog."

Betsy frowned. "Charlotte Gillespie?"

"The dog's name was Jack," I said. "He was a little yellowish puppy with a pointy nose. He'd been poisoned. It was about a week ago."

"Oh, yeah," she said. "He was cute. Wicked sick, though. He died."

"Yes, I know. Was that you?"

"Me?"

"Who returned the dog's body?"

"Why?" She looked up at me, then dropped her eyes. "Did I do something wrong?"

"No," I said. "I just want to know who came for the dog."

"He knew the dog's name," she said. "He said the owner had asked him to come for it. Laura said it was okay to give him the puppy."

"But he didn't give you his name."

"No. He just said he'd come to fetch the dead puppy."

"What did he look like?"

Betsy's eyes darted around the room as if she were looking for somebody to help her. They finally settled on her lap. "I don't remember," she mumbled. "I think he was wearing sunglasses and a hat."

"Was he young or old? Big or small? Fair or dark?"

She shook her head. "I can't remember at all." She looked up at me. "We were wicked busy, and I hardly noticed. I mean, I asked Laura—Dr. Spear—and she said it was okay to get the dog from the fridge and give it to the man, so that's what I did. I hardly even looked at him, you know?"

"You must remember something," I said.

"No," she said quickly. "I don't. Honest."

I nodded. I didn't believe her. It occurred to me that someone who'd leave a threatening telephone message might also find a way to scare a young woman like Betsy into forgetfulness. Betsy seemed frightened, and the last thing I wanted to do was endanger her.

"Well," I said, "thanks anyway." I took out one of my business cards, wrote Alex's phone number on it, and handed it to her. "If you remember anything, maybe you'd give me a call?"

She took the card, glanced at it, and slipped it into the pocket of her smock. "Sure," she said. She smiled quickly. "I'll think about it. But I doubt I'll remember anything."

I was back at Alex's wiping the dust off the swastika on my Wrangler when Sheriff Dickman's truck pulled into the driveway. He got out, opened the back door, reached in, and came out with a big grocery bag. He had to hug it in both of his arms. He looked my way, nodded, and said, "Mornin'." He took the bag to the front steps and put it down. Then he came over to me.

We shook hands. "What's in the bag?" I said.

"Just some stuff from the garden. Hope you can use it." He pointed his chin at my can of Rustoleum, which sat on the Wrangler's hood. "Looks like you're planning to cover up the evidence of a crime."

"The culprit has confessed," I said.

Dickman's eyebrows shot up.

"He did not confess to the No Trespassing sign or the outhouse door," I said. "An ignorant kid who has no idea what a swastika represents."

"Assuming your culprit is telling the truth."

"Yes," I said. "Assuming that."

"So is that why you called this morning?"

"No," I said. "Let's have some coffee. I'll tell you all about it."

Dickman followed me to the house. I hefted the bag of vegetables. I could barely lift it. "We'll be able to feed the whole town," I grunted.

"It'll all keep for a few days. Just don't put the tomatoes in the refrigerator. The cold sucks the sun-taste out of them."

He held the door for me. I put the bag of vegetables on the kitchen table, poured two mugs of coffee, and led him out onto the deck.

Dickman gazed out over the valley and woodlands. "Nice view," he said.

"We get some pretty sunsets," I said. I lit a cigarette and took a sip of my coffee. "Alex had a message on her answering machine last night."

"Huh? What kind of message?"

I repeated it to him.

"Good God," he muttered. "You didn't recognize the voice?"

"No. He whispered, and he spoke very slowly, as if he was reading it."

"I want that tape," said Dickman. "See if we can make anything out of it. How's your lady doing with it?"

"She seems okay today. She wasn't so hot last night." I took another drag from my cigarette. "I also talked with the girl who gave Charlotte's dog back. I figure it has to be the same guy who burglarized that animal hospital. She said it was a man wearing sunglasses and a hat, but claimed she couldn't remember what he looked like."

"Claimed?"

"I think she was lying. She seemed frightened."

I glanced at Dickman. He was smiling.

"What's funny?" I said.

"I bet you're one helluva lawyer, Mr. Coyne."

"Sure," I said. "I'm pretty good."

We sipped coffee and gazed off into the distance for a minute. Then I said, "Something's happened to Charlotte, Sheriff. From the looks of that cabin, she left in a big hurry."

"Or got taken away."

I nodded.

"No sign of a struggle or anything?"

I shook my head. "It just looked like she was reading quietly at the kitchen table and was interrupted."

Dickman nodded. "So you think someone went up there, grabbed her, and painted a swastika on her outhouse."

I shrugged. "Something like that, I guess."

"Or maybe she heard something and decided to skedaddle."

"I don't know what to think," I said. "But something happened."

"Maybe I should put the fear of the law in that spray painter."

I shook my head. "He promised to see what he could find out. Maybe we should give him a couple days."

"What about that girl at the vet's?"

"I don't know," I said. "She might talk to you."

"Sounds like I better go take a look at that cabin myself." Dickman took a sip of coffee, then turned to me. "Normally, I'd tell you to leave law enforcement to those of us who are paid to do it. You've been doing a helluva lot of snooping." He grinned. "I did some checking. You've been in some interesting scrapes, for a man who specializes in family law."

"You checked up on me?"

"I talked to a state police lieutenant down in Boston. Guy named Horowitz." He arched his eyebrows.

"Horowitz and I are acquainted," I said neutrally.

"He told me you were a pain in the ass," said Dickman. "I gathered he admired you. Anyway, I'm inclined to trust you. Work with you, if you're willing."

I held up a hand. "Whoa," I said. "I'm really worried about Charlotte Gillespie, yes. And I do not like having swastikas painted on my car, or threatening messages on my answering machine. But I'm no cop, Sheriff. I've got a busy law practice in Boston. I just come up here on weekends, and that's to spend time with Alex. I drive up on Friday nights and go back Sunday. When I'm here, it's to relax. I like to drive the back roads, chop some wood, do a little fishing. If you think . . ."

He was smiling at me. "Last I looked," he said, "today's Monday."

"Sometimes I stay an extra day."

"Heading back tonight, then?"

"Actually," I said, "I'm taking a couple extra days."

The sheriff nodded. "Horowitz said you couldn't resist getting involved. He also said you'd deny it. He said if it was him, he'd try to keep you in line, but he knew he couldn't." Dickman leaned toward me. "I don't know what we've got going on here," he said, "but I don't like it any more than you do. If I had my way, I'd put a full-timer on this situation and tell him to stay on it until he solved it. Preferably, that man would be me. But I also know that I'm spread all over York County, and I don't have anybody I can spare to investigate a case of petty vandalism."

"But it's hardly—"

He held up his hand. "I know. Swastikas. Plus a missing woman." He sighed. "Except she's not missing. No one's reported her missing. Except you, and you don't count. As far as anybody knows, she's just not home. How can I justify investigating that?" He shook his head. "That's the way it is."

"What about that message? And—"

"You have any idea how many reports of telephone threats we get every week?"

"Sure, but—"

"The point is, Mr. Coyne, the only actual criminal complaint we've received has been the vandalism of a very old and banged-up automobile, and we know who's responsible for that."

"I reported that telephone message to you."

"True. That you did. But—"

"You can't ignore it," I said.

He narrowed his eyes and stared at me for a moment. "You're absolutely right," he said. "I really have to do something." He pushed himself up from the rocker. "Stand up, please."

I looked up at him. "What?"

"I asked you to stand up."

I shrugged and stood up.

"Raise your right hand."

"Huh?"

"Do it."

I smiled and raised my right hand.

"Now," he said, "repeat after me. I, Brady Coyne, do solemnly promise—"

I lowered my hand. "Come on—"

"—to uphold the Constitution of the United States and the laws of the State of Maine, so help me God."

"Listen—"

"Just repeat those words, Mr. Coyne."

I shrugged, raised my right hand again, and repeated his words.

Dickman reached up, took my hand, and shook it. "Congratulations," he said. "Now you work for me." He took something from his pants pocket and handed it to me. It was a thin black leather folder, about the size of a small wallet. I flipped it open. It held a round silver badge with the words "Sheriff's Deputy, York County, Maine" on it, along with a four-digit number.

I looked up at him. "You're joking."

"We sheriffs don't joke about things like this," he said.

"I'm really a deputy?"

He nodded.

"Can I form a posse? Arrest outlaws? Shoot 'em if they draw on me?"

"You can't pick your nose without checking with me first. The pay is lousy—which is to say, nothing—and there are no benefits, unless you consider figuring out what's going on around here a benefit. You can quit anytime. Want to quit?"

I shook my head. "No, I guess not. This is a helluva nice badge."

"Keep it in your pocket. And remember. Now I am your boss. You do what I say, and if I say not to do something, you can't do it. If you learn anything, you've got to tell me. Got all that?"

"I got it," I said. I jiggled the badge in my hand. It had a pleasant weight to it. "Horowitz never tried to deputize me."

"Lieutenant Horowitz," said Dickman, "has never been elected high sheriff of York County." He drained his mug, then stood. "I've got to hit the road. Get me that tape."

Dickman followed me inside. I removed the little cassette from the answering machine and gave it to him, and we went out the front door. He climbed into his truck and started up the engine. Then he stopped and leaned out the window. "You forgot to give me the name of our spray painter."

I shook my head. "I didn't forget. I'm not going to tell you."

"You want to break the record for the shortest tenure as sheriff's deputy in the history of York County?"

"Look," I said. "He's just an ignorant kid. He didn't do the outhouse or the sign. He's going to try to find out who did. I

108

threatened to tell you, and that seemed to motivate him. Once I do tell you, we lose that motivation. So can we leave it that way for now, boss?"

"Ignorant kid, maybe," he grumbled. Dickman put the Explorer in gear. "Suppose you ought to know that we located the place where Ms. Gillespie used to live. It's in Falmouth, just north of Portland."

"How'd you manage that?"

"It took some pretty fancy police work." He smiled. "Looked her up in last year's phone book."

"Mighty clever. Did you search the place?"

"Search it for what?"

I shrugged. "Clues."

"Right," he said. "Clues. Of course." He rolled his eyes. "What we found out," he said, "is that the place is in a nice condo development. She was renting it. She's not living there anymore. It's all rented out to someone else now, so there's not much sense in searching it for clues. Anyhow, Falmouth is in Cumberland County. Out of my jurisdiction." He glanced at his wristwatch and frowned. "Listen," he said. "I do want to know what happened to her. See what you can find out, Deputy."

He backed down the driveway, waved out the window, and drove off.

I slipped my hand into my pants pocket and fished out the leather folder with my badge inside. It felt solid and important in my hand.

I couldn't wait to show it to Alex.

FOURTEEN

After the sheriff left, I gave the hood of my Wrangler two coats of black Rustoleum. Up close, you could still see the outline of the swastika, but from a distance it just looked like somebody had dumped a can of black paint on the hood.

Leon was right. I should've bought three cans and done the whole thing.

I waited until after lunch, when Alex and I were sitting on the deck sipping iced coffee. "Got something to show you," I said casually. I took the badge folder from my pocket, flipped it open, and held it in my palm.

She laughed. "Where'd you get that, from a Cheerios box?"

I handed it to her. "Just heft this sucker. It's made of real metal."

She took it and bounced it in the palm of her hand. "I'll be damned," she said.

"I've been formally deputized," I said. "Sheriff Dickman himself administered the solemn oath." I shook my head. "Cheerios box. Humph."

"Oh," Alex said, fluttering her hand over her heart. "A solemn oath." She shook her head. "Seriously, Brady."

111

"What do you mean, 'seriously'? There are serious things going on around here."

"I know," she said. "Of course there are. But a badge?"

I held out my hand and she put my badge in it. I stood up and slipped it into my pocket. "Well, I got work to do, woman."

She looked up at me and smiled. "Go git 'em, Deputy."

I went inside, found the portable phone, and sat at the kitchen table. I opened my wallet and fished out the business card that Charlotte had been using for a bookmark. Harrington, Keith & Co., Certified Public Accountants. I dialed the number.

A woman answered. "William Keith," she said. "This is Ellen. How may I direct your call?"

"Is this the accounting firm?"

"Yes, sir."

"I'm looking for Harrington, Keith and Company."

"You've got the right place, sir. Mr. Harrington retired. Our name is now William Keith and Company."

"Oh, dear," I said. "How long has Mr. Harrington been gone?"

"Over a year. Can we help you?"

I tried to think. Charlotte Gillespie's bookmark was old and outdated. Suddenly, this business card did not appear to be such a great clue.

But I'd come this far. I decided to push forward anyway. "Well, actually," I said, "I'd like to speak with Charlotte Gillespie, please."

"I'm sorry, sir. Ms. Gillespie is no longer with the company."

"But this is where she worked?"

"Oh, yes. She was with us for over two years."

"Boy, I'm really behind the times," I said. "Do you happen to know how I might reach Ms. Gillespie?"

"I'm sorry. I don't."

"Can you tell me when she left you?"

She hesitated. "Several months ago. May I connect you to someone else, sir?"

"Thank you anyway," I said, and hung up.

I sat there smiling. The sheriff had been smart to deputize me. I was a helluva deputy. I didn't know if it would help me actually find Charlotte, but I knew my duty. I had a case to pursue, and I had to follow every lead, however slim.

I poked my head out onto the deck. Alex was sitting there in her rocking chair with her eyes closed. "Hey," I whispered.

Her eyes fluttered open. She turned her head and smiled. "Hey," she said.

"Wanna go to the big city?"

"New York?"

"Would you settle for Portland?"

"Why?"

"I gotta do some sleuthing."

She pushed herself out of the rocking chair. "It sounds almost like a date," she said.

By asking directions, we found the street in downtown Portland where the William Keith accounting firm was located. I left the car in a parking lot, and Alex and I agreed to meet in an hour at a little café on the corner. She said she intended to go buy herself a frock.

I found the Keith offices in a newish glass-fronted building halfway down a steep hill, on the ocean side. At the foot of the hill stood a row of old brick warehouses that had been renovated into chic bistros and boutiques. Portland, Maine, like Newburyport, Massachusetts, and Portsmouth, New Hampshire, and other old New England cities with "port" in their names, had enjoyed resurgences over the past twenty-five years after a century or more of decline and neglect. Nowadays, these old seafaring deep-harbor cities capitalize on their settings. They thrive on high-tech industry and yuppie trade, and it takes a lot of accountants to keep them going.

William Keith occupied a suite of offices on the first floor. I opened the glass door and stepped into a waiting room decorated with hanging ferns and low-backed sofas and glass-topped coffee tables strewn with *Forbes* and *Business Week* magazines. A string quartet played softly from hidden speakers, and a back-lit aquarium was built into one wall. A receptionist behind a large desk guarded the gateway to the inside offices where, I assumed, an army of accountants marched numbers around on their computer screens.

Her name, according to the plaque on her desk, was Mrs. Sanderson. She had dark hair with some gray in it piled up on her head, reading glasses perched out toward the tip of her nose, and, when I approached her, a well-practiced smile. "Yes, sir? Can I help you?"

"I'm looking for Charlotte Gillespie."

She plucked her glasses off her nose and frowned. I noticed that Mrs. Sanderson did not wear a wedding ring. "Are you the gentleman who called earlier?"

"Yes, I am."

"I believe I told you, Ms. Gillespie no longer works here."

"You did say that, yes. I'm trying to track her down. It's rather important."

"I don't think anybody here knows where she went. We haven't seen her since—oh, back in June sometime."

"Did she quit?"

"Well . . ." She looked up at me and shrugged.

"She was fired," I said.

"Look, Mr.—"

"Coyne," I said. "Brady Coyne."

She nodded. "I really can't talk about it."

"Who can?"

She hesitated for a moment, then said, "Is Charlotte in some kind of trouble?"

" 'Danger,' " I said, "would be a better word for it."

She cocked her head and frowned at me. Then she nodded. "Why don't you have a seat. I'll see if Mr. Keith can talk to you."

"Thank you," I said. I sat on one of the sofas, picked up a copy of *Down East* magazine, and thumbed through it while Mrs. Sanderson spoke softly into the telephone.

After a minute she hung up and said, "Mr. Keith will be able to see you in a minute."

"I appreciate it," I said.

Nearly fifteen minutes later a tall athletic man in his fifties

114

emerged from the offices and approached me. "Mr. Coyne, is it?" he said.

I stood up and held out my hand. "Brady Coyne," I said.

We shook. "Bill Keith," he said. "Come on in."

I followed him past Mrs. Sanderson's desk, through an open room full of copy machines and file cabinets, and into a large corner office. Half a dozen diplomas hung behind his desk, and a shoulder-high bookcase was stuffed with manila file folders, three-ring note-books, and dull-looking volumes similar to the books of case law that lined the shelves in my own office back in Copley Square. On top of the bookcase stood a large framed photograph of a Labrador retriever holding a dead duck in its mouth. A considerably smaller photo—a posed K Mart portrait—showed William Keith about twenty years younger standing with a plain-looking woman and two small boys.

Keith sat behind his desk. I took the straight-back chair opposite him. He leaned forward on his forearms. "Ellen said you were looking for Charlotte Gillespie. She indicated that Ms. Gillespie could be in some sort of trouble."

"Danger," I said. "I used the word 'danger.' "

"Perhaps you could elaborate."

I shook my head. "I couldn't, actually."

"You're a friend of hers, then?"

"This is not personal, Mr. Keith." What the hell, I thought. I slid my deputy's badge from my pocket, flipped open the leather holder, and showed it to him.

He squinted at it, then looked up at me. "How do I know that—"

"Mr. Keith," I said quickly, "this is an urgent matter. I really don't have time to argue with you. If you'd like to call my boss, feel free." I took Sheriff Dickman's card from my wallet and put it on the desk.

He picked it up, looked at it, and put it down. "What do you want to know?" he said.

"Did Charlotte quit, or was she fired?"

"We, um, we accepted her resignation."

"You asked for it?"

He nodded.

"So she was fired," I said. "Why?"

"Her clients complained about her work. They threatened to take their business elsewhere."

"They?" I said. "Several clients?"

"One client, actually," he said. "An important client."

"She was incompetent?"

Keith gazed out his window for a minute. "She was a very good accountant, Mr. Coyne. We'd never had anything but praise for her work." He shrugged. "But . . ."

"One client complains and you fire her?"

"They were quite upset. We're in a very competitive business here in Portland, Mr. Coyne. This client is in a position to . . ." He waved his hand.

"I understand," I said. "So this very competent accountant has a problem with one client and she's fired. She must have done something terrible."

"I can't talk about that," said Keith.

"Who is this client?"

He shook his head. "I certainly can't tell you that, Mr. Coyne."

"No, of course not. I'd need a subpoena for that information." I let the implications of that bluff sink in for a minute, then said, "Actually, that wouldn't be necessary if I could find her. You don't have any idea how I might do that, do you?"

"She lives in Falmouth," he said. "I assume—"

"She doesn't live there anymore."

He shrugged. "In that case, I can't help you. I'm sorry."

"Me, too." I plucked a pen from the mug on his desk, slid a notepad toward me, and wrote my name with Alex's phone number on it. I turned the pad around and pushed it to him. "If you think of something or have a change of heart, you can reach me here. Otherwise, you'll probably be hearing from me again." I stood up and held my hand across the desk to William Keith. "Thank you for your time. I can find my way out."

He half stood and shook my hand, and I went to the door. I put my hand on the knob, then turned to him. "Oh, by the way," I said. "You don't hunt deer, do you?"

116

"Of course I do." He smiled. "Everyone hunts deer."

"Been doing it for a while, have you?"

"All my life," he said. "My father started taking me when I was a kid. Shot my first whitetail when I was twelve. Little spikehorn, about a hundred pounds." He smiled. "Dad smeared its blood on my face and made me take a sip of brandy."

"Do you hunt alone or with friends?"

He cocked his head, and his smile faded. "With friends, usually. Why?"

"Ever hunt around Garrison?"

"Garrison?"

I nodded.

"I've hunted that area a little."

"Do you rent a cabin in Garrison?"

He shook his head. "I don't rent a cabin anywhere, Mr. Coyne."

I nodded. "Thanks, Mr. Keith."

I went out into the reception area and nodded at Mrs. Sanderson, who smiled and said, "Is everything all right?"

"You mean Charlotte?"

She nodded.

"I don't think she's all right," I said. "I think something's happened to her. That's why I'm here."

She frowned, then jerked her chin back in the direction of William Keith's office. "Did you . . . um . . . was it helpful?"

I put my hands on her desk and leaned to her. "Mrs. Sanderson," I said. "Were you a friend of hers?"

She nodded. "Yes," she said softly. "I liked her very much. We used to have supper together on Fridays after work. We're both divorced, and . . ." She shrugged, as if that explained it, which it pretty much did.

I took out one of my business cards, wrote Alex's phone number on the back of it, underlined it twice, and put it on her desk.

She picked it up, glanced at both sides of it, then pushed it away from her. She rolled her eyes back in the direction of William Keith's office. "I just can't," she said softly.

"Charlotte Gillespie is renting a cabin in the woods," I said. "She's been missing for several days. Her dog was poisoned. Someone's making swastikas on her property. I'm trying to find her. I believe something has happened to her. Or might happen to her." I dropped my voice. "I'd like to talk to you."

She looked up at me. "I—"

At that moment, William Keith opened the door. "Oh," he said. "You're still here, Mr. Coyne." He grinned. "Flirting with the help, eh?"

I straightened up and shrugged. "I was just on my way." I looked at Mrs. Sanderson. "It was nice talking to you."

She nodded, and as I turned to go I saw her reach casually across her desk, cover my business card with her hand, and draw it back under some papers.

FIFTEEN

A lex was waiting inside the café when I got there. She was sipping something tall and amber through a straw.

I slid into the chair across from her. It was one of those tippy wrought-iron things with a hard round metal seat. The table had matching wrought-iron legs and a glass top about as big around as a straw hat. The furniture matched the cute-old-fashioned-ice-cream-shoppe decor of the place—hammered aluminum ceiling, checkered black-and-white-tile floor, mirrors and framed *New Yorker* covers on the walls, with several signs in fancy calligraphy that read: "Thank You for Not Smoking."

"What're you drinking?" I said.

"Iced tea. I'm almost done. Let's get out of here."

"Where's your new frock?"

She tipped up the glass and sucked the iced tea from the bottom, making gurgling noises through the straw. "No frock," she mumbled. "I don't want to talk about it." She set the glass down, fumbled in her purse, then dropped a five-dollar bill on the table. "Let's go."

"You don't want to wait for your change?"

"Change?" She blew out a quick laugh. "You know what a glass of iced tea costs in this place?"

"I don't think I want to know. I guess you've got to pay for the ambiance. Those are very classy No Smoking signs."

We walked out, and I took Alex's hand. "What about dinner? I bet we can find a place somewhere in this city that has comfortable chairs and big tables."

She squeezed my hand and gave me a halfhearted smile. "Can we just go home? I know I'm being a grouchy old poop, but really, all I want to do is change into shorts and a T-shirt and bare feet and grill some burgers and drink some beer. I think I'll hang myself if Noah and Susannah interrupt us tonight."

"Home it shall be," I said. "And we will decline all social invitations."

"I'm sorry," she said. "Are you disappointed? Did you really want to go to a restaurant?"

"Hell, no. They've all got No Smoking signs."

During the hour it took us to drive back to Garrison, I told her about my interview with William Keith.

"You actually flashed your badge at him?" she said.

"You betcha. Put the fear of the law in him, I did."

"But he didn't tell you anything."

"Valid point. Still, I could tell he was impressed. I think the receptionist, Mrs. Sanderson, knows something. She was friends with Charlotte, and I think I convinced her that Charlotte is in trouble. I cleverly slipped her your phone number. She hasn't even seen the badge yet. That's my ace in the hole."

"Move over, Wyatt Earp," she said.

After we got home, I went onto the deck to get the charcoal started. When I went back into the kitchen, Alex was standing at the counter making the salad. A bottle of Sam Adams stood beside her. I fetched a hunk of ground sirloin from the refrigerator and took it to the table.

I glanced at her. She was slicing an onion. Her eyes were red. "What's the matter?" I said. "Are you crying?"

"I'm peeling a Bermuda onion, for Christ's sake." She wiped her eyes with her forearm.

120

"Oh."

"Okay, goddammit. I have been sort of crying."

"Sort of?"

"Shit. Crying. Okay?"

I went to where she was standing at the counter and put my arm around her shoulder. "What's the matter?" I said.

"Nothing. Nothing new. You know."

I sighed. "I guess I do."

She shrugged. "It is what it is. You drop in, you stay awhile, and you leave. We talk long-distance on the phone a couple times during the week. Then you drop in again."

"Whose fault is that?"

Her head snapped up. "What's that supposed to mean?"

I took my arm off her shoulder. "It wasn't me who moved to Maine."

She cocked her head and peered at me through narrowed eyes. "I thought we had a commitment," she said.

"We did. We do. We are keeping it. I think we're doing okay under the circumstances."

She nodded. "Yeah, well, I guess the circumstances are getting to me. I mean, even when we have an afternoon together, we're not together."

"You mean the Charlotte thing."

"Yes, the Charlotte thing, and the Susannah and Noah thing. Visiting Arnold Hood and driving to Portland. Those kinds of things. Tomorrow you're going back to Boston, and . . ." She sat down at the table and hugged herself.

"No, I'm not," I said.

"You're not?"

"No. You think I'd let you stay here alone with somebody leaving you threats on the telephone?"

"I can take care of myself, Brady. I took care of myself just fine before I met you."

"I know. I'm staying anyway. I'm going to stay until this is settled."

She looked up at me and shook her head. "The big deputy." She laughed quickly. "Jesus."

"Look," I said. "As soon as we get this business straightened out, let's just take off for a weekend. We can drive up to Acadia. It's great this time of year, after the tourists are gone. We can climb around the rocks at the top of Mount Desert, find us a funky lobster shack, eat a bushel of steamers and a couple of boiled lobsters with big gobs of potato salad and several ears of corn on the cob and a few bottles of cold beer, then crash in a bed-and-breakfast and sleep till noon. We can leave our watches and compasses home, just follow our noses, do whatever we feel like doing whenever we feel like it, no schedule, no goals, and . . ."

I let my voice trail away. Alex had pulled her hand away from mine, folded her arms on the table, and lowered her head to them.

"Bad idea, I guess," I said.

"No," she mumbled into the tabletop. "It's a lovely idea. Except I have to work every day."

"You don't have to. You're the boss. Give yourself a day off. You've earned it."

She lifted her head. Her eyes glistened. "You don't understand, Brady. I'm a very cruel boss. I give absolutely no benefits to my employees. If they ever figured out what they make per hour, they'd quit. I hound them unmercifully. No praise. No rewards for a job well done. Just criticism. I'm always on the verge of firing them. I'm a master at making them feel guilty if they even think about goofing off. The only way they can keep me off their backs is by working hard every single goddam day. Anything else and I make their lives miserable. They know it's not worth it. That's why my employees are so damned compulsive and stressed-out." She sighed heavily. "That's why this book is actually gonna get done. Because I beat the shit out of myself every day. That's why."

"Is this by way of explaining why you didn't buy yourself a new dress today?" I said.

She shrugged. "I guess so. I'm wandering around Portland while you're off sleuthing, and all the time I'm thinking, Where the hell is Brady? Why isn't he here with me? And I'm also thinking that if I were more responsible, I'd be back at my computer writing my goddam book. Shopping for a stupid dress seemed so—so frivolous. So, yes. It's by way of explaining a lot of things, I guess. Why

I'm such a bitch, mainly." She held her hand across the table to me, and when I took it, she said, "I'm sorry. It's just that sometimes—"

At that moment the phone began to ring.

We looked at each other. Alex arched her eyebows.

"Let the machine get it," I said.

She shrugged, pushed back her chair, reached to the counter behind her, and picked up the kitchen extension. She said, "Hello," then paused, frowned for a minute, and handed it to me.

I mouthed the word "who."

She shrugged, then stood up and walked out of the room.

I put the phone to my ear and said, "This is Brady Coyne."

"It's Ellen Sanderson."

"Thanks for calling. Do you—?"

"Like I told you," she said quickly, "Charlotte is my friend. I want to help."

"Well, good."

"Can you meet me?"

"Of course. When?"

"Tomorrow. After work. Say around six?"

"Okay. Name the place."

"There's a clam shack on the Scarborough River, right near where it empties into the bay. There's a parking lot and a boat launch there. You take Route 1 south from Portland and follow the signs to Pine Point."

"I'll find it," I said.

"Look," she said. "I've gotta go."

The phone clicked in my ear.

I hung up, then found a scrap of paper and scribbled "Pine Point" and "Scarborough River" and "Route 1" and "Tuesday, 6:00" on it before I forgot.

SIXTEEN

I found Alex in her office peering at her computer through her big round glasses. I leaned over the top of the bookcase partition and said, "How about those burgers?"

"Let me know when they're ready," she said. She hit a couple of keys, then leaned forward as words scrolled down the screen.

I was dismissed.

I went back to the kitchen, rummaged among the herbs and spices, and selected, more or less randomly, dried sage and basil. I sprinkled some of each onto the meat, added some salt and fresh-ground pepper, then picked up the one-pound glob of chopped sirloin and kneaded it in my fingers. I divided it in half, shaped each half into a ball, then pressed and patted each ball into a thick patty, which I put on a platter. Then I cut two thick slices of extra-sharp cheddar and four slices from a loaf of Italian bread. I slathered one side of the bread slices with butter, sprinkled garlic salt and paprika on them, and piled the bread on the platter, too.

The charcoal was glowing red in the grill on the deck. I laid the two patties on it, then sat in one of the rockers. The sun had set in the west, where it always does, and the pink was fading from the low cloudbank off toward New Hampshire. I lit a cigarette. A friendly bat swooped and fluttered overhead. Every mosquito he nailed was one that wouldn't ram its proboscis into the back of my neck.

Alex was inside. Sulking, I figured. Angry with me, angry with herself. When she was angry, she retreated to her book.

She didn't think it was working.

Maybe she was right. It had been so long since I'd been in a relationship that worked that I'd lost my perspective. How much conflict and discontent could there be in a relationship that still qualified as Good? How good did it have to be before you could confidently and unequivocally call it Good?

Damned if I knew. To me, it was working. But maybe, after years of having no relationship whatsoever, I had no standards.

I snapped my cigarette butt into the yard, got up, and flipped over the burgers. I laid the cheese slices on top of the patties, then put the four slices of bread around the edges of the grill. I kept turning the bread over and moving it around the grill while the burgers cooked and the cheese melted. After years of trial and error, I knew that when the toast was golden brown, the burgers would be pink—but not red—on the inside.

My culinary repertoire is pretty much limited to bachelor necessity. I can heat up a can of baked beans or Dinty Moore beef stew with the best of them, and I'm pretty good with eggs. Grilled burgers with melted cheddar cheese on toasted garlic bread is my specialty.

By the time I slid it all onto the platter, darkness had seeped into the backyard and a whole flock of bats were darting around overhead.

I went inside. "Food," I called to Alex.

"Coming," she answered.

"Beer?"

"Please."

I snagged two bottles from the refrigerator, found a couple of frosted mugs in the freezer, and managed a perfect head when I poured them. Beer from a bottle. Another specialty of mine.

Alex came in and sat at the table. "Yum," she said.

I kissed her cheek, then sat across from her. She spread catsup on her burger and took a big bite. "Delish," she mumbled.

We ate in silence for a few minutes. Then Alex said, "Something's been bothering me, Brady."

"I know," I said. "We can work it out."

She shook her head. "No. Not that. Charlotte Gillespie. She told you she knew me, remember?"

I nodded.

"But I don't know her. Never laid eyes on her, I'm certain of it. From your description, I wouldn't have forgotten her. An African-American woman in Garrison?" She shook her head. "But something niggled at me. And I finally figured it out. That's what I was doing just now."

"What were you doing?"

"Figuring it out."

"I thought you were sulking," I said.

"Not this time." She dabbed at her mouth with her napkin. "I just went through some old files in my computer. I found what I was looking for, and I was right. I've never seen her. But I did talk with her on the phone. It was the name Charlotte that niggled at me. She never said her last name. She called me about my series in the *Globe*. Said it was the first thing she'd ever read on the subject of abuse that rang true to her. I got the distinct impression that she knew a great deal about the subject, but when I told her I was doing a book on it and was interested in interviewing victims, she backed off."

"You sure this is the same Charlotte?" I said.

She shrugged. "I remember her voice had a Smoky Mountains twang to it. But the reason I'm sure it was her is that she told me she lived in Maine, and I remember thinking it seemed odd for someone with her accent. I inferred that whatever her situation had been, she'd escaped it, gone to Maine, and started a new life for herself." Alex peered up at me. "Now here's the really strange thing. This whole conversation happened over a year ago, when I was still living on Marlborough Street."

"Before you moved up here."

"Yes. Before I even started looking for places."

"I don't get it."

"When I realized that she was reluctant to talk about her situation," said Alex, "I changed the subject. You know. To relax her. I mentioned that I was planning to move to a quiet country place to work on the book. When I told her I was thinking about New Hampshire, that I wanted someplace within a couple hours of Boston, she mentioned southwestern Maine. Said she knew an area that was prettier and quieter and cheaper than New Hampshire."

"Garrison?" I said.

"Yes," said Alex. "She specifically mentioned Garrison. And so when I began looking for places, I checked out this area, and . . ."

"*Voilà*," I said. "You're here because of Charlotte."

She nodded. "Thing of it is, we know she wasn't living here then. She was living in Falmouth and working in Portland."

"But this is where she came when she got fired."

"Yes. Garrison is a perfect place to hide out, she said. Those were almost her exact words. A perfect place to hide out. Anyway, the point of it all is, I'm sure from what she said that she'd been abused. That she fled that situation and went to Portland and made a new life for herself."

"Then she fled to Garrison," I said, "and now she's missing. And you think her abusive husband—"

"—or boyfriend or whatever—"

"—tracked her down and . . ."

She nodded. "The legacy of abuse. It's got to be the same Charlotte, don't you think?"

"Unquestionably," I said. I took a bite of my burger, then a sip of beer. "That was excellent detecting, lady. I will suggest to Sheriff Dickman that he should deputize you."

Alex smiled.

"All the time, I thought you were in there being mad at me."

"Oh, I was," she said. "But mainly I was detecting. Computers are excellent for detecting. It's a good thing I'm compulsive about entering all my notes. I typed the word 'Charlotte' and sent my machine on a find mission, and there it was."

I told Alex about my conversation with Ellen Sanderson and my plan to meet her at six the next evening.

"Sounds deliciously clandestine." She smiled. "It's too bad you don't have the same enthusiasm for your law practice that you do for—"

I slapped the side of my head with my palm. "Oh, shit," I said. "Julie. I was supposed to call Julie. She'll kill me."

"If there was something urgent, she knows this number."

"Yeah, but that's not the point."

"The point being," said Alex, "Julie thinks you're irresponsible as it is, and this just confirms it. And despite the fact that you are, in fact, irresponsible, you don't like it when your behavior confirms it."

"Yeah," I grumbled. "Something like that."

After we finished eating and cleaned up the kitchen, I took a deep breath and called Julie at home. When I explained that I'd been out all day on important business, that I was sorry I hadn't been able to call, that it had weighed heavily on my mind the whole time, and that this was the absolute first chance I'd had, she replied with silence.

"Okay," I said. "So I forgot. But then I remembered."

"Well," she said, "nothing happened except that Mr. Jackson and Dr. Adams called, and they both want to go fishing."

"What'd J. W. say? Have the blues started blitzing on the Vineyard?"

"Something to that effect," said Julie.

"What about Doc? What'd he have to say?"

"Oh, he mentioned trout. Sounded wistful. Hardly flirted with me at all."

"That's not like Doc," I said. "I'll call both of 'em when I get back. Which, by the way, won't be at least till next week. See, I've got something—"

"*What?*"

"I said—"

"I heard what you said, Brady." She let out a long dramatic sigh. "I give up. Cancel the rest of the week, right?"

"Reschedule. You know the drill."

She laughed. "Rescheduling clients? That is a drill I know very well."

I found myself smiling. "I expected you to be really upset."

"I saw this coming," she said.

"You did? I didn't."

"I know you better than you do," she said.

I found Alex in a rocker on the deck. I plopped down in the chair beside her and reached for her hand. She held on and we rocked there in silence, watching the bats play on the edges of the floodlit yard.

After a while, I said, "Well, I talked with Julie. We're all set."

"Bet she gave you some shit, huh?"

"Hardly at all, actually. Julie knows me. Said she expected it."

"I'm glad someone knows you," she mumbled.

"We'll take that weekend," I said.

"Promise?"

"Promise," I said. And as I said it, I remembered a lifetime of broken promises and unfulfilled commitments. This seemed like a promise that I'd better keep.

We rocked and held hands and stared off into the darkness, and after a few minutes, Alex said, "You'd better not let me down."

It was spooky how Alex, just like Julie—and, come to think of it, like Gloria, my ex-wife, and like Sylvie Szabo and Terri Fiori and, for that matter, like just about every woman I'd been involved with—how they all seemed to know exactly what I was thinking.

"I know you better than you do," Julie had said. If women understood me so well, how come I never seemed to have the foggiest idea of what was going on in their minds?

SEVENTEEN

⋙━━━━━━━━━━━━━━━━⋘

I'd just started on my second mug of coffee the next morning when Sheriff Dickman called. "I'll pick you up around noon," he said.

"Where're we going?"

"I'll fill you in when I get there. Good-bye." And he hung up. A busy man.

I had the morning to kill, so I decided to go back to Charlotte's cabin, look around again. Maybe she'd even be there. I doubted it, but it was worth trying. While I was up there, I'd take a look at Cutter's Run, the stream that divided Arnold Hood's property from Noah Hollingsworth's.

I never visit water without a fly rod. Maybe some wild brook trout had taken up residence in the pond the beavers had built. So I tossed an old fiberglass stick and my fishing vest into the back of the Wrangler and drove the back roads to Charlotte Gillespie's cabin. I turned in at the No Trespassing sign with the swastika, switched into four-wheel drive, and crept the Wrangler along the ruts to the place where the boulders in the dry streambed blocked the roadway. I parked there and carried my rod and vest the rest of the way up the hill. I walked all around the cabin and checked the outhouse. Everything looked exactly as it had the last time I'd been there.

I went to the front door of the cabin and pushed it open. "Charlotte?" I called. "Are you home?"

There was no answer. I went inside and looked around.

Nothing had changed except that the place seemed even emptier than it had before.

So I carried my rod down the sloping meadow through thigh-high grass and goldenrod and clumps of juniper to the flooded alders and poplars in the crease between the hills.

The beaver pond was shallow and brushy around the edges, and it smelled of mud and decay. Gnawed-off stumps poked up through the water here and there, but I could see where it deepened toward the middle. The stream's channel looked as if it might hold a pretty native brook trout or two.

The deepest part would be down at the foot of the pond. I could kneel on the beaver dam and cast into the good-looking water and, if I was lucky, catch a trout and still keep my feet dry. So I began to circle downstream along the edge of the pond.

I noticed that no lily pads grew in the water, a sign that the pond had been created fairly recently. New beaver ponds usually make better trout water than old ones, because after a few years they begin to fill with silt. They grow shallow and warm and acidic and weedy, and then they no longer provide good habitat for brook trout.

A new beaver pond, on the other hand, is cold and clear and clean, a trout fisherman's treasure. And this appeared to be a fairly new one.

It took me ten or fifteen minutes to weave my way through the briars and alders and fallen tree trunks and mud and mosquitoes to the dam. It was about thirty feet across and nearly five feet high, an amazing piece of engineering, as are all beaver dams. The sticks, branches, and twigs from hundreds of poplars and alders were woven together so tightly and intricately that they held back the unrelenting force of moving water to create a pond deep enough for beavers to build their lodges and raise their young in safety.

The beavers had taken advantage of what they'd found. They'd braced the end of their dam against a big hunk of old concrete that was half embedded in the earth beside the stream. Susannah had said that old man Cutter, for whom the run was named, had operated a tannery on its banks, and that it had used waterpower to turn its machinery. Cutter undoubtedly had used the stream itself to flush away his tanning chemicals and animal parts and anything else he wanted to get rid of, too. That was standard practice in those days, and it might've killed the trout that lived downstream of the tannery. In those days, nobody cared.

That old milldam must have been right here, and the remains of it had given the smart beavers a solid anchor for their own dam.

When I scrambled up onto it, I was able to see that it had backed the water up for a hundred feet or so. The pond, I guessed, covered nearly an acre. The beaver lodge was constructed of woven sticks and mud, like the dam, and it sat in the water off toward Noah Hollingsworth's side of Cutter's Run.

Back through the stumps and trees that poked out of the water on that side, I spotted several hunks of half-submerged crumbling concrete, a section of foundation, and a couple of crumbling brick chimneys. The ruins of Cutter's tannery, I assumed, now half submerged under the beaver pond. A historic place in Garrison, Maine. An archaeological site.

I saw no beavers, which did not surprise me. They would've heard me moving through the woods and slipped into the sanctuary of their lodge through its underwater entry, where they would remain hidden and safe until I left.

The pond's surface was flat and glassy. I squatted there atop the dam to study it. I hoped to see the dimple and ring of a trout sipping an insect off the surface. I saw a few mayflies and damselflies sitting on the water. There were plenty of mosquitoes clouding over it, too.

But for the length of time it took me to smoke a cigarette and belatedly slather some insect repellent on the back of my neck, I saw no evidence that a trout lived there.

I dipped my hand into the water and guessed its temperature to be around sixty. Ideal for brook trout.

As I sat there in the silence of the late-August morning gazing at the pond's smooth skin, I became aware of the gurgle of running water. Beaver dams, of course, are not designed to hold back every drop that flows down a stream. Enough water seeps through the interlaced twigs of even the tightest dam to allow the stream, although greatly diminished in volume, to continue along its course. An absolutely watertight dam, no matter how sturdy it was, would eventually burst from the ever-growing pressure of the water accumulating behind it. Beavers understand hydraulic engineering well enough to build safety valves into their structures.

But when I looked along the length of this dam, I saw that down toward the other end the water had broken a V-shaped chunk out of the top and was cascading through, spilling in a little waterfall to the streambed downstream.

This fissure in the dam, I figured, was slowly draining the pond. It explained the wet mud around the rim. The break was so recent that the mud had not yet dried and hardened. All the relentless force of the held-back pond was focused on this weak point. As gravity pulled on it from downstream, the water would eat away at that vulnerable spot, making it bigger and bigger and releasing more and more water until, if the beavers didn't repair it, it would blow out the dam.

Now the stream below the dam was only six or eight feet across. I judged by the dry rocks and mud that bordered it that it was normally twelve to fifteen feet wide.

I tight-roped my way across the top of the dam to the breach in it. When I knelt down to look at it, I saw the water tear a couple of twigs loose from the dam and carry them away. At this rate, the dam would be blown out the first time a big rainstorm swelled the stream. The pond would then cease to exist, and Cutter's Run would again be twelve or fifteen feet wide, as it had been before the beavers had chosen it for their homesite.

And then it occurred to me that the beavers must have already abandoned their pond and all the labor they had invested in it, because if they still lived here, they would have kept their dam repaired. The legends don't exaggerate. Beavers work hard, and building and tending their dams and lodges is their main job.

I wondered what had happened. A community of beavers eventually eat all the bark and twigs in an area, and then they must move on. But they're smart enough to choose homesites that provide a long-term food supply, and there still seemed to be plenty of delicious poplar trees and alder bushes for them around the edges of this pond. Maybe a persistent predator—a bobcat or a pack of coyotes, or even Charlotte Gillespie's dog or housecats—had convinced them that this was an unsafe place to live. Or maybe a predator had actually killed them.

Beavers are a vital part of Mother Nature's grand ecological scheme. They create wetlands, vital habitat for countless species of flora and fauna. But when beavers build their dams near human civilization, their ponds tend to flood roads and backyards and cellars and septic systems. They contaminate water supplies. Then state fish and wildlife experts are called in to trap them and dynamite their dams.

This beaver pond did not threaten anybody's water supply. Somebody might've trapped the beavers, but no one had destroyed the dam.

Whatever had happened to the animals, their dam was disintegrating, and the pond they had made would eventually disappear. If I was to catch a trout from it, now was the time.

I slipped a fly box from my vest and selected a size 14 Adams, a generic gray-brown floating pattern that vaguely resembled a lot of different insects without looking precisely like anything. An Adams is usually close enough to tempt wild brook trout, which are always beautiful and spooky, but which are not noted for being fussy eaters. I tied the fly to my leader, checked behind me for trees that might snag my backcast, and flicked it out onto the glassy water. It landed as softly as milkweed fuzz, but I knew that any nearby trout would spot it and cruise closer for a better look. I imagined a trout darting toward my fly, then slowing and hovering, suspended directly beneath it, its body tilted slightly upward, its nose just millimeters under it, trying to decide whether to eat it.

Cautiously I tightened my line and gave the fly a tiny twitch. It's alive, I was saying to that trout. Eat, quick, before it flaps its little wings and escapes.

No trout poked its nose through the water's surface and sipped in my fly. After a couple more twitches, I lifted it from the water and cast again, this time beyond where my first cast had landed, so that it would get the attention of any trout that had not seen it where it had settled the first time.

And as usually happens when I'm casting a dry fly onto quiet water and no actual trout are eating it, I caught several imaginary ones, and I was neither bored nor discouraged. I crept along the entire length of the dam, casting here and there, letting the fly sit on the water, twitching it, waiting, and visualizing the trout that might have darted over to eye it.

By the time I had worked my way back to the end of the dam where I had first climbed onto it, the sun was high in the sky. I reeled in, snipped the Adams off my leader, put it back into its proper compartment in my fly box, unjointed my rod, lit a cigarette, and crouched there atop the dam.

I'd just spent a couple of hours catching no trout. I was disappointed that, based on my highly unscientific survey, no wild brook trout appeared to be living in Cutter's Run. But it had been engrossing, and it did not occur to me that I had wasted my time.

I'd had no thoughts of Charlotte Gillespie or swastikas or poisoned dogs or threatening phone calls. I hadn't wondered whether I was losing Alex, and I hadn't felt sad that Noah Hollingsworth was dying.

I'd been fishing. It had completely occupied my consciousness.

People who don't cast flies for trout sometimes tell me they'd like to try it, although they think they lack the patience for it. If they didn't catch a lot of fish, they say, they're afraid they'd quickly become bored. They don't think they're contemplative enough. They've got too much on their minds—implying, of course, that people like me can't have much of anything on our minds, and that we must have a high tolerance for boredom to devote all that time to not catching fish.

I've given up trying to explain how, when I'm fishing, my mind is fully and actively engaged, and that while I may be moderately contemplative, I am also actually quite an impatient man. Casting dry flies for trout is never boring. Trout of both species—real and imaginary—are endlessly fascinating.

I glanced at my watch. It was eleven o'clock. Time to get back and meet the sheriff.

EIGHTEEN

I'd been crouching there on the dam for a couple of hours, and when I stood up—too fast—I felt dizzy and nearly lost my balance. So I squatted there, taking deep breaths against the dull nausea that squeezed my stomach until the dizziness passed. Then I pushed my way through the undergrowth, aiming for the meadow, where the breeze and the sunlight would clear the blurriness from my brain.

I heard a voice and looked up. On the edge of the meadow in front of me stood Arlo, Susannah Hollingsworth's horse. There was no mistaking him for a moose. And when I broke through the thicket into the open, I saw Susannah herself. She was sitting cross-legged on a gray blanket. She wore raggedy low-riding cut-off jeans and a little white halter top that left her flat stomach bare. I couldn't see her eyes behind her sunglasses. A beer bottle sat by her elbow.

She lifted her hand. "Hi."

"Hi yourself."

She plucked off the glasses and smiled. "You're a sight."

"Why thank you, ma'am. You are, too, if I might say so."

"That fishing must be hard work." she said. "Look at you. You're all muddy and sweaty and your neck is bleeding. Grab yourself a beer from Arlo's saddlebag and bring it here." She patted the blanket beside her.

"A beer sounds good." I found three bottles of Dos Equis and some half-melted ice cubes in a soft plastic cooler in Arlo's saddlebag. I fished out a bottle and pressed it against my forehead. The cold was a shock. I thought I might have a fever.

"Hey," said Susannah. "You okay?"

I put my rod and fishing vest on the ground and slumped down beside her. "Just a little light-headed. Too much sun, I guess." I twisted the cap off the beer bottle and took a long swallow. I was very thirsty. The beer felt good all the way down.

She reached over and laid the back of her hand against my forehead. "I don't think you've got a fever." She squinted at me. "But you look kinda peaked, as my mother used to say." She pronounced it "peek-id."

I smiled at her. "You followed me."

She nodded. "Sort of."

I lit a cigarette and held the pack to Susannah. She pushed herself onto her elbows, took one, and steadied my hand as I held my Zippo for her. Then she flopped back onto the blanket.

I took another swig from the beer bottle and said, "So what's up?"

"Up? Nothing's up. Around here, nothing's ever up. I was out on Arlo and saw your car, and I remembered you'd mentioned trying to catch a trout. Thought I'd wander down and see what luck you had."

"No luck," I said. "I don't think there are any trout in the stream."

"I'm not surprised," she said. "I've tried to tell my father that you can't spread chemical fertilizers on a hundred acres of orchard and spray the trees about six times a year without affecting the environment. All that stuff has been leeching into Cutter's Run for decades."

I nodded. "It's happening to trout streams everywhere. Pisses me off."

She smiled. "You could've stayed home, avoided the mud and the bugs and the sun, and caught just as many fish." Her hand moved up to my neck. "What happened here?" She showed me her finger. It was wet with blood.

138

"I don't know. Didn't notice it. Briars, probably. Or maybe it's where I scratched at a mosquito bite."

She sat up, took a tissue from the pocket of her shorts, wet it with her tongue, and dabbed it at my neck. "Nasty scratch," she murmured. Her face was so close to mine that I could smell her perfume. "Looks like a briar got you." She touched my cheek with her fingertips, then sank back onto the blanket. "Can I ask you a question?" she said.

I nodded. "Sure. I guess so."

She propped herself up on her elbows. "Did my father say anything to you?"

"About what?" Noah had told me he was dying. He'd also told me that he hadn't told Susannah.

She shook her head. "I don't know. Something's going on with him. I know him. Something's wrong. But he wouldn't tell me. He'd want to protect me. I thought he might've said something to you. He'd talk to another man. That's how he is."

"What about Paul?"

She smiled quickly and shook her head. "He wouldn't talk to Paul. He thinks Paul's a lightweight." She smiled quickly. "Daddy doesn't trust a man who'd wear an apron."

"Susannah," I said gently, "if Noah had confided in me, I'd have to respect his privacy."

She narrowed her eyes. "I'm his daughter. I've got a right to know." Tears brimmed her eyes. "He did tell you something, didn't he?" She rolled onto her side and laid her cheek on my thigh. I hesitated, then touched her hair. She put her arm around my waist and pushed her face against my stomach. Her shoulders began to tremble, and I knew she was crying.

I stroked her bare arm. "Talk to him," I said. "Tell him what you told me. That you know something's wrong, and that you've got a right to know what it is. I can't tell you. It's between the two of you."

She rolled onto her back. Her head was on my lap, and she looked up at me with wet eyes. She seemed to be studying my face, and a moment later she gave a little nod. "I'm right, aren't I?" she whispered.

I shook my head. "I'm sorry."

She reached her arm up, hooked it around my neck, and drew my face down to hers. I wanted to resist her. I knew I should. But I didn't. Her mouth opened under mine, and I felt the flick of her tongue, and her lips were soft and encouraging. Then a little cry came from her throat, and she pulled me down beside her on the blanket. I tried to think of Alex. But Alex was fuzzy and distant, and Susannah was pressing against me, with her fingers in my hair and her hips moving on me.

I forced myself to slide my mouth away from hers. "Hey," I whispered, tilting my head back to look at her.

I read sadness in her eyes. "I'm sorry," she said. She flopped back on the blanket. "God, Brady. I am sorry."

I shook my head. "It's my fault."

She closed her eyes. "He's really sick, isn't he?"

I touched her cheek, and her hand came up and held it there. Her eyes opened and peered into mine, and I nodded.

She tried to smile, and the tears came again. She grabbed the front of my shirt and pulled me down, and this time her mouth and the taste of her felt familiar, and when she lifted herself against me, my arm went around her as if it had its own will, and my fingers began to stroke her back, exploring the skin under her halter top and along her shoulders, touching the side of her breast, then moving down along the knuckles of her spine until I was holding her butt and guiding her rhythm as her hips rolled against me, and then it was Susannah who put her palm on my chest, twisted away, gave me a gentle push, and whispered, "Wait."

I flopped onto my back and blew out a long breath. "Jesus, Susannah."

"I did not intend for this to happen," she said. She sat up, picked up her beer bottle, and took a long swig. Her throat worked as she swallowed, and a trickle of beer dribbled down her chin. She lowered the bottle and wiped her mouth with the back of her wrist. "Want to get me another one?"

"Sure." I stood up, steadied myself until a moment of dizziness passed, fished out another beer from Arlo's saddlebag, and brought it back to her.

140

"Thanks." She pressed the wet bottle against the side of her neck. "I came here hoping I'd find you," she said quietly. She was sitting cross-legged, staring down at the blanket.

"To seduce me?"

She frowned at me. "Of course not."

I shook my head. "I'm sorry. That was uncalled-for. It was my fault, not yours."

She gazed off into the distance. "No," she said quietly, "maybe you're right. Maybe I did think about kissing you." She took a sip of beer. "I apologize. It's our secret. No harm, no foul."

"I've got to tell Alex," I said.

"Don't be silly."

"It's not good to have secrets."

"Everybody has secrets, Brady. It was just a kiss, for God's sake. Nothing happened."

I shook my head. "That was not just a kiss. Something happened."

Susannah nodded. "Do what you think you have to do. Just keep in mind that Alex is my friend, and if you tell her that we—that you kissed me—I'll probably lose her friendship. And I know," she said quickly. "We should've thought of that before."

I sipped from my beer and said nothing.

"It was nice, though," she said after a minute. "Wasn't it?"

I nodded. "Yes. It was nice."

She smiled at me. "Would you kiss me again?"

I shook my head. "I don't think so."

Her hand slithered under my shirt and crept up my back. "Hey," she said softly.

I looked at her, and she tilted up her face, and I touched her cheek and bent to her, and I kissed her again, and this time it was gentle, almost sexless, and when we broke it off, I kissed her eyes and hugged her against me. "Noah does want to talk to you," I said into her hair. "He will if you make it easy for him."

She nodded.

I pushed myself to my feet and picked up my rod and vest. My light-headedness seemed to have passed, but I felt weak and faintly nauseated. "Come on," I said to Susannah. "Give me a ride back to my car."

She told me she had put the saddle on Arlo for my benefit, so I grabbed the reins and mounted him and she scrambled up behind me. She wrapped her arms around my waist and laid her cheek against my back, and Arlo began to meander up the sloping meadow.

"I'm sorry you didn't catch any trout," she said. "Was it pretty? The beaver pond, I mean?"

"It was perfect. I think the beavers have deserted it, though. There's a break in their dam, and they haven't fixed it. They built it exactly where the old dam used to be. I saw some of the ruins of the old tannery. I'd like to look at it sometime. Old broken things interest me."

"Nothing much to see," said Susannah. "It's been gone a long time. Fire and flood and time have taken it all away. There's nothing left but briars and mosquitoes and a few random hunks of concrete and brick." She hugged me from behind. "Anything new on Charlotte Gillespie?"

As Arlo carried us up the meadow, past the cabin, and down the roadway to my car, I told Susannah about the vile phone message we'd had waiting for us on Sunday evening. I told her about talking to the girl at the animal hospital, and my visit from Norman and Paris LeClair, and how Sheriff Dickman had deputized me. I told her how I had met with William Keith at the accounting firm where Charlotte had worked, and I finished my story just about the time Arlo stopped beside the Wrangler.

Susannah slid off Arlo's back, and then I dismounted.

"What about Paul?" I said to her.

She cocked her head and frowned at me. "What about him?"

"You going to tell him about . . . about what just happened?"

"Of course not."

I shrugged. "I just thought . . ."

"Look," she said. "Paul Forten is a nice guy. He's amusing and smart. He seems to care for me, in his own self-absorbed way, and he believes he can persuade me to care for him. That's his term—'care for.' He says, 'Susannah, I care for you.' And I want to go,

'Paul, I wish you weren't such a damn romantic.' " She blew out a long breath. "It's as if entering into a relationship is this logical decision I've got to make. He buys me gifts. He waits on me. Hell, he does the dishes." She smiled. "And I let him do it. I know that's not nice. But it's easier than arguing with him."

"I figured women nowadays went for that stuff," I said.

"Not me." She looked into my eyes. "Paul Forten is not my type of guy." She laughed quickly. "Actually, I think he likes Daddy more than he likes me. He—he's persistent, Brady. I just don't have the energy to tell him to stop coming around. I certainly don't owe him any explanation for anything, never mind an apology."

"Well," I said, "it's different with me and Alex."

She nodded. "I know." She stepped toward me and wrapped her arms around my waist. "Maybe we'll run into each other again."

She tilted up her face. I kissed her forehead, then put my hands on her hips and gently pushed her away. "I hope not," I said.

NINETEEN

I bumped slowly over the dusty roads, heading back to Alex's house. I had to tell her what had happened with Susannah, and I had to say it the right way, explain it so that she understood. I did not want to lie or distort or exaggerate or minimize.

I practiced my speech, tried to play out the scenario, to visualize Alex's face as I spoke to her. "I kissed Susannah Hollingsworth this morning. I kissed her several times, and I wanted to make love to her. I didn't, but I wanted to. I thought of you, and I kissed her anyway. Two of them were deep, long, passionate kisses, and she had her body pressed against mine, and I responded to her. I touched her breast and I held her ass in my hands. I broke away from two of those kisses. But one of them, it was Susannah who pushed me away. If she hadn't done that, I don't know if I would have stopped."

Alex would be staring into my face as I spoke, and she would not reveal what she was thinking. I would tell her: "Before today, I believed I was a good, strong, faithful man. I think you believed the same thing. I want you to know that I am not that good or that strong, and today I was not faithful."

And I would also have to tell Alex that if a similar situation arose in the future, I could not promise that I would be good or strong or faithful enough to resist kissing Susannah again. Another time I might make love to her.

I would tell Alex that I had wanted to make love to Susannah, that she had aroused me and excited me. Even now, riding in my Jeep over the back roads, I realized that part of me still wanted to make love to Susannah Hollingsworth.

I would talk to Alex right away, just as soon as I got back, while I still had the courage to do it. She'd be at her desk working on her book, and I'd have to interrupt her.

"Later, honey," she'd say, leaning forward, peering at her computer monitor, barely registering what I was saying.

"It's important," I'd tell her. "I wouldn't interrupt your work if it wasn't important."

Then she'd shake her head, turn to look up at me, and give me a frown, because I should know better than to interrupt her work.

But then she'd see my face and recognize the importance of what I wanted to say to her. She'd nod. "Okay," she'd say quietly. "What's up?"

And then I'd tell her.

And then it would never be the same with us again.

When I got there, Sheriff Dickman's green Explorer was parked in Alex's driveway. I pulled in beside it, got out, retrieved my rod and vest from the back, and went inside. I stowed the fishing gear in the closet and went into the kitchen. When I peeked out through the glass sliders, I saw Dickman and Alex sitting out on the deck.

They were sipping what looked like iced coffee. Both of them had their heels propped up on the railing and they were rocking and gazing off toward New Hampshire. Dickman was talking and gesturing, and Alex kept glancing at him through her big glasses in that endearingly myopic way of hers that makes you think you are the only person in her world. She cocks her head and thrusts her face forward slightly, and through her glasses her eyes look big and childlike, and you can see that she's fascinated with the wit and intelligence of what you're saying to her. A little half-smile plays on her mouth while you talk, and her lips sometimes move, as if

146

she's silently repeating your words to herself so that she will remember every single one of them.

Alex listens with her entire face, and her hands, too. Her hands are restless. They stroke whatever she might be holding, and when you say something clever or sad or profound, she touches your arm or grabs your sleeve. She keeps poking her glasses up onto the bridge of her nose with her forefinger, as if it's very important for her to keep you in focus.

I noticed all these things about Alex the first time I met her. But I had never before really noticed that she looks at everyone that way when she's engaged in a conversation. I'd always thought it was only me.

Now, as I stood in the kitchen watching her through the glass door while Dickman talked to her, I saw her shift her gaze from the horizon to Dickman's face, and I saw her flash him a quick smile. She was moving her finger up and down the side of the wet glass she was holding as she peered into Dickman's eyes. And then, without shifting her gaze away from him, her finger, the one that had been caressing the glass, moved up to her mouth. The tip of her tongue darted out to touch it, and then her lips closed around it, and it looked like she was kissing her fingertip.

It was painfully intimate, achingly erotic, and I felt like a voyeur, standing there in the kitchen watching Alex sucking her finger and peering into Sheriff Dickman's eyes.

I wondered if Dickman saw Alex the way I did.

I went into the bathroom and splashed cold water on my face. That strange light-headed sensation had passed, but I still felt a bit wobbly and very thirsty. I dried my face, popped three aspirin, washed them down with water, and went back into the kitchen. I filled a tall glass with ice cubes, then took the jug of iced coffee from the refrigerator and poured it over the ice. I gulped down half of it, then refilled it.

I opened the sliding door and went out onto the deck.

They both looked up at me. "Sorry if I'm late," I said to the sheriff. I bent down and kissed Alex on the puckered mouth she held up to me, then shook hands with Dickman. I sat in the empty rocker beside Alex.

She was grinning. "Look at you," she said. "You look totally wiped. You must've hooked a monster."

"I hooked nothing, actually. There are no trout in that beaver pond."

"Wait a minute," said Dickman. "You trying to say that because you didn't catch one, there aren't any there? Are you that good?"

"Trust me," I grumbled. "I know when there are trout in a fucking stream, whether or not I actually catch any."

Dickman frowned and held up a hand. "Whoa," he said. "No offense intended, my friend. I was just kidding."

I shook my head. "Sorry. I know you were. I had a nice morning, and maybe there are some trout there. But I couldn't catch any of them."

"Well, it looks like you've been battling Moby Dick," said Alex. "And Moby won. You look awful."

"Why, thank you kindly, ma'am," I said to her.

"No, seriously," she said. "Do you feel all right?"

I nodded. "Sure. I'm fine."

"Well," she said, "tell us about your adventure."

So I told Alex and Dickman about checking out Charlotte's cabin again and my fruitless visit to the beaver dam. I left out the part about Susannah being there when I stopped fishing. That was the important part of my story, but it was for Alex, not the sheriff.

After I finished my tale of incomplete truths, she stood up. Dickman started to rise, too, but she put her hand on his shoulder and said, "I've got to get back to work. You go ahead and have your law-enforcement conversation with your trusted deputy, here." She touched my cheek. "You've got a nasty scratch on your neck, Brady. Wash it and put a Band-Aid on it. You don't want it to get infected." She squeezed my shoulder, said "Bye" to Dickman, and slipped inside.

Susannah had dampened a tissue with her tongue and dabbed at that scratch on my neck. I had to tell Alex about Susannah, but now was not the time.

I realized that I felt relieved.

I turned to Dickman. "So what's up, Sheriff? Or did you come here to ogle Alex?"

He smiled. "She's easy to ogle, my friend. I asked her about that phone call, of course. She seems okay with it. Tough lady."

"You listened to the tape?"

He nodded. "Couldn't make any more out of it than you did. It's a threat, that's about all I could say for sure. How seriously we should take it . . ." He shrugged.

"I've decided to stick around for a few more days," I said. "I know Alex is tough, and when she's writing you couldn't distract her with a nuclear explosion. But still . . ."

"She's certainly absorbed in her book," said Dickman. "She told me about it, and then picked my brain on the subject of abuse. I told her that it's not uncommon in rural Maine, but rarely gets reported. Husbands beat wives, mothers and fathers and stepparents and grandparents beat kids, and when kids get older, they keep the tradition alive with their own kids. Sometimes kids beat their parents and grandparents. No one talks about it much, so we law-enforcement types generally hear about it secondhand—if we hear it at all—and we hardly ever get a complaint. It's amazing how many people show up in the emergency room with black eyes and broken noses and cracked ribs from slipping and falling. This was of great interest to Alex. She said that based on her research, what I see around here is what's happening everywhere. Urban slums, rural slums, rich suburbs. You name it."

"Alex thinks Charlotte Gillespie might've been the victim of abuse," I said.

He nodded. "She mentioned that. Certainly worth checking."

I told him about visiting William Keith and how I'd be meeting with Ellen Sanderson that evening.

"That's good work, Deputy," said Dickman. He reached down and picked up a manila envelope from the deck beside his rocking chair. "I wanted to show you this." He handed it to me.

I opened the flap and slid out half a dozen nine-by-twelve glossy black-and-white photographs. I flipped through them quickly. They were grainy and blurry, as if they'd been shot hastily from a great distance through a poorly focused telephoto lens, but they were plenty clear enough for me to see what was going on.

They had captured a sequence of the same general scene: a milling crowd, several uniformed policemen, a dozen or so men wearing white robes with their fists raised, some of them waving hand-lettered signs. The signs bore clever slogans such as "Segregation Forever," "End Affirmative Action," "Christians Against Queers," "White Supremacy."

In the background I recognized the plaza in front of the JFK Federal Building in Boston's Government Center.

I looked up at Dickman. "The KKK?"

He nodded. "This was a few years ago at some kind of civil rights rally. There were several arrests for disorderly conduct."

"I remember," I said. "It was big news in our city for a day. The Klan came from Illinois or somewhere, proclaiming their constitutional rights to free assembly and free speech. Hateful sons of bitches, of course, but they knew their rights, by God, and they knew a juicy publicity opportunity when they saw it. They were hoping they could antagonize the good Boston liberals, make them lose their cool. Which they did. There were fights and arrests. As I recall, none of the white sheets got arrested."

"No, they didn't," said Dickman. "They're quite crafty that way. But it was still a productive event for the FBI, because when the melee started, several of the 'robed demonstrators'—which is what Alex's paper delicately called the assholes—had their hoods ripped off their heads. Look."

He leaned toward me, paged through the photos until he came to the one he was looking for, and tapped it with his finger. "Indiana," he said. "It wasn't Illinois, though there are Klans there, too. But this contingent was from Indiana. A month before they arrived, they told the press they were coming to Boston, and the Associated Press picked up the story. It was in most of the papers. They drove all the way in private automobiles with 'KKK' painted on the doors and Confederate flags flying from the antennas, and they arrived the night before the rally. They stayed in the Marriott in Newton, apparently quite disappointed that they weren't turned away. A couple of them actually wore their robes into the restaurant, and they weren't turned away there, either."

"Which must've pissed them off," I said.

"Oh, yes. Nothing the Klan loves better than being the victims of prejudice and discrimination. Anyway, it seems that there are at least a few New Englanders who yearn for a better-organized Klan around here. Some of them suited up and joined the Indiana contingent there at Government Center that day. Here. Look at this."

Dickman's finger moved over the photo and came to rest just beneath a blurry face.

I bent close and squinted at it, then looked up at him. "Should I recognize him?"

"Try this one." Dickman found another photo, peered at it for a minute, then jabbed his forefinger at another face.

I studied it, then looked up at him. "How in the world did you—?"

"The FBI ID'd him," he said quickly. "You recognize him, don't you?"

"Sure," I said. "I met him the other day. He rented out his hunting cabin to Charlotte Gillespie. That's Arnold Hood."

TWENTY

Arnold Hood," repeated Dickman. He laid his head against the back of the rocker and gazed up at the puffy afternoon clouds. "Forty-one years old. Never married. Born in Garrison, Maine, where he's lived all his life in the same house. Calls himself self-employed on tax returns, on which he has never declared an income over seventeen grand a year. Honorably discharged from the Army, 1981, having attained the exalted rank of corporal. Both parents dead. Belongs to the VFW and the Dublin Rod and Gun Club. Arrested twice for drunk and disorderly, '82 and '84, no convictions."

"Arnold Hood is in the Klan?" I said. "I find that hard to believe."

Dickman tapped the photograph. "See for yourself."

"I didn't exactly take him for a genius or a philosopher," I said. "But he seemed like a nice enough guy. Quiet-spoken, kind of ingenuous. Simple, really."

"Probably a pretty accurate profile of your typical Klansman, if the truth were known. Look," said the sheriff, leaning toward me. "This is unlikely to be a coincidence. I mean, those swastikas, Ms. Gillespie being African-American, and Mr. Hood wearing sheets to Klan rallies. Agreed?"

I nodded. "Agreed."

"You're worried about her," he said, "and I'm worried about her, too. I'm also very interested in skinheads and Klansmen. So. Shall we?"

"Shall we what?"

"Pay Mr. Arnold Hood a visit, of course."

"You and me?"

"Sure. The two of us. We'll double-team him."

I smiled. "I'm no cop, Sheriff. I've never double-teamed anybody."

"You're a lawyer, aren't you?"

"I guess I am."

"Never cross-examined anyone? A hostile witness, maybe?"

"Sure."

He lifted the palms of his hands up in front of him. "Easy as that."

"A cross-examination is never easy."

"Then you should find this a snap." Dickman pushed himself up from the rocker. "Besides, it's about time a deputy sheriff learned some tricks of the trade." He put his hands on his hips, arched his back, and groaned. "Before we drop in on Hood, I want you to take me to that cabin. I'd like to see these swastikas for myself."

I went inside. I could hear writing sounds from Alex's cubicle—the hum of her computer's fan, the muffled clack and clatter of keys being tapped, the squeak of her swivel chair. I tiptoed past her and up to the bedroom, shucked off my mud-stained fishing clothes, and pulled on a clean pair of chino pants and a light cotton shirt. Then I went back downstairs. I hesitated, then peeked over the bookcases into Alex's workspace. She was sitting there with her back to me, stiff-necked, tense and alert, with her head jutting forward at her computer. "Hey," I said softly.

"Hi," she mumbled without turning around.

"The sheriff and I are going to do some sleuthing. I'll be back, but I've got to be in Portland at six, don't forget. Will you be okay?"

Still peering at her monitor, she lifted one hand and waved backward at me. "Have fun, Deputy."

"I'll lock the doors behind me," I said.

I stood there for a moment, looking at her, thinking of what I had to tell her.

But not now.

I locked the slider onto the deck, grabbed two apples and two cans of Coke from the refrigerator, and joined Dickman in the driveway, locking the front door behind me. I gave him an apple and a Coke. "Lunch," I said.

He nodded and took a bite out of his apple.

"What car do you want to bring?" I said.

"Oh, definitely mine. It's got a big light bar and a classy official logo on the door. Let's make an impression on that boy."

Heavy wire mesh separated the backseat of Dickman's cruiser from the front. He had a cellular phone and a police radio for entertainment and a pillow to sit on. The floor under my feet on the passenger side was littered with Styrofoam cups and candy bar wrappers and Dunkin' Donuts bags. Typical cop car.

"I dropped in on the animal hospital on the way over this morning," he said, as we headed for Charlotte's cabin.

"I thought you said you didn't have the time or the resources to investigate cases of petty vandalism and nuisance phone calls."

He shrugged. "So I changed my mind. I talked to that Betsy. She's either a scatterbrain or she's scared. Hard to say which. She told me what she told you—that the man who came for the dog was wearing sunglasses and a hat. That's as much as she'd say."

"Like a disguise," I said.

"Like someone who didn't expect to be recognized in the first place," he said, "but was taking no chances."

"A dead end, then?"

He shrugged.

I directed Dickman down the dirt road to Charlotte's driveway, and he stopped directly beside the No Trespassing sign. It still sported its big red swastika. He gazed at it for a minute, then shook his head. "I guess if you don't understand what it means," he said quietly, "it is just petty vandalism."

"Throw it into four-wheel drive," I said. "We can drive in a ways further. When I left my car here, it ended up with its own swastika."

"Nobody would dare vandalize the sheriff's vehicle," he said. He glanced sideways at me. "Joke," he said.

I nodded.

He drove down to the rocky streambed and parked there, and we walked the rest of the way. When we arrived at the meadow that sloped down to the beaver dam on Cutter's Run, my stomach flipped. I had been here just this morning. With Susannah Hollingsworth. Right down there, toward the bottom of the slope, was where I had kissed her, lying on her gray blanket. It all came flooding back, all those complicated and contradictory feelings, and I was reminded again that I had not yet confessed to Alex.

Dickman headed around to the back of the house where, his logic told him before I had the chance to, he'd find the outhouse. I followed him, and when we rounded the corner I caught a glimpse of orange and white flitting through the bushes along the meadow's edge. It was one of Charlotte's cats.

The cat stopped, crouched, and peered at us from under a bush, then squirted away and disappeared into the woods. I looked for others, but saw none.

Dickman stood there with his arms folded and peered at the big swastika on the outhouse door. He gave his head a little shake, but said nothing, and neither did I. After a minute we headed back to the cabin.

"You searched the place?" he said.

"Twice," I said. "I went in there again this morning. Nothing has changed."

He went to the cabin door, knocked loudly, paused, and pushed it open. Then he bent down, picked up the note I'd left, glanced at it, and put it down again. He stuck his head inside and called, "Ms. Gillespie? Charlotte? Are you home?"

She wasn't.

Dickman turned to me. "Just take a peek, tell me if anything looks different."

"I told you. I went in this morning. Nothing had changed."

"Humor me," he said.

I went inside and moved slowly from room to room. Nothing looked different.

"She hasn't been back," I said when I rejoined Dickman outside. "Everything's exactly as it was."

He nodded. "Then let's mosey over to Mr. Hood's house, see what he's got to say for himself."

We didn't talk during the stroll back to Dickman's car. After we climbed in, he sat there with both hands gripping the steering wheel, staring out through the windshield. Then he blew out a long breath and patted his shirt pocket. "Got a smoke?" he said.

"Didn't know you smoked, Sheriff."

"I don't anymore. Gimme one."

I took out my pack and held it to him. He plucked out a cigarette, lit it, exhaled through his nose, and said, "I lost an uncle and an aunt and an infant cousin at Buchenwald. I have trouble being objective about certain things."

"Forgivable," I said.

"Maybe, maybe not. Depends."

"You don't intend to arrest Arnold Hood, do you?"

He shook his head. "No. Not unless he's broken the law. But if he's got anything to do with those terrible symbols, by God, I'll be sorely tempted to do something."

"I may be a lowly deputy," I said, "but I'm also a lawyer. If you feel compelled to take action, you should consult me regarding Mr. Hood's civil liberties first."

He turned to me, grinned quickly, and started the car, and ten minutes later we pulled up in front of Arnold Hood's big square farmhouse.

His Dodge pickup truck was parked in the same place beside the house and Hood was up on the roof, just as he had been two days earlier when I'd come here with Susannah and Alex. In fact, it looked like he was still tacking down the same shingle he'd been working on then. Arnold Hood was a slow worker.

When Dickman and I slid out of his Explorer, we heard a woman bleating a country tune—or western, I never did know the differ-

157

ence—at full volume. The music had apparently drowned out the sound of our arrival, because Hood did not look down at us as we approached the house.

"The radio's on the windowsill in the kitchen," I told the sheriff. "I'll go turn it off. That'll get his attention."

I moved around to the side of the house. The kitchen window was open and an elderly black plastic plug-in radio sat on the sill, about chest high from the ground. I reached up to switch it off, then hesitated as I glanced into Arnold Hood's kitchen.

A Confederate flag hung on the wall over the table.

The lawyer in me tried to recall precedent, old cases that might be used to argue whether something seen through a window would constitute admissible evidence, or would be thrown out as the product of an illegal search. My recollection of civil liberties case law was too fuzzy to produce an answer.

It was a moot question anyway. There was no law against nailing a Confederate flag to your kitchen wall. As far as I knew, there was no law against wearing a sheet in public, either.

I turned off the radio and went around to the front of the house, where the sheriff was gazing up at the roof.

Hood was shading his eyes and looking down at us. "What do you boys want?" he said mildly. "I was listenin' to that."

"I need to talk to you, Mr. Hood," said Dickman. "Come down here."

"Come back when I ain't working," he said. He turned and tacked down a shingle.

"Don't make trouble for yourself," said the sheriff.

Hood did not respond. He pounded in another shingle tack.

Dickman stood there with his hands on his hips for a minute, staring up at Arnold Hood. Then he turned to me. "Come on."

I followed him to where Hood's paint-spotted aluminum ladder rested against the gutter above the second-floor windows. "Give me a hand," said the sheriff, grabbing onto the ladder.

I nodded, and we pulled the ladder away from the house and let it topple backward. It crashed onto the ground.

Arnold Hood was frowning down at us. "What in hell're you doin'?"

"Just want to know where we can find you," said the sheriff. "You go ahead and finish up your work. We'll be back."

"Put that goddam ladder back where it was. You can't do this."

Dickman grabbed my arm and said, "Come on, Deputy. We've got work to do."

We turned and began to stroll toward the sheriff's Explorer.

"Okay," yelled Hood. "Okay. I'll come down. For Christ's sake, put that ladder back."

Without turning, Dickman raised his hand and wiggled his fingers. "We'll be back, Mr. Hood," he said. "You just sit tight."

He opened his car door, then looked at me. "Well, Deputy. Don't just stand there with your face hanging out. Let's go."

I shrugged and slid into the front seat. Dickman got in, started up the car, and pulled away.

I smiled at him. "Can you do that?"

"I guess I could've pulled my nine-millimeter on him, or threatened to come back with a warrant or to bring him downtown, the way they do on TV." He grinned. "Sometimes I love this job." He turned the corner, then pulled to the side in the shade of a big oak tree and stopped. He reached over and patted my shirt pocket. "Gimme another smoke, Deputy Coyne."

TWENTY-ONE

W e finished our cigarettes and continued to sit there in the shade of the oak. The car windows were open, and a dry breeze blew through, bringing with it the mingled scent of moss and ferns and pine needles and road dust. The breeze felt cool on my face.

Dickman mentioned that he was a Pirates fan, and I said that as long as it wasn't any team from New York such as the Mets, whom I'd never forgiven for 1986, or the Yankees, whom I had hated long before 1978, we could still work together, although we probably should've clarified those vital matters of compatibility before I got deputized.

"Bill Buckner," he said.

"Yes. And Bob Stanley. That was '86. In '78 it was Mike Torrez. He gave up the home run to Bucky Dent. The villains were the New York teams, but we Red Sox fans always blame our own guys. We're kind of masochistic that way."

He smiled and changed the subject to gardening, and then I talked about fly fishing, and after a while he glanced at his watch. "What time did you say you had to be in Portland?"

"Six. I don't want to be late."

He nodded. "Okay. Maybe Mr. Hood is ready to come down, talk with us now."

161

So we drove back, stopped in front, and got out. Arnold Hood was squatting up there on the roof where we'd left him, staring down at us. Dickman leaned his elbows on top of his car and called, "What do you say, Mr. Hood?"

"I'm about done up here," he said. "So if you'll kindly put that ladder back for me, I'll fetch us some iced tea. It gets hot up on this here roof in the afternoon."

Dickman and I wrestled the ladder up against the gutter and steadied it for Arnold Hood while he backed his way down.

When he got to the bottom, he hitched up his jeans, looked first at me and then at Dickman, and said, "I'll be right with you. Gotta take a leak, then I'll bring some tea."

He disappeared around the side of the house. Dickman and I sat on the front steps.

"I don't think I mentioned that he's got a Confederate flag hanging in his kitchen," I said.

Dickman turned and nodded. "That fits," he said.

"I don't know as the Klan uses the swastika for one of its symbols," I said. "I thought they were mainly into crosses, preferably fiery ones."

Dickman shrugged. "You might be right about that," he said. "But from everything I've read, your neo-Nazis and your Klan share a lot of ideology. Either of them would serve a bigot's psychological needs the same way. They call a swastika a twisted cross, don't they?"

I nodded and was about to ask him how he wanted to proceed with our interview with Hood when his eyes widened slightly. Suddenly, he grabbed my arm and yanked me sideways. We both toppled off the side of the steps into the shrubbery just as a loud explosion sounded, and at the same moment I felt something hot and sharp jab into my right calf.

My first thought was that a wasp had nailed me. But then I realized that Dickman was pushing against my back, holding me down flat on my belly, and that the explosion had to have been a gunshot.

I twisted away from Dickman's grip and got up onto my knees.

"Stay down," he hissed. "He's got a shotgun."

"He got me," I said.

"You all right?"

"My leg. It smarts."

"Good," he said. "It's when you can't feel it that we worry." He cleared his throat, then called conversationally, "Come on now, Arnold. Throw down that old pumpgun before you do something really dumb. We just want to have a conversation here, and I was kind of thirsting for some of your iced tea."

"Nobody leaves Arnold Hood up on a roof without a ladder," came Hood's voice.

I peeked over the steps but couldn't see him.

"Keep your head down," said Dickman. He had his 9mm automatic in his hand.

"Where is he?"

"Around the corner of the house. If we stop hearing his voice, you turn around and watch our backs, in case he circles around." Then he called, "I guess we're even, Arnold. Throw that gun out on the lawn where I can see it, and then you come on out here where I can see you."

"I don't want no trouble," Hood said. "I was mindin' my own business, just shinglin' my roof."

"Yes, that's a fact," said Dickman. "And if you'd come on down when I asked you the first time, nothing would've happened. So like I said, we each got in a poke, and now we're even."

"You gonna arrest me?"

"What for?"

"Well, shit," said Hood. "Nothin', I guess."

A moment later I saw a shotgun clatter onto the ground by the corner of the house. "Okay?" said Hood.

"Okay," said Dickman. "You just come on out here where I can see you, and I'd feel a whole lot better if you had both your hands clasped together behind your neck."

Hood appeared. He stood there with his hands pressed against the sides of his face as if he had a double toothache. He was looking at the ground.

The sheriff stood up and moved toward him, his automatic in his hand. I followed close behind.

"You're not carrying another weapon, are you, Arnold?" said Dickman.

Hood shook his head. "No, sir," he mumbled.

Dickman went behind him and patted him down quickly, then holstered his gun and said, "Well, put your hands down, then. You look silly."

Hood dropped his hands. They dangled there awkwardly at the ends of his arms, as if he didn't know what to do with them.

The sheriff picked up Hood's shotgun from where he had tossed it onto the ground. A band of duct tape was wound around the stock, and the barrel was shiny where the bluing had worn off. Dickman ejected three shells onto the ground. He bent down, picked them up, squinted at them for a minute, then dropped them into his pocket. He looked up at Hood, gave him a smile, and swung the gun by its barrel, smashing the heavy wooden stock against the side of Hood's knee.

Hood muttered, "Shit," and went to the ground. He sat there rubbing his leg and frowning up at the sheriff. "What'd you do that for?" he said. "You coulda busted my leg."

"I should arrest you," said Dickman softly. "That's a pretty serious thing, shooting at police officers."

Hood managed a lopsided grin. "Well, shit, Sheriff. A man's got the right to protect his own property. Anyways, it was just birdshot. Guess I shouldn't've done it, but I was pissed at you. Didn't mean nothing by it. You didn't have to hit me."

"You could've put out somebody's eye."

Hood shook his head. "I wasn't aimin' for your eyes. If I'da been, I guess I would've put out more'n one of 'em. I was just shootin' at the ground."

"You got me in the leg," I said.

He shrugged. "Sorry. It musta ricocheted."

"Why don't you go fetch us some of your iced tea," said Dickman. "I don't want to see any more guns. I'd hate to have to plug you."

"That old pump's my only gun. It useta be my daddy's." Hood pushed himself to his feet. He bent over and rubbed his knee where Dickman had whacked it. "You boys want sugar in your tea?"

"No," said Dickman. "Brady?"

I shook my head, and Hood turned and limped back toward the kitchen.

"I think that was a mistake," I said.

"What? Letting him go?"

"No," I said. "Declining the sugar. His tea's pretty bitter."

Dickman cocked his head and peered at me. "I know what you're thinking."

"You do?"

"Yep. You're thinking I shouldn't have whacked him. You're thinking the Klan thing made me lose my cool. You're thinking I'm a brutal policeman."

"Actually," I said, "I was wondering why you don't arrest him."

"I might yet do that," he said. "If it serves our purpose. We'll see."

Hood was back a couple of minutes later with three glasses and the same blue plastic jug he'd used when I'd been there with Susannah and Alex. We sat on the front steps, and he poured each glass full.

"Your leg okay, there, Mr. Coyne?" he asked.

I rolled up my pantleg. The pellet was actually visible, a little black dot just under the skin. A tiny droplet of blood had oozed out, and the area had reddened.

"Lemme take care of that," said Hood. He pulled a folding knife from his pocket, opened it up, wiped the blade on his jeans, and used its tip to pry out the pellet. He held it in the palm of his hand. It was about the size of a pinhead. "See?" he said. "Number nine birdshot. It's what I keep in that old gun for scarin' off the kids when they come around drunk, throwin' beer cans on my lawn, yellin' names at me."

Dickman took a sip of his iced tea, then put his glass on the step. "Arnold," he said, "I'm afraid we've got a problem. I'm hoping you can clear some things up for us."

Hood shrugged. He was holding his glass in both hands and looking at Dickman over its rim. "I figure this has somethin' to do with Miz Gillespie." He glanced quickly at me, then back at the sheriff. "I told Mr. Coyne here everything."

165

"You didn't tell him about the Klan, Arnold."

"That ain't—" He stopped himself, took a sip of tea, then shook his head. "I don't know what you mean."

Dickman pushed his face close to Hood's. "Don't fuck with me, Arnold. You fuck with me, I'm gonna cuff you and take you in for shooting at us. I'm gonna call it attempted murder, and Mr. Coyne here is a damned honorable witness to it, with a wound in his leg to prove it. I should remind you that unless you've got a couple hundred thousand dollars laying around so's you can hire yourself a real lawyer, you're gonna end up with young Johnny Boynton for your PD, and that boy hasn't won a case in three years. That what you want, Arnold?"

"You fuckin' hit me, man," he mumbled. "I can bring charges."

"I don't remember hitting you," said Dickman. "Do you remember anything like that, Mr. Coyne?"

I shrugged. "I didn't see anything."

Hood frowned at me for a minute, then shook his head. "Yeah, okay. I joined up."

"The Klan, you mean," said Dickman.

Hood shrugged. "But I changed my mind, so I quit."

"Why'd you join?" said Dickman.

He shrugged. "You know."

"No. Tell me."

Hood glanced at me, then looked out toward the woods. "Niggers," he mumbled.

"I didn't hear you," said Dickman.

Hood turned to him. "Niggers, for Christ's sake. Why would anybody join the Klan?"

"That," said Dickman, "is a question I've often asked myself. Never could come up with a good answer. So tell me. Who else around here belongs?"

Hood shook his head. "I don't know nothin' about it. I told you, I quit."

I touched Dickman's arm, and he glanced at me and gave me a little nod. "Mr. Hood," I said, "when we talked the other day, you told me that Charlotte Gillespie's color didn't bother you."

"I told you," he said, "that I didn't know what color she was when I rented my cabin to her. I told you we did the deal over the phone and she mailed me a check."

"Actually," I said, "you told me it didn't matter to you whether she was green or purple—I believe those were the colors you mentioned—as long as you got your check."

Hood shrugged. "Maybe I said that."

"Now you're saying it did matter?"

He shrugged and looked down into his glass.

"So when you saw her and realized she was—"

He looked up at me. "A nigger?"

"When you realized that," I said, "how did you feel?"

"Stupid," he said.

"Angry?"

He shrugged. "I guess I felt like I'd been tricked."

"She made you look like a fool."

He nodded. "Maybe."

"She should have mentioned it to you."

He nodded again.

"That she was black."

"That she was a nigger."

"So when you saw her . . ."

"I didn't do nothin'," he said. He turned to Dickman. "I ain't done nothin', Sheriff. So, okay, I went to a couple meetings and they give me a hood. Big laugh, right? Ol' Hoodie's got his own hood? But I ain't broken any laws. First Amendment says I can join whatever I want to join, and then I can quit if I want. And that's just what I done."

"And you want us to believe that you never laid eyes on Charlotte Gillespie until after she moved into your cabin?" I said.

"I guess you'll believe what you want to believe, Mr. Coyne. But that's the way it was. When I seen her on the road, seen that she was a—a colored lady, I said to myself that she'd be outa there in six months, and meantime, I didn't need to have nothing to do with her. I was waitin' for her to complain about that old water pump, which don't work right, or the propane hot water heater, which ain't too good either, or the fact that there's no place to plug in the TV, or maybe the mice or the porcupines. Then I'd tell her she could shove off if she wanted to. But she never complained."

"So you tried to scare her away," said Dickman.

"What, them swastikas?" Hood shook his head. "I didn't do that."

"You didn't."

"No, sir. I didn't."

"But you know who did."

Hood frowned. "If I'da knowed who done that, I guess I'd've plastered his ass with a load of number nines. That's my property up there, regardless of who's livin' in it."

"You're saying you don't know who made the swastikas?" said Dickman.

Hood nodded slowly. "Yup-suh. That's what I'm sayin'. That's just what I'm sayin'."

"You quit the Klan, huh?" I said.

He nodded.

"Then what's that Confederate flag doing in your kitchen?"

"You lookin' into my house? You can't do that. That's my fuckin' house, and what I got in it ain't nobody's business."

"So you still are with the Klan, is that it?" I said.

"Nope. I quit. Don't mean I can't keep that flag there if I want. Anyways, what if I didn't quit? So what?"

"We are gravely concerned about Charlotte Gillespie," said Dickman. "We are hoping that she is all right. Because if it turns out that she isn't all right, we will round up every goddam white sheet in York County. And before we let them go, we'll be sure that every one of them knows we had some long conversations with Arnold Hood." He tapped Hood on the leg. "Do you get my drift, Arnold?"

"I guess so," he said mildly.

"So if you happen to know anything that might help us in this very important investigation, you had better unburden yourself." Dickman leaned toward Hood, so close that their noses almost touched. "Because if I should find out that you knew something but didn't tell me," he said softly, "I will be very upset. And I assure you, Mr. Hood, that the weight of the law will fall on your shoulders so hard it'll drive you into the ground clear up to your tits. Do you understand me?"

"Yes, sir," Hood mumbled.

Dickman stood up. "I want you to give some serious consideration to what I've told you," he said. "Then maybe we'll have another conversation."

Hood looked up at him and nodded.

"Come on, Deputy," said Dickman. He put his hand on my shoulder, and we started toward the car.

"Deputy?" said Hood. "You didn't tell me you was no deputy, Mr. Coyne."

I turned around. "And you didn't tell me you were a Klansman, Mr. Hood."

We were almost to the car when I touched Dickman's arm. "Wait a minute," I said. I went back to Hood, who was still sitting on his front steps watching us. "Something's been bothering me," I said to him.

"Something's been bothering me, too," he said. He jerked his head in Dickman's direction. "You boys. You're what's been botherin' me."

I smiled. "The other day you told me that you didn't meet Charlotte until after she'd moved in, right?"

"That's right."

"You never showed her the place ahead of time, or took her up there when she was ready to move in?"

"No."

"That's a hard place to find if you don't know it's there," I said. "You must have drawn her a map or given her directions."

"Nope," he said. "She never asked, and I never offered."

"That's hard to believe," I said.

"Well," he said, "I cain't help that. I'm tellin' you, I didn't know she was a nigger when I rented it out to her, and I admitted to you that if I'd've known, I wouldn't've rented it to her. But when I seen her, I didn't do nothin'. I didn't make those damn swastikas, and I don't know where she's at, and that's the truth."

I nodded. "Okay. Thanks for your help."

I started back for the sheriff's car.

"Hey, Mr. Deputy," called Hood.

I stopped and turned to face him. "What?"

He was grinning. "You taken a poke at Susannah Hollingsworth yet?"

I shook my head. "Jesus Christ," I said.

" 'Cause if you ain't," he said, "you're about the only man in York County. Had a piece of her myself, oh, back damn near twenty years ago when she was still sweet and tender."

I looked hard into his eyes. "You'd better be careful, Mr. Hood," I said.

He arched his eyebrows, thrust out his lower lip, and nodded thoughtfully. "You, too, Mr. Coyne."

"Is that a threat?"

He shook his head. "Nope. A friendly warning, that's all. Miss Susannah ain't that tender anymore. And she sure as hell ain't sweet."

TWENTY-TWO

We were creeping over the back roads heading back to Alex's place, and I was staring out the side window pondering what Arnold Hood had said about Susannah, when Dickman said, "Well? What do you think?"

I turned to look at him. "About what?"

"Mr. Arnold Hood's story."

"I think that pulling a shotgun on us was incredibly stupid," I said. "I think that Arnold Hood is an ignorant, crude, bigoted man. But I don't think he made those swastikas, and I don't think he did anything to Charlotte Gillespie."

"Why not?"

I shrugged. "I guess he strikes me as too stupid to be a convincing liar."

"He lied to you the first time you met him, didn't he?"

I nodded. "He did."

"And you believed him then."

"You're right. I did."

"Arnold Hood is crude and bigoted, all right," said the sheriff. "But I don't think he's stupid."

"So what do you figure he was lying about?" I said.

He shrugged. "A good liar mixes in truth with the lies. Figuring out which is which is the trick. A mildly self-incriminating truth,

171

like admitting to prejudice and using the word 'nigger,' makes the lies sound plausible. I'd start with the reason he pulled that shotgun on us."

"He didn't intend to kill us or anything," I said. "Hell, it was loaded with birdshot. He said he was mad because we removed his ladder. Makes sense to me."

"A good lie does make sense," said Dickman. "You didn't see him when he came around the corner of his house. He was holding that pumpgun down alongside his leg, and I've got the feeling that if we hadn't scrambled into the bushes, he would've kept coming until he had us point-blank. A load of birdshot at ten yards makes a pattern about six inches wide. Blow one helluva big hole in a man."

"You think he *did* intend to kill us?" I said.

"I don't know. Maybe."

"Not because of the ladder."

"Well," said Dickman, "if it wasn't because of the ladder, it was something else."

"Like Charlotte Gillespie."

"Maybe."

"Here's what's bothering me," I said. "Hood says that Charlotte just called him up out of the blue and asked to rent his place. She wasn't from around here. He didn't advertise the place. So—"

"So you're wondering how she knew about it?" said Dickman.

"Yes. If Hood's telling the truth . . ."

"Those deer hunters," he said. "The ones who rented it. They were from Portland."

"She could have known one of them," I said.

Dickman smiled. "That's pretty good thinking, Deputy. Arnold should be able to give us some names." He shrugged. "Not sure where that would lead us. But worth a follow-up. I'll take care of it. I want you to steer clear of Arnold Hood for a while." He glanced at me. "Got it?"

"What?"

"You stay away from him, Deputy." He pulled into the driveway and stopped beside my Wrangler. He left the motor running and glanced at his watch. "You've got just about enough time to get to Pine Point without breaking the law. It wouldn't do for a York County deputy sheriff to get nailed for speeding."

I nodded and got out of the car. I bent to the window and said, "I'll fill you in."

"Damn right you will. Why do you think I deputized you?"

He shifted into reverse, lifted his hand, and backed out of the driveway. I turned and went into the house.

Alex was not behind her bookcase partitions. I found her on the deck with her heels up on the railing and her rocking chair tilted back. A sheaf of papers lay on her lap, and her head rested against the back of the chair. She was wearing sunglasses, so I couldn't see her eyes. I figured she was napping and decided not to disturb her.

I went upstairs, washed my face and hands, and combed my wet fingers through my hair. It was a few minutes after four-thirty. I didn't want Ellen Sanderson to have to wait for me at Pine Point.

Downstairs I snagged a Coke from the refrigerator, then went out onto the deck. Alex sat forward, slipped her sunglasses down onto the tip of her nose, and looked up at me over the tops of them. "I was just going over some stuff," she said, putting her hand on the papers on her lap. "Guess I dozed off. The sun feels good. So how'd you and the sheriff make out?"

"Well, it turns out that Arnold Hood belongs—or once belonged—to the Klan. He tried to shoot us. I got hit in the leg. I'll tell you all about it. But now I've gotta go meet Ellen Sanderson. Don't want to be late."

I bent to kiss her, but she twisted away from me. "Not so fast," she said. "You tell me you got *shot*—and then you think you can breeze out of here without telling me the story?"

"Sorry," I said. "I'm all right, and it's really kind of a funny story. When I get back, I'll tell it to you with all the proper embellishments. Okay?"

"I guess I have no choice." She thrust out her lower lip in a parody of a pout.

"If you're good, I'll even show you my wound," I said.

"Wow," she said. "There's an incentive."

I glanced meaningfully at my watch, and this time when I leaned down, Alex gave me a good shot at her mouth. When I kissed it, her arm hooked around my neck and held me there, and I couldn't help remembering how Susannah's mouth had tasted, and how her lips and tongue worked differently from Alex's.

And I knew I was a despicable man for comparing them. Returning Alex's kiss felt like a lie.

I gently put my hands on her shoulders and broke it off. "Keep that up," I said in what I intended to be a cheerful tone, "and I'll never get to that meeting."

She nodded and smiled. "Well, good luck, Deputy."

"Be sure to lock the doors and—"

"Don't worry about me, Brady."

"Well, I do."

She nodded. "Sure you do."

I kissed the top of her head and got the hell out of there. I hadn't really lied to her yet. But I had not told her some important truths, which amounted to the same thing, and it left me with a knot in my stomach and an acid taste in my throat.

Some people, I knew, could lie without compunction. Their only worry was getting caught. Perhaps Arnold Hood was like that. But I was not. I had, of course, told my share of lies, and regardless of the fact that I had rarely been caught, every one of them had managed to punish me.

I followed Route 160 out of town, hooked onto Route 25 heading east, and followed it over the gently rolling landscape through Kezar Falls and Limington and Standish, and as I drove I tried to put thoughts of Alex and Susannah out of my mind and focus on my upcoming interview with Ellen Sanderson.

Route 25 passed under Interstate 95 in Westbrook. Following the directions Ellen had given me, I continued on to Route 1, headed south, and after a few miles came to a left turn marked by a sign that read "Pine Point and Prouts Neck."

Ten minutes later I pulled into a parking area that fronted a narrow beach along a tidal river. On the left a large gray-shingled building crowded against the high-tide line. This, I assumed, although I saw no sign, was the clam shack. An open veranda faced the water overlooking a small marina. A few sportfishing boats and sailboats and other recreational craft were moored there.

I climbed out of my Wrangler and headed toward the building. Running alongside it into the water was a concrete boat ramp, where a pair of guys with long-billed caps were wrestling a Boston Whaler up onto a trailer. A few fly rods bristled from the Whaler, and I was tempted to go down and ask about the fishing. I'd heard there was excellent striped bass fishing in this area.

Then I heard a voice calling, "Mr. Coyne?"

I turned around and made a visor of my hand against the low afternoon sun.

"Over here."

I looked up to the veranda on the back of the clam shack and saw a hand wave. I waved back, then climbed the stairs and sat down across from Ellen Sanderson.

When I'd met her in her office, she'd had her hair up in a complicated bun, and she'd been wearing a dark blue business suit with a silk blouse underneath. Now she was wearing jeans and a bulky sweatshirt with "Colby College" on the front and long dangly silver-and-turquoise earrings. Navajo, I guessed. Her dark hair, which was lightly streaked with gray, hung down her back in a loose flowing ponytail, held in place with a turquoise silk kerchief that matched her earrings.

If she hadn't waved and called my name, I probably wouldn't have recognized her. I held my hand across the table to her, and when she took it and smiled, she looked younger and prettier than I'd remembered.

"Thank you for coming," I said.

"No," she said. "Thank you. I called you, remember?"

Her eyes matched the turquoise in the earrings and the kerchief. They crinkled when she smiled. She was sipping from a dewy glass through a straw. "What're you drinking?" I said.

"Gin and tonic," she said. "It's about my only indulgence. Isn't that sad?"

"Everybody needs a few indulgences," I said. "The best kinds are those that don't bother anybody else." I looked around and spotted a college-age girl wearing a white T-shirt and black Bermuda shorts standing near the wall and holding a tray. I waved at her, and she nodded and came over. "Drink, sir?"

175

"Gin and tonic sounds good," I said. I turned to Ellen. "Ready for a refill?"

"Sure," she said. "I don't mind."

When the waitress left, Ellen said, "For courage, I guess."

"The drink?"

She shrugged and nodded.

I leaned forward. "In the first place," I said, "I'm a lawyer. Nothing you say to me will get back to the wrong people. I promise you that. In the second place, I'm sort of a temporary law-enforcement person. I have just one case. I'm trying to figure out what's happened to Charlotte. I hope you can help."

"I trust you," she said. "I trusted you when I met you the other day. Otherwise I wouldn't be here. But I really don't know if I can help you or not." She reached down beside her and pulled a big leather bag up onto her lap. She rummaged inside it, slipped something onto her lap, and put the bag back on the floor. She glanced around the veranda. Then she picked up her napkin, dabbed her mouth, and put the napkin on her lap. She darted her eyes around again and then picked it up and put it on the table between us. "It's under the napkin," she said. She gave a small nervous laugh. "I'm being silly, I know."

"It's good to be cautious," I said.

I waited for a minute. Then I reached for her napkin, felt something small and square under it, picked it up inside the napkin, and put them both onto my lap.

When I looked down, I saw a floppy disk. I looked up at Ellen. "For me?"

She nodded.

I slipped it into my pants pocket. "What's on it?"

Ellen glanced up. Our waitress deposited gin and tonics in front of us. "Something to eat?" she said.

I glanced at Ellen, who shook her head. "Not yet," I said to the waitress. "Maybe later."

After she left, Ellen said, "I think I mentioned to you that Charlotte and I used to go out after work on Fridays. Not every Friday. But more often than not. In the summer, as a matter of fact, we liked to come here. We never saw anybody we knew here. We liked

176

that." She bent to her straw and sipped her drink. "The day she got fired, she left the office around noon. She'd been in a meeting with Mr. Keith all morning, and when she came out, she just said, 'He fired me. The Mexican place at six, okay?' When I met her there, she gave me that disk. Asked me to hang on to it for her. Didn't say why, didn't say what was on it. And I didn't ask. And stupid me, it didn't really occur to me that it was her way of saying she was worried, that she might be in some kind of danger, that the disk was—I don't know—insurance, or something. Not until you came in the other day. Remember what you told me?"

I nodded.

"You said you thought she was in danger," she said. "Or that, God forbid, something had already happened to her. Then I remembered. And I thought about it. And then I decided I'd better call you." She shrugged. "And here we are."

"What's on the disk?"

She smiled. "Charlotte didn't specifically forbid me from looking at it. But I figured it was none of my business. After I called you, though, I booted it up." She shook her head. "I only glanced at it. It's accounting stuff. Just a lot of numbers. Means nothing to me."

"Nothing?"

"I'm only a secretary, remember? Maybe you can figure it out."

"Well," I said, "I'll try." I took out my cigarettes and held them to Ellen. She shook her head.

"Do you mind?"

"Not as long as we're outdoors," she said.

I got one lit. "Tell me about her getting fired. Your boss told me one of her clients complained about her work. He said he had no choice but to let her go."

She nodded. "That's basically what Charlotte told me. She didn't tell me which client or what the complaint was about. That was Charlotte. Discreet no matter what the situation. But I gather that she was preparing their quarterly figures, and the client wanted her to fudge them. She refused, of course. That would violate the ethics of her profession. So the client complained to Mr. Keith—gave him an ultimatum, according to Charlotte—and he went along with it."

"And presumably assigned the account to one of your firm's other accountants who had fewer compunctions about fudging figures."

Ellen shrugged.

"Did Charlotte seem frightened that night when she'd been fired?"

"Frightened?" She looked down at her nearly empty gin and tonic. "No, I wouldn't say frightened. Angry, depressed, stunned. Betrayed, mainly. That was the big emotion I recall. She told me that after the client complained, she was eager to meet with Mr. Keith, explain the situation to him. It was reasonable for her to expect his support."

"And instead of commending her for a job well done and for sticking to her guns," I said, "he canned her."

Ellen nodded. "I don't like him. If jobs weren't so scarce . . ."

I noticed our waitress hovering nearby. "How about some supper?" I said to Ellen.

"I wouldn't mind. Gin and tonics make me hungry."

We both ordered lobster rolls and a side of onion rings. Beer for me. Ellen switched to Diet Coke.

When the waitress left, I said to Ellen, "Could you find out who that client was?"

"The one that got Charlotte fired?"

I nodded.

She studied her hands, which were rotating her empty gin-and-tonic glass. When she looked up, she nodded. "I'll have to wait till Mr. Keith is away from the office. The billing records should do it. Each accountant bills his own clients, so I can check Charlotte's old accounts, see who's got them now, and work at it from there. Ask a few innocent questions, cross-reference the correspondence." She nodded. "It might take a day or two. But, yeah, I think I can do it."

"Don't get yourself in trouble," I said.

"At this point," she said, "I don't care. It hasn't been much fun since Charlotte left."

"Be careful anyway."

"Oh, I can take care of myself," she said. "Believe me."

A few minutes later our waitress came with our lobster rolls and onion rings. While we ate, Ellen told me about her friendship with Charlotte. Both women had been divorced fairly recently when Charlotte joined the firm a little more than two years earlier. Two fortyish divorcées working closely together naturally became friends. They didn't actually socialize with each other except for their Friday after-work outings. "Charlotte is a very private person," said Ellen, giving a little emphasis to the present-tense verb. "She sometimes talked about personal problems or issues, but she always managed to keep them vague and general, as if they were someone else's problems. For example, for a while she was involved with a man, and it was bothering her, making her unhappy. But she never let her hair down and just spilled it out to me, or asked for my advice or anything. When it ended, she didn't even tell me for over a month. And I was never clear who broke it off, or why."

"How soon was that before she was fired?" I said.

Ellen looked up at the sky, which had become dark while we'd been sitting there. "Oh, quite a while. Last summer sometime."

"That man," I said. "It wasn't . . . ?"

"Mr. Keith?" She smiled. "I really, seriously doubt it. He's just not Charlotte's type, and I don't think she's his, for that matter. Anyhow, he's married. Charlotte would never get involved with a married man."

"So you have no idea who it might've been?"

"I think it was a client."

"The one who—"

"Who got her fired?" She shrugged. "That would fit, wouldn't it?"

I nodded. "Did she ever go away with that man?"

"What do you mean?"

"Like for a weekend, or for a vacation?"

Ellen looked up at the sky, which was darkening overhead. Then she turned to me. "I think she did, yes. Last summer. She was gone for a week, and it was soon after she came back that she mentioned that she was no longer involved with that man."

"Who might've been a client."

She nodded.

"Who got her fired," I said.

Ellen shrugged. "I don't know any of this. But, yes, that would fit."

"She didn't tell you where she went for that week, did she?"

She shook her head.

"A cabin in the woods, maybe?"

"She didn't talk about it. Charlotte never talked about her personal life with me." Ellen smiled. "I'm sorry. I really don't know. Like I said, Charlotte was super-discreet, and I never pressed her for details. Our friendship wasn't like that."

"What about her former husband?" I said. "Did she ever talk about him?"

"All I know," she said, "is, he abused her."

TWENTY-THREE

It was a beautiful late-summer evening out on the patio at Pine Point, and Ellen Sanderson and I lingered there after we ate, sipping coffee and watching the tide change directions in the river. I asked her a few more questions about Charlotte, but she couldn't think of anything else to tell me. So we lapsed into long silences, which were not uncomfortable.

A few fishermen came in, backed their trucks down to the water, and trailered their boats. A few others arrived and untrailered theirs for a try at night fishing.

When one of those comfortable silences was interrupted by our waitress, I accepted a coffee refill, took a sip, lit a cigarette, and said to Ellen, "You're a woman."

She smiled. "Why, thank you for noticing."

"I'd like a woman's perspective. Hypothetical situation."

"Sure." She nodded. "Hypothetical."

"Okay," I said. "Suppose a guy is involved in a relationship. He's married, say. He's not looking for it, but he finds himself attracted to another woman. This other attraction takes him by surprise, and he—he responds to this other woman."

Ellen was watching my face. A little smile played around her mouth, as if she wanted to laugh but thought it would be rude. "Responds to her," she repeated. "What do you mean?"

"Oh," I said, "say he kisses her a couple times. Deep, passionate kisses."

"And?"

"That's it."

"They don't . . . ?"

"No. Just the kisses. But these are not what you'd call chaste kisses. He is aroused. He wants to. She does, too. But they don't."

"Then what?" she said.

"That's all. He's had this encounter. What does he do?"

"Easy," she said. "He avoids seeing this other woman in any situation where they might get intimate. Assuming, of course, that he cherishes his relationship with his wife."

I waved my hand. "Sure," I said. "But what does he say to his wife?"

Ellen reached across the table and put her hand on top of mine. "You're feeling pretty guilty, aren't you?"

I shrugged. "Yeah."

"Do you want to confess? To your wife, I mean?"

"I feel like that would be the right thing to do."

"Why?"

"Because we've always had an honest relationship. Because I'm too grown-up to play games. Because I don't want secrets between us."

"And because you'd feel a lot better if you confessed," she said.

"Well, sure."

"How do you think—Tell me your wife's name."

"We're not married. A friend of mine says I should call her my virtual spouse. Her name's Alex. Alexandria."

"Pretty name," said Ellen. "So how do you think Alex would feel if you confessed to her?"

"I think it would hurt her terribly. She knows this other woman. Susannah's her name."

"Do you want to hurt Alex?"

"Of course not."

"It was a serious question," she said. "Think about it."

I looked at her. "I understand what you're getting at," I said.

"No. I really don't think I want to hurt her. I have no reason to hurt her."

"So spilling it all out to her would hurt her but make you feel better."

"There's more to it than that."

She smiled. "Sure there is. You're attracted to this other woman, and you've got to figure out what that means. But, okay. You asked for a woman's opinion. I don't pretend I can speak for all women. But if it was me, I can tell you this. I would not want to know. If you were actually having an affair with—Susannah, is it?—with Susannah, then I would definitely want to know. If you were in love with Susannah, if you were sneaking around behind my back, if you'd stopped loving me and wanted to leave me to be with Susannah, you're damned right I'd want to know. But if you'd kissed Susannah, gotten aroused, felt guilty about it, knew you would not pursue it—hell, no. Don't tell me. Call it ancient history. Let it pass. Let me keep being happy."

"You're saying I shouldn't tell her?"

"Hey, I'm not Alex. I'm not Solomon, either. I'm not even Ann Landers. But I'll tell you what." She patted my hand. "I'd bet a hundred dollars that Alex has something she's decided not to tell you. And she's probably wrestled with her conscience, just like you are."

"It's hard for me to think that Alex would have a secret from me."

"And it's hard for her to think you've got a secret," she said. "Sure. But we all have secrets. And some of them should always be secrets. Even if it's painful to keep them. Even if confession is good for the soul, it can be bad for the relationship."

"I should just suffer in silence, then."

"You're the one who sinned," she said. "Why should someone else suffer for it?"

I leaned back in my chair and shook my head. "You are either one very wise lady . . ."

She smiled and nodded. "Or else I'm completely full of kaka."

"You've given me something to think about," I said.

"I know. And truthfully, I'm glad it's your dilemma, not mine." She shook her head. "Although I sure wouldn't mind having a virtual spouse in my life."

I pondered what Ellen had told me and watched the river flow by, and when I glanced at my watch, it was after eleven. I looked up and saw her smiling at me. "I've kept you up after your bedtime," she said.

"It's been a nice evening," I said. "And instructive as well. But I think I'd better get going. I've got an hour's drive ahead of me."

I paid the bill and we headed for the parking lot. Ellen held on to my arm, and when we got to her car, she turned to me and held out her hand. "I had fun," she said. "Even if the circumstances are unfortunate, this was the nicest date I've had in years."

I took her hand. "Me, too. I enjoyed talking to you."

"Sometimes," she said, "it's easier to talk to someone who you don't know that well. Someone who doesn't have any stake in it. You know what I mean?"

I nodded. "I don't think I could have had that conversation with a friend."

"Does that mean we aren't friends?"

"I'm sorry," I said. "That's not what I meant. I'd be honored to consider you my friend."

"Me, too." She unlocked her car door, then turned to me. "Keep me posted on Charlotte, okay?"

"Sure," I said. "And if you can figure out who that client was . . ."

"I'll figure it out," she said. "You'll hear from me."

I held the door for her as she slid in. She looked up at me. "I hope it works out. With Alex, I mean."

I nodded, touched her shoulder, then closed her car door. She smiled at me through the window, started up the engine, turned on her headlights, and pulled out of the parking lot. I waved, and she tooted her horn as she disappeared around the corner.

Then I climbed into my car and headed back to Garrison.

It was close to twelve-thirty when I pulled into the driveway. Except for the porch light, Alex's house was dark.

I closed the car door quietly, slipped inside, and took off my shoes. I went into Alex's office, sat in front of her computer, turned it on, and slid in the disk Ellen had given me, and when the icon appeared on the screen, I double-clicked it.

In a few seconds I saw what Ellen had described—columns of figures and meaningless acronyms. Accountant stuff. I scrolled through it all. It did not name people who spray-painted swastikas on outhouse doors or poisoned dogs or took women from their homes.

But I hadn't expected it to.

If I was going to make any sense of it, I'd have to study it, think about it, execute some deductive reasoning worthy of a York County deputy sheriff. Even then, I probably wouldn't be able to make sense of it. But I'd give it a shot.

I copied the disk onto the hard drive, ejected it, turned off the computer, and tiptoed back upstairs. I undressed in the bathroom.

Then I went into the bedroom. In the silvery light from the skylight, I could see that Alex's eyes were open and following me as I approached the bed.

"Still awake?" I said.

She nodded.

I sat on the edge of the bed. "Are you okay?"

"Sure," she mumbled. "I'm fine."

I heard it in her voice. "He called again, didn't he?" I said.

She let out a long breath. "I was asleep. He said, 'If you know what's good for you, you'll tell your boyfriend to turn in his badge.'"

"Was that all?"

She nodded. "I said, 'Who is this?' But he hung up."

"Was it—?"

"The same voice, yes. It sounded the same."

I reached for her, and she rolled to me. I lay down on top of the covers and held her head against my chest. "I'm sorry," I said. "I shouldn't have gone."

185

"He would've called anyway," she mumbled. "It's okay. I'm not afraid."

"It's okay to be afraid."

"Well, I'm not." She tilted her head back. "Brady, who knows you've got that badge?"

"In this town? By now, everybody, probably."

She nodded. "I want to go to sleep now."

"Okay." I stood up, shucked off my clothes, then slid in beside her. I kissed her cheek, and she rolled onto her belly. A few minutes later her breathing slowed and deepened.

I stared up through the skylight for a long time listening to the quiet rhythms of Alex sleeping beside me.

The ringing of the telephone interrupted a muddled dream, which I forgot instantly. As I climbed out of sleep, I became aware of Alex muttering, shifting her position, groping for the phone, then saying, "H'lo?"

I sat up quickly and watched her face. She was nodding at the telephone and running her fingers through her hair. It was somebody she knew, I realized.

I slumped back onto my pillow. Through the skylight I saw that the sky overhead was pewter, the way it is just before the rising sun turns it blue. I glanced at my watch. It was a little after six. I yawned, rolled over onto my side facing away from Alex, and closed my eyes.

I felt her shifting, hitching herself up against the headboard. Then she murmured, "Oh. Oh, my God, no."

I felt the tension in her body, and I turned to her. She was sitting straight up, but her head was bent so that her hair bracketed her face. She was gripping the phone so hard that the veins on the back of her hand stood out. She was holding her free hand over her mouth, and her eyes were full.

I touched her arm and mouthed, "What?"

She met my eyes, and at that moment hers brimmed over. She gave her head a small shake, then looked down. "What can we do?" she said into the phone.

She listened, then nodded. "Of course." She glanced at me, then said into the phone, "Yes, he's right here. . . . No, it's all right. Hold on."

Alex looked at me, then held the phone out to me. "It's Susannah."

I took the phone from her and held it for a moment, trying to read Alex's expression.

All I saw was sadness.

Fragments of my lost dream flashed in my head. It had been a guilt dream.

I put the phone to my ear. "Susannah?"

I heard a quick exhale. "Oh, Brady . . ."

"What is it?"

She hesitated for so long that I glanced at Alex and arched my eyebrows. She turned her head away.

"I'm sorry," said Susannah, in that husky soft voice of hers. "It's Noah. My father, Brady. Shit. I can't . . . Damn him . . . I found him. He's . . . he died."

TWENTY-FOUR

W hat happened, Susannah?" I said. "Can you talk about it? Where are you?"

"I'm here," she said. "Home. It's—I'm all alone now. They came and took him away, Brady, and now it's terribly empty here. Alex said you'd come over. The two of you. Can you? I don't think I could stand to be alone right now."

Alex had slipped out of bed and gone into the bathroom. "Of course," I said. "We'll be right there."

O n the ride over to Susannah's, Alex said, "It's flattering, isn't it? That she called us, I mean."

"She told me she couldn't think of anyone else to call."

"She must know a million people," she said. "I mean, there's Paul, for God's sake. Wouldn't you think . . . ?"

"Maybe she tried him." I shrugged. "You don't expect someone to act logically under those circumstances. Hell, she just found her father's dead body. Anyway, my impression is that she and Paul are not exactly . . ."

"In love?" said Alex.

I nodded. "I don't sense much passion between them." I was thinking of what Susannah had said about Paul while we were lying

189

on a blanket beside Cutter's Run, the passion I had felt between us, the passion she'd denied feeling for Paul.

"I think he feels strongly for her," said Alex. "But, yes, she seems to be tolerating him. She bosses him around, and he obeys her like a little puppy dog, almost too eager to please."

When we pulled up in front of the Hollingsworth Orchards farmstand, Susannah was sitting on the porch steps holding a coffee mug. Alex and I got out of the car, and she got up and came toward us.

Alex met her halfway and opened her arms, and they hugged each other. Susannah was several inches taller than Alex. She laid her forehead on Alex's shoulder, and Alex patted her back and murmured to her.

After a while, Alex gave her a squeeze and Susannah kissed Alex's cheek. They stood apart, and Susannah came to me and put both of her arms around my waist. I hugged her against me. "I'm sorry," was all I could think of to say, and she held on to me and said nothing for what seemed like a long time.

Finally Susannah broke away and said, "The coffee's hot."

The three of us walked around to the back of the house and climbed up onto the deck. "I'll get the coffee," said Alex.

She slipped in through the sliding glass doors. Susannah and I sat at the table, gazing out toward the orchard. The early-morning sun was burning through the fog, and the low-angled light painted it in blurry shades of green, yellow, and red and caught droplets of dew on the grass. It looked like a field of diamonds.

"This is where it happened," she said.

"Here? On the deck?"

She nodded.

"Do you want to talk about it?"

"Yes," she said. "Yes, I really do." She took a deep breath and gazed out at the orchard. "He went to bed earlier than usual. Around nine. Said he was tired. He went out on Arlo yesterday afternoon, after—" she looked up at me and gave me a quick smile—"after I got back."

I nodded. After she got back from her encounter with me, is what she meant.

"He hadn't done that for a long time," she said. "After my mother died, he seemed to lose all interest in riding Arlo or checking out the orchard. But yesterday, for some reason, he did. Anyway, I guess it tired him out. I'd hoped to talk to him about—about what you and I talked about. But he went to bed. I figured, okay, I'd confront him tomorrow, make him talk to me, find out what's going on with him." She smiled quickly and shook her head.

"He was dying," I said. "He told me he had maybe eighteen months."

She nodded. "Yeah, well, that's pretty much what I figured. But I didn't want to guess. I wanted to know. I wanted him to tell me." She shrugged. "Anyway, I went to bed around eleven, read for a while, and went to sleep. Sometime later I heard him get up, so—"

She looked up. I turned. Alex was standing on the other side of the glass door holding a tray. I got up and slid it open for her.

"Thanks," she said. She put the tray on the table. It held a carafe and three mugs. She poured the mugs full, then sat with us. "Sorry to interrupt," she said.

I reached for her hand. "Susannah had just started to tell me what happened."

Alex gave my hand a quick squeeze, then let go. She picked up her mug in both hands.

Susannah took a sip of coffee. "Daddy gets up two or three times a night. He clomps around, bangs the sliding doors, and goes out on the deck to relieve himself. Even in the winter he insists on peeing off the deck in the middle of the night." She glanced at Alex and smiled quickly, as if to say, "Men, you know?"

"He wakes me up every time," she continued. "And I always lie there until he comes back inside, bangs the sliders shut, and then slams his bedroom door. Then I go back to sleep. Well, this time—last night—he didn't come back in. I lay there, and I was thinking maybe I'd dozed off and didn't hear him. But I knew I wouldn't get back to sleep until I was sure he was back in bed. So I went downstairs. His bedroom door was open. I peeked in, and he wasn't there. So I went into the kitchen and looked out on the deck, figuring I'd see him standing there in his long johns, peeing off the

191

edge." She smiled. "He wore those red flannel long johns to bed every single night, right through the summer." She shook her head. "Anyhow, I didn't see him. So I went out there. The sky was full of stars last night, and the moon was about half full, and my first thought was how bright and pretty it was, and maybe Daddy had decided to go for a little stroll in the moonlight. Which was dumb. He wouldn't do that. But it's what I was thinking. Anyway, I walked over to the edge—right over there." She pointed at the place Noah had called his "pissing platform," where he could aim at an old rusty harrow that lay in the weeds. "And then I saw this—this red on the ground."

Susannah took a deep breath. She looked at Alex, then at me. She blinked a couple of times, then bent to her coffee mug.

"Susannah," I said. "You don't have to—"

"No," she said quickly. "I want to. It was Noah, of course. Noah in those dumb red flannel long johns. He was so still. The minute I saw him, I knew. That he was dead, I mean. And you know what my first thought was?" She looked at me.

I shook my head.

"My first thought was, 'You old bastard. You went and died on me without talking to me first. You talked to Brady, but you didn't talk to me.' That seemed so unfair." She gave her head a quick little shake. "Anyway, I went down and poked at him and yelled at him, and he didn't move. He wasn't breathing. I finally had enough sense to check for a pulse, and I couldn't find one." She picked up her coffee mug, took a quick sip, and put it down. "So I sat there beside him in the goldenrod and milkweed, me in my nightie and him in his red flannels, and I told him it wasn't fair for him to die like that, out there in the weeds at night while I was upstairs. After a while I went in and made my phone call. They sent an ambulance, and one of the EMTs checked him and said he was dead, and they put him on a stretcher and loaded him into their wagon. They said I could go with him if I wanted to, and I said, 'Why?' And they just shook their heads, because there was nothing I could do. So they drove away with him, and I sat here on the deck, and after a while the birds began singing and the sky started to get light, and finally

192

I figured it would be okay to call you." She smiled. "The only thing I could think of doing was calling you guys."

"You should have called right away," said Alex. "We would have come over."

"It was okay," said Susannah. "I had some thinking to do. Things I had to settle with Noah. It was good. I think I'll be okay now." She smiled, first at me and then at Alex. "I really appreciate this. You're good friends. Listen. How about some breakfast?"

"Let me get it," I said.

Susannah started to speak, but Alex reached over and touched her arm. "Brady makes a good breakfast, if you're into cholesterol."

"I really don't know what we've got," said Susannah.

I stood up. "I'll forage."

I went into the kitchen. I found some eggs in the refrigerator and a bag of raisin bagels in the freezer and a big cast-iron skillet in the drawer under the oven. Further exploration yielded a wedge of cheddar cheese, orange juice, margarine, and milk.

I scrambled the eggs and cheese, toasted the bagels, and poured three glasses of orange juice. Then I went to the sliding doors. Alex and Susannah were leaning over the table toward each other, talking intently. I slid open the door and cleared my throat. "Come and get it," I said.

"Smells great," said Susannah.

"The trick to gourmet cooking," I said, "is to be sure everybody's really hungry."

Alex came in, loaded her plate, and took her eggs, bagel, and juice out onto the deck. Then Susannah helped herself.

"You okay?" I said.

She nodded. "Yes. Alex is pretty special. You're lucky." She broke off a piece of scrambled egg with her fingers and put it into her mouth. "Delicious," she said. "You're a bundle of surprises, Brady Coyne. I guess Alex is pretty lucky, too."

"Alex is a good cook," I said. "We generally take turns."

"I wasn't really talking about your cooking," she said.

We sat at the table on the deck. Susannah took a couple of small bites, then put down her fork and stared out at the orchard. After a minute, she shook her head, picked up her fork, and began eating again, and just about the time we were dabbing our mouths with our napkins and patting our stomachs, we heard a car door slam out front.

"Oh, shit," mumbled Susannah. I glanced at her. Her eyes were wide and watery. She was shaking her head. "I don't think I can . . ."

I stood up. "I'll see who it is."

"I don't want to talk to anybody," said Susannah. "Tell them to go away."

I nodded, then went around to the front of the house. Sheriff Dickman was standing on the porch. "Hey," I called to him.

He turned and came to me. "I heard about Noah," he said.

"You were friends?"

He shrugged. "Not quite. Acquaintances would be more accurate. He was a curmudgeonly old bastard. I liked him better than he liked me. He once told me he'd never voted for me. Said I was a waste of taxpayers' money." He smiled. "Sometimes I think he was right. Anyway, I've got to talk to Susannah, and I do not look forward to it."

"She's doing pretty well," I said.

"Yeah, well, she might not be doing so well when I get done with her. Gimme a smoke."

I gave my pack to him. He fumbled out a cigarette and then I held my lighter for him. He lit up, blew out a long plume of smoke, and peered at me through narrowed eyes. "See," he said, "I'm the one who's got to tell Susannah that it looks like her father was murdered."

TWENTY-FIVE

Dickman sat heavily on the front steps, and I sat beside him. "The EMTs screwed up big-time," he said. "Noah was dead when they got here. They should've left him there, called my office or the state police. Unattended death. Standard procedure." He took a drag off his cigarette, then waved his hand at the smoke. "Whatever. It was dark, middle of the night. Old guy who keeled over." He shrugged. "Still, inexcusable. Anyway, when they got him to the hospital, they needed a doctor to pronounce him dead. Doc Blanchard was there, and when he took a look at Noah he called me, woke me up—it was about four A.M.—told me I better haul my ass on over there. Taciturn old coot wouldn't tell me anything more on the telephone. When I got there, he took me to where they had Noah's body and peeled back the sheet. It wasn't that apparent until Blanchard pointed it out to me." The sheriff dropped his half-smoked cigarette on the ground and ground it under his heel. "There were red marks on his throat."

I frowned. "You telling me he was strangled?"

He nodded. "We need an autopsy to make it official, of course. But I can't wait around. I've got to talk to Susannah."

"That'll be hard for her to hear," I said.

Dickman sighed. "No harder for her than for me," he said. "I'm the guy who's got to ask her the questions."

"If he was strangled," I said, "wouldn't Susannah have noticed? I mean, wouldn't his face be purple or his eyes and tongue bulging out or something?"

Dickman shook his head. "Doc Blanchard thinks he actually died of a heart attack or stroke."

"Induced by being strangled," I said.

"Something like that." He stood up. "It's still murder. I gotta talk to her."

"Want me to sit in on it?"

"Play lawyer for her, you mean?"

I shrugged. Noah had asked me to help Susannah with legal matters after he died. "Play friend for her," I said.

"How's about you play deputy sheriff for me," said Dickman. "Pay attention and keep your mouth shut."

We walked around to the back of the house. Alex and Susannah were sitting at the table. They turned to watch us as we approached. Dickman went up onto the deck, nodded and smiled at Alex, then turned to Susannah, took off his hat, and said, "I'm very sorry about your father, Susannah."

He held out his hand, and she took it. "You came to extend your sympathies?" she said. "That's very nice."

"Noah could be an irascible old goat. Opinionated, hardheaded, and I don't think I ever knew a man tighter with a dollar." Dickman smiled. "I liked him a lot." He pulled out a chair, sat at the table, and looked at Alex. "Any more coffee?"

"Sure. I'll get it." She glanced at me, then picked up the empty carafe and went into the kitchen.

I sat beside Susannah. Dickman leaned forward. "Susannah," he said, "I've known your father for many years."

"Yes," she said softly. "You'd drop by on some pretext or other and Daddy would give you a bag of apples."

"I always tried to pay for them. He'd never let me. I kept telling him I couldn't accept handouts. Against my ethics. He told me not to be stupid." Dickman smiled. "I ate a lot of apples while I was driving around York County." He reached across the table and put his hand over Susannah's. "Noah was murdered," he said quietly.

Her eyes widened. "What did you say?"

"Somebody killed him."

She hugged herself. Her eyes kept shifting between Dickman and me as if she was waiting for one of us to admit it was a joke. Then she shook her head. "But I saw him," she said. "There was no . . ."

"He was strangled," said Dickman. "There were marks on his throat."

"I didn't see any marks."

He nodded. He was gazing kindly at her. Studying her, it seemed to me.

Susannah turned to me, then shifted her gaze to the sheriff. "Who . . . ?"

"We don't know," he said.

"It was the middle of the night," she said. "I was the only one here. I would've heard something."

"You didn't? Voices? A car door slamming?"

She shook her head. "No. Nothing. My bedroom's in the front of the house. I heard him get up and go out back, like he does every night. I—I didn't hear him come back in, so I went down there. And—I found him."

"Tell me what happened," he said.

She told Dickman exactly what she had told Alex and me. In the middle of her recitation, Alex came out with coffee. She put the carafe on the table and went back inside.

When Susannah finished her story, Dickman said, "So who would want to kill your father?"

Susannah shook her head. "Nobody. That's crazy. He knew everybody in York County. Not everybody loved him, I know. But my father had no enemies. Certainly not the kind who'd want to kill him." She narrowed her eyes at Dickman for a moment, then turned and looked at me. "He thinks I did it," she said.

"Now, Susannah," he said softly. "I think no such thing. Somebody did kill him, and since we have no suspects, everybody is a suspect, and the more information we can get, the easier it will be to eliminate some of them."

"Right," she said. "And did anything I told you eliminate me from your list?"

He shook his head. "I guess not. That doesn't mean I don't believe you. I want you to give more thought to who his enemies were and who might stand to gain from his being dead."

"Besides me," she said.

Dickman lifted his mug and took a sip. "Anything you can think of, you tell me."

She shrugged. "What happens next?"

"The state boys'll be along soon," he said. "I'm afraid this crime scene's pretty messed up, but they'll do their forensics, maybe get lucky and find a bootprint or cigarette butt that doesn't match any of ours. They'll want to question you all over again. They'll talk to the neighbors, folks in town. People Noah did business with, who owed him money, who he owed money to, anything like that." He took another sip of coffee, then put down his mug, picked up his hat from the table, and stood. He looked from Susannah to me. "Anybody you talk to, just leave it that he died. It's not much, but right now the fact that only us and the one who did it know he was strangled gives us a little edge." He hooked his sunglasses over his ears. "I am sorry, Susannah. Sorry about Noah, and sorry to have to ask you these questions. But you want to know something?"

Susannah was looking up at him without expression. "What?" she said softly.

"Somebody *did* kill him," said Dickman. "And I'm going to figure out who." He turned to me. "Want to walk me back to my vehicle, Deputy?"

I got up and followed him. When we got to his truck, he leaned against the fender and squinted at me. "Did she talk to you about it before I got here?"

I nodded. "She told it the same way to you as she did to me."

"No contradictions?"

"None."

"Like she'd rehearsed it?" he said.

"No. Like it was the truth."

He gave his head a little shake. "She *is* the most logical one, Brady."

"That's ridiculous," I said. "She took care of him. I can tell you, she loved him. She's heartbroken."

He shrugged and held up his left hand with three fingers extended. "Means," he said, bending down his left forefinger with his other one. "She's a strong girl, he was a weak, spindly old man. It'd be simple enough for her to do it." He folded down another finger. "Opportunity. She was there. As far as we know, the only one who was. And—" he bent down the third finger—"motive. Well, who knows? Insurance? His property? An argument? A family thing?" He shrugged. "Usually, of course, it's money. He was a widower, she's an only child."

I shook my head. "Christ, Sheriff."

He gazed off into the distance. "It's hard to imagine that Susannah did this," he said. "But that doesn't mean she's not a good suspect." Then he narrowed his eyes at me and shook his head. "Hell, Brady. You're a lawyer. You know how it goes. Anyway, we got something to ponder, you and I."

"I know," I said. "We've got to ponder whether there's a connection between Noah's murder and Charlotte Gillespie's disappearance."

He grinned. "Wish to hell my regular deputies were as quick as you. Look. We got swastikas and we got a member of the KKK who shoots at people with his shotgun and we got a missing woman and a poisoned dog, and now we got a murdered old man, and any one of them is a once-in-a-decade sort of thing for a quiet little town like Garrison. I'm not much for coincidence, Brady. I believe in reasons and explanations and connections."

"We've also got two threatening phone calls," I said.

He looked at me. "Two?"

I nodded. "Alex got another one last night while I was away. He said I should turn in my badge."

"Well, I'm damn sorry about the phone calls. But on the other hand, it sounds like we're getting to somebody."

"Arnold Hood?" I said.

He shrugged. "Could be. Somebody's spooked. It sure seems to confirm that something did happen to Ms. Gillespie, all right."

"And now Noah."

Dickman nodded. "Okay, Deputy, give me a scenario."

I gazed up at the sky. "Noah and Charlotte?" I looked at him and smiled. "Maybe . . . ?"

He shrugged. "He was a widower. Lived alone, except when his daughter visited. Charlotte was living alone, too, and right next door, practically. A pair of lonely people. She was good-looking, you said. He was—well, maybe a woman would've found Noah attractive. Hardly the world's most bizarre scenario. Then what?"

"Somebody found out about it," I said. "And didn't like it. Killed them both."

He arched his eyebrows.

"Like Susannah, you're thinking," I said.

"It's possible."

"Charlotte was divorced," I said. "There's an ex-husband somewhere. Alex thinks Charlotte had been abused. There's an ex-boyfriend, too. Maybe more than one."

Dickman sighed. "See? The world is full of suspects."

"Maybe Noah intended to marry Charlotte, make her his heir, deprive Susannah of her rightful patrimony. . . ." I shook my head. "That's dumb. Susannah didn't do this."

Dickman was smiling at me. "Go ahead," he said.

"Well," I said, "maybe somebody didn't like what was going on between them, and killed them both."

"Someone who didn't approve of a white man and a black woman."

"Sure," I said. "Or maybe Noah . . ."

Dickman nodded. "Maybe Noah killed Charlotte."

"But why?"

He shrugged. "Who knows?"

"And then somebody else, avenging her death, went after Noah." I shook my head. "Jesus, Sheriff. It must be terrible to have to think this way for a living."

"You're the one doing the thinking here," he said. "And you're doing a damn good job of it, for a city lawyer. But listen. If it's not Susannah, whoever it was must've known that Noah went out on the deck to take a piss in the middle of the night. He—or she— was waiting for him. He was old and weak. He'd be easy to kill."

"I've got the feeling that everybody in Garrison knows everything about everybody else," I said.

Dickman smiled. "True enough."

"Why didn't you ask Susannah about Noah and Charlotte?" I said.

He shook his head. "That seemed . . . indelicate, under the circumstances. I gave her the chance to volunteer Charlotte's name, and she didn't." He put his hat on, turned, and climbed into his car. He squinted up at me through the open window. "Now you listen to me, Deputy Coyne."

"What?"

"Noah Hollingsworth's murder is not your case. You understand?"

"Even if it's connected to Charlotte's disappearance, and those phone calls we're getting?"

He nodded. "Absolutely. Remember, we still don't know she's disappeared. There's no evidence whatsoever that she's the victim of anything except somebody spray-painting a vile symbol on her outhouse door. Your case is about swastikas, and that's all it's about. This one here's about murder."

"What if we find out Charlotte was murdered?"

"If we learn she was, then that won't be your case, either. Don't forget. I am the sheriff around here, and you are my deputy. I give the orders, and I order you to keep your nose out of murder cases." He slid on his sunglasses and adjusted them around his ears. "And stay away from Arnold Hood."

"What if I quit?"

"You can't quit unless I say you can. I'm the boss."

I smiled. "What if I don't tell you what's on the floppy disk Ellen Sanderson gave me last night? What if I decide not to tell you who got Charlotte fired because she refused to fudge some numbers, cover up something for them?"

Dickman reached out through his car window and grabbed my wrist. "You better tell me, pal. Right now."

"Right now, I don't know," I said. "Want me to try to find out?"

"Bet your ass I do."

"Then," I said, "you'd better be nice to me."

TWENTY-SIX

After Sheriff Dickman drove away, I went around to the back of the house. Through the glass doors I could see Alex and Susannah in the kitchen cleaning up the breakfast mess. Mostly it was my mess. I'm a sloppy and inefficient cook. I use more utensils than I need to, I tend to spill things, and I hate to clean up.

Alex was at the sink rinsing dishes and loading them into the dishwasher. Susannah was gathering them from the table and counters and piling them beside her. They worked slowly with frequent pauses, and I could see that they were talking about serious matters.

I sat on the steps and lit a cigarette, and a few minutes later Alex came out and sat beside me. "I'm going to stay with Susannah for a while," she said.

I shook my head. "I don't—"

"Not you," she said quickly. "I think it would be best if it was just me. She's got a lot on her mind. I think it would be easier for her . . ."

"Sure," I said. "A girl thing."

"She needs to talk," said Alex, as if that explained it. Which I suppose it did.

I nodded. "Okay. I've got plenty to do." I stood up. "I'll go say good-bye to Susannah."

Alex put her hand on my arm. "You okay?"

"I'm sad about Noah," I said. "I'm sad for Susannah. I'm sad for all of us. Angry, too." I smiled. "Otherwise, sure. I'm fine."

I went into the kitchen, gave Susannah a hug, and said I'd be back. She held on for a minute or two, and when she pulled back, her cheeks were wet.

Alex followed me to the car. "Give me a call later on," she said.

When I got back to the house, I put on some coffee. Then I went to Alex's office, turned on her computer, and inserted the disk Ellen Sanderson had given me. A minute later the screen was again filled with rows and columns of numbers and combinations of letters that looked like acronyms. It probably would've made logical sense to an accountant, but none of it made any more sense to me now than it had the night before.

I went to the kitchen, poured a mug of coffee, brought it back to the computer, and studied those numbers and letters some more. I wondered if there was some secret code embedded in them. That struck me as unlikely.

I scrolled through it slowly, and then, at the very end of the file, I found: "Account #147. First quarter, 1997. C. Gillespie, CPA."

Ellen had guessed that the disk was "insurance" for Charlotte. If so, then this one—number 147—must have been the account that had gotten her fired, and somewhere in those numbers a trained person could probably find the discrepancy that Charlotte had refused to change.

I picked up the phone and dialed the Keith agency. When Ellen Sanderson answered, I said, "It's Brady. Can you talk?"

"Yes," she said. "For a minute. Look, I'm sorry, but I haven't had a chance—"

"It's account number one forty-seven," I said. "The first-quarter report. On that disk you gave me. As you said, it's all just a bunch of numbers. I can't make any sense of any of it. But I'd like to know what account this is."

"Okay," she said. "It's almost lunchtime. I'll call you back within an hour. Knowing the account number will make it easy. You said one forty-seven, first quarter?"

"Right."

"If you don't hear from me," she said, "send the cops. It means they caught me."

"Jesus, Ellen. Don't take any chances."

She laughed. "I'm just kidding. Don't worry about me."

After I disconnected from Ellen, I went upstairs, retrieved my personal phone directory, and jotted down Skip Churchill's e-mail address.

Churchill is an accountant who works out of his home in Belmont, just outside Boston. I handled his divorce for him a couple of years ago, and as usually happens with my clients, we became friends. He always said if I ever needed a favor of the accounting variety, I should call on him.

So I downloaded the contents of the disk to a file and e-mailed it to Skip. Then I took the phone and a mug of coffee out onto the deck, where I slumped in a rocking chair. I called Skip, got his answering machine, and told him to check his e-mail and give me a call.

I rocked and gazed at the countryside. More and more autumnal color was showing up every day, little patches of gold and auburn and crimson splotched against the green. New England autumn, of course, can be spectacular to look at. But it always depressed me. It was the season of death.

I pondered what I knew. The cabin on Arnold Hood's property was down the hill, over Cutter's Run, and up the next hill from Noah Hollingsworth's orchard. If Charlotte Gillespie had been murdered—and so far, I reminded myself, there was no actual evidence either to prove or disprove it—that made two murders within about a week and barely a mile of each other. And that, as Sheriff Dickman had said, was not the kind of coincidence one could easily swallow.

I could come up with theoretical villains easily enough. Arnold Hood and Susannah made two, and there was William Keith, who'd fired Charlotte. Any of them could've had the means and the opportunity to murder Charlotte and Noah.

But I couldn't think of a motive for any of these suspects to kill both of them. Maybe Hood had killed Charlotte simply because he hated African-Americans. Or William Keith, because she threatened his business. But I couldn't think of a reason for either of them to kill Noah.

On the basis of a complicated and highly unlikely set of scenarios, I supposed I could make Susannah the killer of both Noah and Charlotte. But I'd have to ignore one thing that I didn't believe she ever could have faked—her obvious devotion to her father.

I had seen Susannah cry for Noah, out of love and frustration and worry. I had kissed her then, and she'd responded to me. As illogical as it was, I found it impossible to imagine that a woman I had kissed could be capable of patricide.

But hell, I'd been wrong plenty of times before. Especially when it came to women.

I'd been sitting out there for fifteen minutes or so when the phone rang. "It's Ellen," she said.

"That was quick. What'd you find?"

"Account number one forty-seven is, in fact, the firm that got Charlotte fired. It's called SynGen, Inc. They're right here in Portland, and we've had their account for several years. It's a research laboratory. They have some ties to the University of Southern Maine, here in Portland. They're financed mostly through government grants and contracts with the university and a couple of private foundations."

"Yeah," I said. "That makes sense. Some of the acronyms on that disk—USOME, for example. The University of Southern Maine, I bet. And UMORO—U. Maine Orono. All those acronyms contained five letters. I remember thinking USFDA might be the Food and Drug Administration."

"SynGen has dealings with them," said Ellen. "So I'm helping you, huh?"

"You're a secretary," I said. "Secretaries always know a lot."

"Oh, I don't know much," she said. "But I know how to find it. What else can I tell you?"

"You sure it's safe there?" I said.

"Here? In the office?" she said. "Right now, yes. Everybody's gone to lunch. It's just me, guarding the phones. I've got the SynGen file up on my screen. I can delete it in one second."

"Does that file give you any names?"

"At SynGen? Sure. Hang on. Just let me punch that up.... There. Okay. The president and CEO is a guy named Gerald Stasio. Two VPs—Roland Passman and Arthur Tate. Passman's head of operations, and Tate's the CFO. They've got seventeen employees, nine of them full-time, and two unpaid interns from the university."

"Have you met these three guys?" I said.

"I've greeted them, brought them coffee, taken their phone calls. We secretaries don't exactly get introduced to the clients, you know. Not as if we were real people. They come in a couple times a year to meet with—well, to meet with Charlotte, and since then, the three of them were in one time to see Mr. Keith. Who, by the way, has taken over that account. Mr. Keith and Stasio are hunting buddies from way back, I know that. When Stasio set up his firm, he retained Keith and Harrington to do his accounting. After they got it up and running, Mr. Keith turned the account over to Charlotte."

"Hunting buddies," I repeated.

"Oh, you know. They go out on Casco Bay in December, when it's ridiculously cold, and shoot sea ducks so Mr. Keith can show off Raisin."

"Raisin?"

"His black Lab. Mr. Keith is awfully proud of that dog. I guess he's a pretty good retriever. They go deer hunting every fall, too. Far as I know, they've never actually shot one. I think they just go to drink and play cards and tell jokes about women's breasts. Guy stuff."

I wondered if they rented a certain cabin in Garrison from Arnold Hood for their guy stuff. Keith had denied ever renting a hunting cabin. To Ellen I said, "Would you know who Charlotte would've dealt with at SynGen?"

"That would be the CFO," she said. "Tate." I heard a sharp intake of breath, and then she said, "Whoops. I gotta go."

"Hey," I said. "Wait a minute." But the phone had gone dead.

I gazed off toward New Hampshire. Three more names that I could, without much imagination, add to my list of suspects in

Charlotte Gillespie's disappearance—or whatever had happened to her. Tate, the CFO, was probably the one who got her fired.

On the assumption that Charlotte and Noah were linked, the SynGen guys could be suspects in Noah's murder, too.

When I called Susannah's number, Alex answered. "The Hollingsworth residence."

"It's me," I said. "How's it going?"

"Okay," she said. "The state police were here poking around and asking questions. I expected yellow crime-scene tape, with photographers and forensics experts swarming all over the place dusting for fingerprints and looking for tire tracks and footprints and cigarette butts, grilling Susannah, playing good-cop-bad-cop. But there were just two of them, very polite young men. I served them coffee, and they talked with Susannah and sleuthed around for maybe a half hour, tipped their hats, and left. Paul got here a little while ago. He and Susannah are out on the deck now." She dropped her voice. "Remember what we were saying?"

"About their lack of passion?"

"Yes. It's pretty obvious. He's very solicitous of her. Says all the right things. When he got here, they hugged each other, and he kissed her cheek, and she thanked him for coming, and . . ."

"No passion."

"Yes."

"Brother and sister."

"Sort of. First thing he said was he can't stay long."

"Being dutiful," I said. "How's Susannah doing?"

"I admire her a lot, Brady. She is completely blown away by the idea that someone would murder Noah. But I think she's been preparing herself for his death for a long time."

"I've got to speak to her for a minute."

"Sure. Hang on."

A minute later, Susannah said, "Hi, Brady."

"How're you doing?"

"I'm okay, considering. What's up?"

"I know this isn't a good time, but I wondered if I could run a couple of names past you."

"Names?"

"Yes. I'm wondering if these men were people Noah might've known."

"You think—"

"I don't think anything, Susannah. Here are the names. Gerald Stasio?"

"Um . . . no. I don't recall Noah ever mentioning that name."

"Roland Passman."

"No."

"Arthur Tate."

"I don't . . . no, I don't think so." She paused, then said, "Who are these people, Brady? What's going on?"

"Probably nothing is going on that has anything to do with what happened to Noah. They used to be Charlotte Gillespie's clients. They're officers of a firm in Portland called SynGen."

"SynGen," she repeated. "Sure. They're some kind of research outfit."

"Well, I believe they're the ones who got Charlotte fired. These guys might've rented Arnold Hood's cabin for deer hunting."

"I guess it's possible my father could've run into them if they were using Hoodie's cabin and hunting around here," said Susannah. "But I don't remember him ever mentioning any of those names." She laughed quickly. "You are taking your deputy duties seriously, aren't you?"

"I don't like it when my friends are . . ." I let my voice trail off.

"Murdered," she said. "It's okay. You can say it. I know what happened. And Brady?"

"Yes?"

"I'm not making fun of you. If you can find out who did this to my father, I will love you forever."

Several responses came to my mind. Twenty-four hours earlier I had kissed Susannah and she had pressed her body against mine, and the memory of it was still vivid. "And if I can't?" I said.

"Oh, I guess I'll love you anyway," she said.

"Susannah . . ."

"Alex is a lifesaver," she said. "I love her to pieces."

"Me, too," I said. "Why don't you let me speak to her again."

"See you later?"

"Yes. Of course. Say hello to Paul for me."

"Sure. I'll get Alex."

A moment later Alex said, "What're you up to this afternoon?"

"I don't know," I said. "I'm trying to figure it out. Want me to come over?"

"Not yet. Call later on. Okay?"

"Sure. You take care."

"You, too."

I disconnected from Alex, put the phone on the deck, yawned, and slouched down in the rocker. I tried to concentrate on what I knew, make the connections, play out the possibilities. But the sun was warm on my face, and with my eyes closed and my heels up on the rail I discovered that I could rock gently with no effort, and I was aware of my mind losing its focus . . .

I was jarred awake by the slamming of a car door, and before I could sit up straight, young Paris LeClair, with his greenish-yellow hair and his earrings and his skinny arms and baggy pants, had bounced up onto the deck. "Hey, hey there, Mr. Coyne," he said. He was blinking fast and flapping his hands around. "You gotta come with me, man. I got something to show you."

TWENTY-SEVEN

❖━━━━━━━━━━━━━━━❖

I waved my hand toward one of the rockers. "Have a seat," I said to Paris. "Relax, son. Calm down. How about a Coke or something?"

He smacked his fist into his palm. "Shit, man. Come *on*, willya?"

"Can't. I'm waiting for a phone call."

He skipped over to me and grabbed the front of my shirt. His yellow-green hair was flying around his face and his eyes were small and glittery. "Fuck the phone call. This is important."

I looked down at his hand until he let go of my shirt. "Tell me what this is all about," I said. "Did you find out who made those swastikas?"

"No," he said. "And I don't *know* what it's all about. I gotta show you. Okay?"

"Paris," I said, "what've you been smoking?"

He rolled his eyes. "Oh, man," he said. "Are you stupid or something?"

"It's not about those swastikas?"

"No." He punched his thigh. "I'm trying to tell you—"

"So tell me."

He shook his head. "Just come with me." He hesitated, then smiled. "Please, okay?"

I smiled. "That's better." I pushed myself up from the chair.

Paris skittered around to the front of the house, and I followed him. A battered old brown Volkswagen Rabbit was parked at an awkward angle in the middle of the driveway. He went over to my Wrangler. "We better take yours," he said.

I shrugged, and we got in. "Where to?"

"Head for the place where I . . . you know. Where I messed up your car."

I backed down the driveway. It occurred to me that Paris could've been leading me to someone who made swastikas and strangled old men and didn't like snoopy deputy sheriffs. I shook the thought away. "You going to tell me what this is all about?" I said.

"I gotta show it to you."

I pulled onto the road and headed down the hill. "Did you watch *Schindler's List* yet?"

"Three times," he said.

"Well?"

"I can't talk about it," he said quietly. "Every time I think about it I feel like I can't breathe."

"Did you get the point?"

"Oh, man," he whispered. "I didn't know that stuff. Honest to God, Mr. Coyne. If I'd known that I never would've . . . you know." He laughed quickly. "After the first time, I tried to get my old man to watch it. He came in, took one look, and said, 'Hell. This is black-and-white. I don't watch no black-and-white movies.' He's an asshole."

We bounced over the dirt roads, and when we came to the long driveway into Charlotte's place where the No Trespassing sign still sported its red swastika, Paris said, "Not here. Keep going. It's right down this road."

The road was barely wide enough for two cars to pass. A mixture of pine and oak arched overhead, and underbrush grew thick along both sides. We seemed to be weaving through a narrow, dark tunnel. About a quarter of a mile past Charlotte's driveway we came to a wooden bridge. It had no railings and was just wide enough for a single car. A stream passed under it. I stopped halfway over the bridge and gazed down at the water. "Is this Cutter's Run?" I said to Paris.

"Yeah."

Sunbaked rocks and gravel and sand lay exposed along the creek's banks. A thin trickle of water flowed in the channel. The beaver dam upstream was still doing its job.

About a hundred yards past the bridge, Paris said, "Here. Stop here."

I pulled over against the bushes, leaving barely enough room for a car to squeeze past. Paris wiggled out and came around to my side. "This way," he said. "Come on."

I got out. Paris was already striding down the road, turning as he walked to see if I was following. When I caught up to him, he was standing by a break in the stone wall that paralleled the road, and I could see that an ancient tote road twisted up into the woods. It was on the other side of the stream from Charlotte's driveway. This old woods road, Cutter's Run, and the driveway up to Charlotte's cabin formed three roughly parallel lines.

"This way, man," said Paris, pointing into the woods. "An old tannery used to be up there. This was the road that went into it."

"Cutter's tannery," I said. "I tried to catch a trout from the beaver pond yesterday. I noticed some old pilings and the remnants of the milldam. Doesn't look like this old road's been used for fifty years."

We started into the woods, following the tote road. It was just a pair of old ruts. Knee-high weeds grew in it, and alders hugged close against both sides. We'd gone no more than fifteen or twenty feet when we had to step over the trunk of a thick poplar tree that had fallen across it.

"Come on," said Paris. The woods pushed against us from both sides and arched over our heads, and the smell of damp earth and decaying leaves and lush, overripe foliage was strong. From off to the left came the faint gurgle of water trickling over stones. Cicadas buzzed in the trees. Dust and pollen and tiny insects floated in the narrow beams of sunlight that filtered down through the canopy overhead.

213

We'd gone another fifty feet or so into the woods when we came to a heavy chain barring the way. It was attached at both ends to thick concrete pillars with iron rings embedded in them. The chain was rusty and obviously old. It looked like it had hung there since the tannery shut down.

Paris went over to one end of the chain and scooched down. "Come here," he said. "Take a look at this."

I went over and squatted beside him. He was holding a large padlock that linked the chain to the ring in the concrete pillar. The padlock was rusty and old, too. But when I looked closer, I saw scratches on its surface, as if it had been used recently.

"This is what you wanted to show me?" I said to Paris.

"Listen," he said. "I went up to that cabin. I wanted to see the outhouse, you know?"

"The swastika," I said.

He nodded. "I didn't make that swastika. I told you that. I been tryin' to find out who did, like I promised." He shrugged. "No luck so far. So anyways, I went up there—night before last, it was. Monday. I parked in the driveway and walked in. It was late, about midnight. I used a flashlight on the way in, but when I got up there on the hill I turned it off. There was enough moon to see okay, once my eyes got used to it. Anyway, while I'm up there looking at the outhouse, I think I hear voices. It was spooky, man. I mean, there's nobody living anywhere around there. Except the lady. Charlotte. I'm thinking about spooks, like I did something bad, making that swastika on your car, and now her ghost is after me. These ghosty voices, you know?

"So anyways, I look in the direction of the voices, and then I see lights flashing and flickering in the woods. And they're coming from the old tannery. And then I hear an engine down there. Sounded like a truck or a tractor or something. So I creep down the hill a ways so I can see better."

Paris looked up at me. "I couldn't see much, with the leaves and everything in the way. But something was going on at the tannery. That's where the lights and the voices were." He shook his head. "So I watched for a while, I don't know how long. It seemed like an hour, man, but it might've been only ten minutes. Spooky as

214

shit, you know? Anyways, after a while the lights start moving down along the stream. Truck lights, see? And they're following this old road—this one here—just kind of jiggling along, real slow. After a while, they're gone. No more voices, no more lights. Nothing. I waited for a while, and then, man, I got the hell out of there."

"And you came to me," I said.

He shook his head quickly. "No. That was two nights ago. The next day—yesterday—I come back. I see this road and I figure it's the one they were using. I start walking, like we're doing, and I find this lock, and it's pretty obvious that somebody's using this road. I mean, that tree back there that's across the road? You can move it. Someone chopped it down. You can see the ax marks on the end of it. It's just to make it look like no one uses it. Last night I went back up the hill. I waited till about one A.M., but nobody showed up. Which was okay with me.

"Anyway," he said with a shrug, "I figured I better tell you."

"Why?"

He frowned. "Huh?"

"Why did you figure you should tell me? What do you think is going on here?"

He looked at me blankly. "I don't know. I mean, I had to tell somebody. I'm not gonna tell my old man. He'd just give me a backhander for snooping around. I came by your house this morning, but nobody was home."

"You saw the lights and heard this truck or whatever it was on Monday?" I said.

He nodded.

"But not last night."

"No. But I remembered one night last week Weezie and I were out driving around, and we were on this road sometime after midnight and we had to pull over because a truck was coming at us. Coming from this direction." He shrugged. "It could've been coming from there. Who else'd be driving these roads that time of night?"

"What day was that?"

"When I saw the truck on the road?" He frowned, then said, "Wednesday. I'm pretty sure it was Wednesday."

"A week ago today."

He nodded.

"So what do you figure?" I said.

Paris shook his head. "I don't know, Mr. Coyne. I just thought, that lady and all . . ."

I stood up and lit a cigarette. Cutter's old tannery was on Noah's property. Anyone who would wait until midnight to use it, who would disguise his use of the old tote road by felling a tree across it, and who would bar the way with a chain and a strong padlock, was clearly intent on not being observed.

Charlotte Gillespie could easily have seen lights and heard voices from her cabin. Perhaps Noah had, too. His "pissing platform" faced in this direction.

Was that what had got them killed?

Paris touched my shoulder. "Come on," he said. "Let's check it out."

I shook my head. "No. Not now. Let's clear out of here."

"What?" he said. "You scared?"

"Sure," I said.

He frowned at me, then shrugged.

"My car's parked right there on the road," I said.

"Oh," he said. "Right."

We followed the old tannery road back out. Here and there I noticed oil stains on the goldenrod that grew between the ruts. Crankcase oil, I guessed. And where the tote road ended at the dirt road, I found a bare patch of sand that held the faint imprint of a tire.

Paris skittered ahead of me, and he was already sitting in the Wrangler when I got there. I climbed in beside him and fumbled out a cigarette.

"Gimme one of those, huh?" he said.

I held the pack to him. He took a cigarette and I held my Zippo for him. His hands were twitching.

"Relax," I said. "You did the right thing. Now you don't have to worry about it."

"It was way spooky, man," he said. "So what do you think's going on?"

"I don't know."

I started up the car, turned around, and headed back.

When we pulled into Alex's driveway, Paris said, "You got your car painted, huh? So what do I owe you?"

"Five bucks."

He looked at me and grinned. "Come on, Mr. Coyne. I told you I'd pay for it."

"I used the expensive stuff. Rustoleum. That's what Leon recommended. You can pay me in installments if you want."

He peered through the windshield at the hood. "You did a crummy job. It needs another coat. Get another can of paint. I'll give you ten bucks next time I see you."

He started to get out. I grabbed his arm. "You did good," I said. "What you showed me might be important."

He shrugged. "I figure I owe you. And that lady. I didn't understand about swastikas, you know?"

I nodded.

"But that movie . . ."

"Now you do understand."

"Oh, yeah. I understand, all right."

"Listen, Paris," I said. "You stay away from that tannery."

"Right." He grinned. "Pretty spooky, huh?"

"Absolutely." I held out my hand, and he took it. "You're a good man," I said.

He rolled his eyes. "Sure."

"I mean it."

"Yeah, well, so're you, Mr. Coyne."

We got out of the car and I followed him over to his Volkswagen. Paris climbed in.

I leaned my hands on the roof and bent down to his window. "My son Billy got his ear pierced when he was about your age."

"Yeah?"

I nodded. "Yeah. That was four or five years ago. Some girl talked him into it. He wore a little diamond stud in it for a while. Then he let the hole grow back in."

"What happened to the girl?"

I smiled. "I don't know. Billy's had lots of girls."

Paris touched his ear. "My old man thinks earrings are faggy."

"That why you got them?"

He cocked his head, then grinned. "Nah. Some girl talked me into it."

"The hair, too?"

"See," he said, "I *know* the hair looks dumb. I did *that* for my old man. I actually kinda like the earrings."

Paris turned the key in the ignition. The Rabbit coughed and sputtered for a minute before the engine caught. He shifted into reverse and I stood back.

But he didn't back down the driveway. Instead, he leaned his head out the window. "Uh, Mr. Coyne," he said.

"Yes?"

"Can I ask you something?"

"Sure."

"You got a son, huh?"

"Two sons, actually."

He looked down toward his lap for a moment, then turned back to me. "Suppose one of your sons, um, got a girl . . . you know?"

"Pregnant?"

"Yeah. I mean when he was in high school."

I looked at Paris for a moment, and I remembered worrying about Joey, who'd had the same girlfriend throughout high school. He and Debbie had always seemed to have an unnaturally mature relationship for teenage kids. I assumed they'd been intimate, though I never asked directly. I'd ventured a few suggestions about AIDS and pregnancy, and Joey had always laughed. He knew all about that stuff.

And Billy, my older, had had dozens of girlfriends. Billy liked the pretty girls. The sexier the better. He'd gone out with seniors when he was a sophomore, and I'd worried about him, too.

The fact was, I never stopped worrying about my boys. Getting their girlfriends pregnant was always one of those worries.

I leaned against the side of Paris's car. "You know what the options are," I said.

He nodded. "She says it's too late for an abortion."

218

"What about putting the child up for adoption?"

He shook his head. "She wants to keep it."

"What does your father say?"

"He doesn't know." He let out a long breath. "Can I tell you something, Mr. Coyne?"

"Of course."

"When she—Weezie, my girl—when she told me, I was, like, proud. I mean, my old man treats me like a baby, like I got no brain, like he knows everything. So I'm thinking, hey, I'm a man. I guess I'm a man if I can . . . you know? And Weezie's like, okay, we get married and I get a job and she cooks and takes care of the baby, you know, and it's like we're grown up and we don't have to live with our parents, and at first it sounds good to me. I can work for my old man, we can rent a trailer and save up for maybe a house."

He looked up at me, and then he looked away. But I saw the glitter in his eyes. "The truth is, Mr. Coyne, I don't love Weezie and she don't love me. And I don't want to quit school, and I don't want to be a fuckin' plumber's helper. I was always thinkin' of college. Learning something. Getting out of Garrison." He turned away from me and brushed the back of his hand across his eyes. "I don't know what to do," he mumbled.

"You and Weezie have to tell your parents," I said.

"My old man'll kill me. I know that."

"You might be surprised," I said. "Any man who would insist that his boy own up to vandalizing someone's property has the makings of a good father. What about her parents?"

Paris smiled and shook his head. "She's only got a mother. I think Weezie's mom got knocked up herself. She's—Mrs. Palmer, I mean—she has a lot of men coming around. 'Guests,' she calls them. It pisses Weezie off, how these guys come to their trailer and drink beer and spend the night and then never show up again. But you know what, Mr. Coyne?"

I shook my head.

"I think Weezie wants to be just like her mother," he said. "And it scares the shit out of me."

"Tell your father," I said. "Tell him what you've told me. Expect him to be upset. Be patient with him. Let him get over it. You and Weezie can't handle this all by yourselves."

"He'll kill me, I'm telling you."

"I doubt it," I said.

Paris looked at me for a minute. Then he nodded. "Thanks, Mr. Coyne," he said. "Your sons are lucky." He backed out of the driveway, poked his arm out the window and waved, and headed down the road. I could hear the roar of his rusted-out muffler for a long time before it finally faded in the distance.

TWENTY-EIGHT

❖————————————❖

It was a few minutes after four in the afternoon. I went inside and checked Alex's answering machine. Its red light glowed steadily. Skip Churchill had not returned my call.

I took the portable phone to the kitchen table. Skip's number rang three times before his machine clicked in. "You've reached Churchill Accounting Associates," came Skip's voice. "Our office hours are nine to five Monday through Friday. Please leave a message and we'll get right back to you."

After the beep, I said, "It's four and today's Wednesday, so where the hell are you? It's Brady, and if you're sitting there smirking at your goddam machine while I'm—"

There was a click and a few seconds of buzzing feedback, and then Skip's actual unrecorded voice said, "Okay, okay. I'm here. If I answered the phone every time it rang I'd never do any certified public accounting, you know? Listen, I got that file, and I'll take a look at it as soon as—"

"Do it now," I said. "Didn't you get my message?"

"Sure," said Skip, "and I know you said you were in a hurry. Hell, in this business everybody's in a hurry, Brady. Gimme a break."

"If I told you it was a matter of life and death . . ."

221

"I'd accuse you of flaunting clichés. Come on. This is a spread-sheet, for God's sake. What could be more boring? Hell, I'm an accountant, and even I have trouble getting a hard-on over a spread-sheet."

"Skip," I said, "trust me on this, okay? I really want to know what's on it, and I really do need it pronto."

He sighed. "Maybe you'd better tell me what it's all about."

"Actually, I think it'd be better if I didn't. I want to know what catches your trained and expert eye, if anything. I'll pay you for your time, of course."

"Screw that. I know you didn't bill me for half the time you spent on my divorce."

"Don't you dare ever mention that to Julie," I said. "She obsesses on billable hours. She'd kill me."

He laughed. "Okay. Give me an hour. I'll get back to you."

"I'll call you," I said. "I've got some things to do. How long will you be there?"

"My home is my office. You know that. I'll be here all night. I'm always here. Just start talking to the machine. I'll pick up."

I got a Coke from the refrigerator, then returned to the kitchen table and pecked out Charlie McDevitt's number. Charlie is my old law school roommate. We were best friends then, and now, more than twenty years later, we still are. Charlie's the one man on earth I absolutely trust. Back at Yale, when I aspired to argue civil liberties cases before the Supreme Court, Charlie dreamed of sitting on that Court. He used to say that he'd have to recuse himself from any case I brought to him. The only thing he holds in higher regard than the law is loyalty.

I feel the same about him.

I, of course, ended up in Boston negotiating divorces and writing wills, and rarely do I argue anything before any court. I spend most of my time with clients and other lawyers, and if I do my job right, I submit a *fait accompli* to a judge, who affirms it with grateful alacrity.

Charlie's been a prosecutor for the Department of Justice for his entire career. He works out of the JFK Building at Government Center in Boston, a twenty-minute stroll from my office in Copley

222

Square. He never has admitted it, but I suspect that he asked for the Boston assignment so that he and I would be close enough to play golf and fish for trout together now and then.

When we reminisce about our law-student dreams, Charlie just laughs. "What the hell did we know?" he says. "Yale was a fountain of knowledge—and we were there to drink."

After I negotiated my way through the federal government's automated answering maze and pecked in Charlie's four-digit extension number, Shirley, his secretary, answered the phone.

Shirley is plump and white-haired, a grandmother about a dozen times. She's a dead ringer for the woman whose face appears on the package of a popular brand of frozen pastries.

"It's Brady, darlin'," I said. "And how have you been feeling this summer?"

She said her neuralgia was no better, but no worse, thank the Lord, then mentioned several people by their first names, on the false assumption that I remembered which were her children and which were the nieces and nephews and all their respective spouses and children. "Jerry's Becky, don't you know, is expecting again, bless her soul, and Kelly and Randy are back together, thank the Lord. It was breakin' poor Lloyd's heart, it was, Mr. Coyne, and if it weren't for little Abigail comin' back home after that terrible time she had . . ."

What I loved about Shirley was that she gave me undeserved credit for keeping track of them all and remembering. She never failed to ask after my two boys, and if I skimped with the details, she insisted that I elaborate.

When she finally connected me to Charlie, he said, "So what can you do for me today?"

"Buy you a bowl of Marie's minestrone," I said. "With a platter of those deep-fried calamari you love on the side."

"Oh, oh. What is it this time?"

"I need information on a company based in Portland, Maine, called SynGen, Inc.," I told him. "And anything you can find out about its board of directors." I gave him the three names that Ellen Sanderson had given me and summarized the events of the past couple of weeks in Garrison, Maine.

When I finished, Charlie was chuckling. "You're doing it again, Coyne," he said.

"Doing what?"

"Snooping."

"I told you, I'm a sheriff's deputy. This is my job."

"Oh, boy," said Charlie. "That sheriff must not have heard of Grabel's Law."

"Who in hell is Grabel?"

"Grabel had a law of mathematics named after him. Grabel's Law states that two is not equal to three, even for very high values of two."

"You mean, you can't make chicken salad out of chicken shit."

"Exactly. And you can't make a lawman out of a lawyer." He gave a big phony sigh. "But, of course, I will see what I can learn about SynGen, Inc., and these guys Stasio, Passman, and Tate. I will breach several government security systems to ferret out this information, and I will get back to you."

"When?"

"Huh?"

"When will you get back to me?"

"Don't push me, Coyne. Marie's calamari isn't that good."

"The mention of it makes you drool and you know it," I said. "This is urgent, Charlie. Climb into that monster mainframe of yours. We've got one and probably two murders up here, and both of them were people I liked. Not to mention a poisoned dog and swastikas."

"Swastikas, huh?"

"Yes."

"Jesus," he muttered. "Okay. Give me a couple of hours. But remember something, okay?"

"What's that?"

"He who dies with the most toys is still dead. And that's the truth."

After I hung up with Charlie I got into my Wrangler and drove to the Garrison Veterinary Hospital and Kennels.

Three people, one dog, and two cages that might've held cats sat in the waiting room. Betsy slouched in the swivel chair behind the counter, talking on the telephone and admiring her fingernails. I put my elbows on the counter and leaned forward, looking at her, trying to catch her eye.

She glanced up without any hint that she remembered me, then returned her attention to her nails.

I cleared my throat loudly, and she turned her head my way again. "I need to see Dr. Spear," I said.

She covered the receiver with her hand, rolled her eyes, and waved her hand at the waiting area. "Have a seat," she said. "There's people ahead of you."

Then she swiveled around, turning her back on me. I reached over the counter, unhooked the gate, walked through, and opened the door that led to the back.

"Hey," said Betsy. "You can't go in there."

I ignored her and kept going. I found myself in a small examining room with a waist-high stainless-steel table and glass-fronted cabinets that held bottles and bandages and swabs and a variety of other medical supplies. The room was empty, so I pushed through the door on the other side, which opened onto a narrow green-tiled corridor. As I stood there looking around, a door opened on my right and Dr. Spear appeared.

She was peeling latex gloves off her fingers. When she saw me, she cocked her head, frowned for an instant, then smiled. "Did Betsy send you back here?" she said.

"No. She told me to wait my turn."

Dr. Spear nodded. "Betsy loves animals, but she's not much good with people. Come on."

I followed her into an office barely large enough to hold a small metal desk and a couple of wooden chairs. Bookshelves crammed with serious-looking volumes lined the wall on the left, and the opposite wall was hung with framed diplomas and a large calendar that pictured a litter of irresistibly cute kittens all tangled together in a basket.

The back wall was dominated by a large window that overlooked the side parking lot and, beyond that, a meadow that sloped away to a second-growth hardwood forest.

225

Dr. Spear slumped behind the desk and gestured at one of the chairs.

I sat down. "Doctor . . ."

"Oh, call me Laura, Mr. Coyne. Please." She removed her glasses, laid them on the desk, pinched the bridge of her nose between her thumb and forefinger, and closed her eyes. When she opened them, she said, "I understand Ms. Gillespie is still missing."

I nodded.

"I heard about those swastikas," she said. She shook her head. "It all goes together, doesn't it? With her poisoned dog, I mean."

I shrugged. "I believe it does."

"The sheriff was by the other day. He talked to Betsy. I guess it's important who picked up the puppy." She shook her head. "I blew it."

"You didn't know," I said. "I have a question for you."

She nodded.

"You've lived around here for a long time, right?"

She smiled. "All my life, except for college."

"You know Cutter's Run?"

"Sure. There used to be a tannery there."

"I went fishing there yesterday," I said. "Didn't catch a thing. And I felt a little woozy afterward. I figure the water's still got old chemicals in it, and maybe runoff from the orchards, you know, chemical fertilizers, the insecticides they spray on the trees, and—"

"I know what you're thinking," she said. "You're thinking that little puppy drank from the stream and that's what poisoned him. It's possible, of course, but I doubt it. Not the way that poison acted. He died so fast. I think he got into something undiluted and powerful and—and unusual." She smiled at me. "Dogs can drink almost anything, you know. Stuff that would make us vomit for a week doesn't even faze them."

I shrugged. "It was just a thought. Nothing lives there, and—"

"You didn't catch anything, so you think nothing lives there?" She smiled.

"It seemed dead," I said lamely.

"I don't think they stock it," she said. "It warms up too much in the summer for trout." She glanced at her watch. "I'm sorry . . ."

"I apologize," I said. "You're busy. Thanks for your time."

"I wish I could be of more help."

As we walked back into the waiting room, she said, "Did you hear about Noah Hollingsworth?"

"I heard he died."

"A nice man," she said. "I treated his horse. He gave me a basket of apples every fall."

TWENTY-NINE

W hen I walked into Leon's store, Pauline was sitting on the stool behind the counter with her arms folded over her chest and two deep vertical creases carved into the middle of her forehead. She watched me suspiciously over the tops of her wire-rimmed glasses as I approached her, and before I could say anything, she reached under the counter and slapped two newspapers onto the counter. "We run out," she said, her voice dripping with accusation. "Leon insisted we hold 'em for you, even though we had to turn down folks who come in askin' for one. I say first come, first served. But Leon says you always come for your paper. Well, you wasn't in yesterday, so I told him he's full of it. Anyways, here's your papers. The news ain't very new anymore."

I smiled. "Thank you for holding them, Mrs. Staples. I do appreciate it." I handed her a dollar bill, and she slipped it into the cash register.

I folded the newspapers and tucked them under my arm. "Is Leon around?" I said.

She snapped her chin toward the back of the store. "S'pose to be countin' stock. Probly sneakin' in a nap."

"Mind if I speak to him?"

"Help yourself," she said with a shrug.

"Thanks." I started for the stockroom out back.

"Excitement up at Hollingsworth's this mornin', Mr. Coyne," said Pauline. "Hear they carted old Noah away."

I stopped and turned around. Pauline Staples was frowning and nodding. "Hear the first person Miss Fancy Pants called was you, Mr. Coyne," she said. "Hear it wasn't no accident, neither, what happened to Noah."

"What else did you hear?" I said.

"Oh, I ain't the kind to spread rumors, don't you know. Anyways, you was there." Her eyebrows were arched expectantly.

"I don't really know anything about it," I said. I lifted my hand to her, then went out past the woodstove and its semicircle of chairs and pushed open the door into the back room.

It was lit by a single bare sixty-watt bulb screwed into a ceiling socket and two dusty windows that bracketed the back door. It smelled of dirt and mold. All four walls were lined with sagging wood-plank shelves crammed with cartons, bags, bottles, and cans. Cardboard boxes and wooden crates were piled randomly over most of the floor space. Leon was sitting on one of the crates. He had a clipboard on his knee, a lump of tobacco in his cheek, a Styrofoam cup in his hand, and a pencil over his ear. He was looking at me as if he'd been expecting me and I was late. He patted the crate beside him. "Take a load off, Mr. Coyne," he said. "I was just gettin' away from that old witch for a few minutes."

I went over and sat beside him.

"Ain't seen you in a couple days," he said. "Been savin' them papers for you."

"Yes," I said. "I appreciate it."

"Ain't had a chance to congratulate you."

I frowned. "What did I do?"

"Some folks're wondering how a fella from away gets himself deputized." He pursed his lips, lifted the Styrofoam cup to his mouth, and spit voluptuously into it.

I shook my head. "It's just Sheriff Dickman's idea of a joke, Leon."

"Folks're thinkin'," he said, turning to look at me, "what's a slick lawyer from Boston doin', snoopin' around other people's property, stickin' his nose in places it don't rightly belong."

"In the first place," I said with a smile, "I'm not all that slick, Leon. Anyway, I'm not a real deputy. I found that swastika on my car and reported it to the sheriff, and . . ." I flapped my hands to suggest the foolishness of it all.

He shrugged. "I don't make no judgments, mind you. But that ain't the way Hoodie sees it."

I cocked my head. "How does Hoodie see it?"

Leon reached over and patted my leg with his big rough hand. "Now, Mr. Coyne," he said. "Don't you get me wrong, okay? Hoodie's been needin' a thrashin' for some time, and most folks around here are probably clappin' and cheerin' for what you and the sheriff done to him. You ask me—"

"What," I said, "did we do to Arnold Hood?"

Leon shifted his chaw to the other cheek. "I guess you drug him out of his house and whacked him around some. Serves him right."

"Arnold told you this?"

"He come limpin' in yesterday just before we closed up, pissin' and moanin'. I ask him what was the matter with his leg. He said you done it to him."

"Me?"

"Yes, sir."

"Did he say why I did it?"

Leon grinned. "Hoodie says he's mindin' his own business— which I don't believe, Mr. Coyne—and you and Dickman go bargin' into his kitchen, grab ahold of his shirt, and haul him outdoors. Start askin' questions about Miz Charlotte, which he says he can't answer, and you shove him down and start thumpin' his leg with a tire iron. He says—you gotta pardon the expression, but it's how Hoodie put it—he says he guesses you got a hard-on for Charlotte." He shook his head. "Anybody got a hard-on for anybody, it's Hoodie. Like I said, I don't believe him. But he did say you showed him a deputy's badge. Hoodie ain't got enough imagination to make that up."

I smiled. "That's quite a story, Leon."

"It's Hoodie's story, not mine," he said. "You want a beer?"

"I wouldn't mind," I said.

He pushed himself up and went to an old refrigerator beside the back door. He came back with two cans of Coors and handed one to me. I snapped it open and took a long swallow.

Leon settled back onto the crate beside me. "I tell you this," he said. "Hoodie's had it comin' for a long time, and I doubt many folks around here are feelin' bad for him. Especially Miz Palmer. No, sir."

"Who's that?"

"You never met Janine Palmer?"

I shook my head.

"Lives in a trailer with that girl of hers out to West County Road past the old dump. Brings her food stamps here. Janine ain't never had it easy, but whenever she's got a spare dollar she tries the lottery, and every time she does, she tells me she expects she's gonna win, and then she's gonna move her and her little girl back up to Calais where she come from, buy a house near her folks." He paused to pop the top of his beer can. "I don't spread gossip, Mr. Coyne. Pauline does, but not me. This ain't gossip. It's the truth, and I guess there's no harm in sharin' what's true." He turned and arched his eyebrows at me.

"The truth isn't the same as gossip," I said.

Leon tilted up his head, lifted his beer can to his mouth, and took a long swallow. Then he squinted at me. "Hoodie likes girls," he said.

I shrugged. "Nothing wrong with that, I guess."

"No, I mean *girls*. Not women."

"Young girls, you mean," I said.

"Yup, suh." He nodded emphatically. "I sure'n hell don't get it. Hoodie's not too bright and not very good-lookin' and he ain't got any money." He shrugged. "Must be hung like a gorilla, only thing I can figger. Anyways, poor Miz Palmer, tryin' to raise that wild little thing of hers all by herself, and that Louise, twitchin' her butt around in them painted-on dungarees of hers at anybody with a lump in his pants." Leon took another long swig of beer, and I noticed that he did it without removing the tobacco from his cheek. When he lowered the can, he looked at me and said, "Louise is tellin' everybody it's the LeClair boy. But most folks figure it's Hoodie."

232

"Wait," I said. "Louise—that's Paris LeClair's girlfriend?"

He nodded. "Hoodie wanted nothin' to do with her once he knocked her up."

"Paris calls her Weezie," I said. "Is that who you mean?"

"Yes, sir. That boy's braggin' on how he shoved a biscuit in her oven, and she ain't contradicting him. But that's Hoodie's biscuit, and I guess young Paris LeClair is about the only one in town who don't know it." He tilted up his beer can again, and I watched his throat work as he drained it. Then he said, "But you come back here for a reason, Mr. Coyne, and I don't guess it was to find out who's gettin' who pregnant around here."

"No," I said. "Actually, I wondered if you know anything about the old tannery."

"Cutter's?" He shrugged. "What's to know? It shut down before I was born, and Noah Hollingsworth's daddy bought it up." He cocked his head and narrowed his eyes at me. "I s'pose you heard about Noah. Damn shame. Knowed him all my life. Good fella, Noah. Knew how to mind his business, always paid cash."

"I liked him a lot," I said.

"Hear they think Miz Susannah might've done it."

"Leon," I said, "is there anything you don't hear?"

He shrugged. "People come in here, they tell you stories. Ambulance picks up somebody in Garrison, I hear about it. Sheriff shows up, then some state cops, don't sound like no heart attack to me. Gotta figure there's something to it."

"Well, I doubt if Susannah is a suspect," I said. "What about the tannery?"

He shook his head. "Nothin', far as I know. Why?"

I shrugged. "I just wondered if it was being used for anything."

"Now why would you wonder a thing like that? That tannery's been shut down since they brung in electricity. Nothin' but falling-down concrete and a few holes in the ground." He sucked on his lips for a minute, then looked up at me. "Though I understand Hoodie had some interest in it a while back."

"What kind of interest?"

Leon shook his head. "Hoodie figured Noah ought to deed it over to him, since it was next to his property there and no good to

Noah." He flapped his hand. "That's Hoodie. Always lookin' to get something for nothin'."

"But why would Arnold Hood want it?" I said.

Leon picked up his Styrofoam cup and spit into it. "Beats the hell out of me." He examined the inside of the cup, then turned and peered at me. "And why would you care about that old place?"

"No reason," I said. "I tried to catch a trout out of the beaver pond there yesterday and saw the remains. I'm interested in old historic places, that's all."

Leon laughed. "Nothin' historic about that place. What I hear, old man Cutter never did make any money at it. Anyways, I guess it's Miz Susannah's now. Maybe Hoodie can convince her to sign it over to him. That Hoodie's got a way with women." He held up his empty beer can. "Another?"

I glanced at my watch. It was nearly six-thirty. "No, thanks." I stood up and held my hand out to him. "I've got to run, Leon. Thanks for the beer."

He nodded. "Anytime. Listen, though. Pauline's givin' me a lot of shit about holdin' your newspapers."

"It's very considerate of you. But hereafter, if I'm not in by noontime, you go ahead and sell them."

He smiled. "Appreciate it. I gotta choose my fights with Pauline, and much as I'd like to oblige you, holdin' your paper for you ain't one of 'em."

THIRTY

When I got back to Alex's house, I found the red light on the
answering machine blinking. One message. I pressed the button,
the tape whirred, beeped once, and then I heard Charlie's voice.
"Coyne," he said. "You'd better call me."

I didn't like the sound of that. Even when he's leaving a message
on my answering machine, Charlie rarely fails to insult me, or crack
a bad joke, or mention trout fishing or the Red Sox bullpen or a
new Italian restaurant he's discovered. On the few occasions when
he has failed to, it's invariably meant bad news of some kind.

I sat down, lit a cigarette, and poked out his number, and when
Shirley answered and I told her it was me again, she said, "Oh, yes,
Mr. Coyne. Mr. McDevitt is waiting for your call."

When Shirley is all business, something's definitely up.

"Brady," said Charlie when Shirley connected us, "what in hell
is going on up there?"

"I thought I explained——"

"Yeah, you did," he said. "You're not telling me everything."

"I told you everything I know. You'd better tell me what this is
I'm hearing in your voice."

He cleared his throat. "Maybe I'm in the process of being shit-
canned here, and this is their way of letting me know. Otherwise . . ."

"Otherwise *what*?" I said when his voice trailed off.

"Otherwise I would probably be risking my neck to tell you. But fuck it. Listen. Normally, getting the dope on someplace like SynGen, Inc., is simple. Tap into the IRS files and I can scan their tax returns. Department of Commerce gives me the terms of their incorporation, history, clients, employees, board of directors, who they buy stuff from and sell it to, anything I want to know about their business. Anything I still don't know, I can slip into the State of Maine files by hitting about three keys on the computer. You hear what I'm saying?"

"I think so," I said.

"Access denied," said Charlie. "All across the board. I type in 'SynGen, Inc.,' and I run into a brick wall. I tried a few roundabout routes, because this kind of thing both pisses me off and scares me. I tried those guys—Passman, Tate, Stasio. Same fucking thing, Brady. Listen, I can get Saddam's shoe size if I want it. I can get the names of every woman the president's ever looked at, and what cigarettes they smoke and whether they like their martinis stirred or shaken. See, it's not as if these guys aren't in the computers. There are files on them, all right. I just can't open them. You getting the picture here?"

"Maybe," I said slowly, "you'd better spell it out for me."

"Okay. Read my lips, here, and I'll make it simple for you. Stay away from SynGen. Steer clear of Tate, Passman, and Stasio. Just forget it. Okay?"

"Why?"

I heard Charlie blow out a quick breath. "Why? Because, my naive but nevertheless beloved friend, I want to keep my fishing partner around for a while. I want to collect that plate of Marie's calamari. Because, goddammit, I am sincerely afraid that something bad will happen to you if you don't back off."

"Charlie, wait—"

"No. You listen to me. Sometimes you are too damned curious for your own good. And sometimes you are just so—so *stupid* that I want to slap some sense into your face. Curiosity and stupidity are a very dangerous combination, Brady. Access denied. Do you understand?"

"Yes," I said. I hesitated. "What about you? Are you in trouble, Charlie?"

I heard him sigh. "I don't know. It's for damn sure that they'll know I tried to get into the company's files. Well, that by itself probably wouldn't set off too many alarms. But then, stupid me, I went after those three guys. They'll see that. What the hell is McDevitt after? they'll be saying. What's he know? Of course, I don't know anything, or if I do, I don't know what I know, which doesn't help. So I'm sitting here trying to think up a story for them when they come around asking. Got any bright ideas?"

"No," I said. "I'm sorry. Obviously it's got something to do with Charlotte Gillespie and Noah Hollingsworth, but whatever it is . . . Who's 'they'?"

"Huh?"

"Who's the 'they' who'll know you were trying to access those files? The 'they' who might come around to interrogate you?"

"Well, hell," he said. "If I knew that I'd be halfway there, wouldn't I?"

"Listen," I said. "I gave a SynGen financial report to an account-ant friend of mine to look at. If he finds anything, I'll let you know. It might help you deal with . . . with whoever you'll have to deal with."

"Oh, boy," muttered Charlie. "Now there's a financial report floating around. Oh, boy."

"It's not floating around. It's—"

"Get it back. Send it to me. No. Cancel that. Just burn it. Okay?"

"It's on a computer disk. I e-mailed a copy of it to Skip Churchill and copied it onto Alex's hard drive."

Charlie laughed. I heard no humor whatsoever in his laugh. "Terrific," he said. "So it's out there in cyberspace somewhere for anybody to snag. And now you probably got Skip in the soup, too. Jesus, Coyne."

"I'm sorry, Charlie," I said. "I didn't know."

"Ah, shit, I know you didn't know. Don't worry about it. Just do what I tell you. Stay the hell away from those guys and that SynGen place. Destroy that disk and erase it from Alex's computer and tell Skip to trash whatever he got from you pronto. Okay?"

"Sure. Okay."

"I mean it, Brady."

"I'll do it, Charlie."

He sighed. "Why do I not quite believe you?"

"Because you think you know me," I said. "But you know I would never do anything to put my friends in jeopardy. I'll talk to Skip right away. I promise."

"And?"

"What do you mean, 'and'?"

"And you'll stop snooping? And you'll destroy the disk?"

"Sure," I said.

He laughed. "You're a fucking liar, Coyne. Look. Be careful, will you?"

"I promise you that," I said.

After I disconnected from Charlie, I tried the sheriff. The dispatcher said she couldn't reach him but would tell him I had called. I asked her to patch me through to his cruiser and mentioned my rank of deputy, but that didn't seem to impress her. I told her it was pretty important, and that didn't impress her, either.

I tried his home number, got his machine, and told him I needed to talk to him. "I've heard some things," I said, trying to sound mysterious.

The phone rang about ten seconds after I hung up. "It's Skip," he said when I picked it up. "I've been trying to reach you for the last fifteen minutes."

"Sorry," I said. "Does this urgency mean you found something?"

"Well, I found something. I don't know what it means, and I wouldn't know if it was urgent or not."

"Tell me," I said.

"Basically," Skip said, "this is the raw data an accountant used to prepare a corporate quarterly report. It's not the report itself. It's the accountant's equivalent of a scratch pad. Income, expenses, taxes, inventories, capital depreciation, salaries, benefits, all that stuff, broken down into categories. In this format, I couldn't tell you what all those categories are, though I can make some guesses.

If I had, say, the previous quarter's report, I could nail all of them for you."

"What would that tell you?"

"That," said Skip, "would tell me where this corporation is cheating."

"What do you mean, cheating?"

"Hell, Brady. I don't know. Like I said, this is all in the accountant's shorthand. It's like code. Acronyms and abbreviations that don't make any sense to me. But they'd make sense to a financial officer in the corporation, and they'd sure as hell make sense to a squinty-eyed IRS accountant who had the other records handy."

"Can you make a guess?" I said. "What's your hunch?"

"We accountants," he said, "don't know from hunches. We crunch numbers, not guesses."

I laughed. "Jesus, Skip."

"Well, it's true," he said. Then he laughed, too. "My guess would be wild and irresponsible. But, hell, accountants can be as wild and irresponsible as, say, a lawyer, when their client isn't paying them." He hesitated. "What it looks like to me is that somebody's stealing this firm's inventory."

"Stealing?"

"Yes. Or destroying it, or using it in a manner that they want to hide. See, in a report like this one, everything's got to be accounted for. That's why they hire accountants. To account for things. And whoever prepared this data found something they couldn't account for."

"Help me out here," I said. "Can you give me a for instance?"

"For instance," he said, "they buy a dozen computers, and they end up with three of them. No place here does it account for the nine missing computers."

"So they used them up," I said. "Or they broke. They threw them away."

"If we were talking about paper or pencils, you'd be right. But paper and pencils are categorized differently. So is office furniture. Carpets, which need cleaning and wear out, fall into a different category from desks, say, or magazine subscriptions. What we've got here, if it was computers, is the company buying them and then either somebody steals them and keeps them or sells them and pockets the money."

"Computers," I said.

"Nah, it's not computers. That was my for instance, my feeble effort to make it understandable for an ignorant layman like you. What we got here is something purchased in large numbers and at great expense, most of it during the quarter but some of it held over from last year's inventory, that's nearly gone by the end of the quarter, with no accounting for where it went."

"And it's not some kind of office supplies."

"No. Like I said, that'd be in a different category."

"But you can't guess what it could be."

"Nope. I need more information."

"But somebody with that information—"

"Could nail it," he said.

"If you were the accountant who was preparing this report, what would you do?"

"I'd show it to the CFO of the company," he said. "I'd tell him that we've got a discrepancy in the data that needs to be cleared up. I'd tell him it looks like someone's stealing or destroying stuff. Something's not, um, *accounted* for, and it needs to be."

"And suppose this CFO said to the accountant: 'Of course there's a discrepancy. Fix it.' "

"Fix it?" said Skip.

"Hide it. Cover it up. Make it look like there isn't a discrepancy."

"You shitting me? That's illegal and unethical and a violation of everything our noble profession stands for."

"What would you do if they fired you when you refused?"

"Do? I wouldn't do anything. I'd have to get by without that account."

"You wouldn't turn them in?"

"Oh, I get it," he said. He paused for a minute. "Well," he said finally, "it would depend. I probably wouldn't turn anybody in. Someone else might. It's something like you lawyers and your clients. There's a confidentiality, a client privilege, though it's not so clear-cut. If it was something blatantly illegal . . ."

"Okay," I said. "I want you to do me a favor."

"I haven't already done you a favor?"

"Another one. Put what you've just told me into an e-mail for me here at Alex's. Point out exactly where in the data those contradictory numbers are and explain what they mean to you, what your hypotheses are. Send me the e-mail and then trash everything I sent you."

"Trash everything, huh?"

"Yes. Everything."

"Okay," he said. "No problem. But are you gonna tell me what's going on here? Who is this company, anyway?"

"I'm not going to tell you."

"Some client of yours, huh?"

"No," I said. "Definitely not a client. Just don't ask, okay?"

He chuckled. "Sounds mysterious, Brady. You know, there are times when I wish I was a lawyer. You guys have all the fun."

"There are times," I said, "when I wish I was an accountant."

As soon as I clicked off with Skip I called Charlie back and summarized what Skip had told me. He didn't interrupt.

When I finished, Charlie said, "So you think SynGen killed their accountant because she caught them cheating and refused to fudge the numbers?"

"Yes," I said. "Because they were afraid she'd report them."

"But she *didn't* report them," he said. "Something like six months went by before she . . . disappeared, and she didn't do anything."

"Not that we know of." I hesitated. "Maybe—"

"She was blackmailing them," he interrupted.

"I don't know," I said. "I only met her a couple times, but—"

"But she didn't seem like that kind of person." Charlie laughed. "For a hard-bitten lawyer, old buddy, you can be awfully naive."

"She came up here to hide from them," I said. "It took them six months to track her down, and when they did, they killed her."

"Because she refused to cheat for them, and then tried to blackmail them?"

"Maybe she'd decided to blow the whistle on them," I said.

"Then those swastikas . . ."

"Red herrings," I said. "To make it look like a racial thing."

"That missing inventory," said Charlie quietly. "I wonder what it was."

"Charlotte knew." I found myself nodding. "I bet I know someone else who figured it out, too."

"Who?"

"Noah Hollingsworth," I said.

"The guy who—?"

"Yes," I said. "The man who was murdered last night."

Charlie was quiet for a long moment. Then he said, "Your friend Noah was probably snooping around, huh?"

"I don't know."

"They apparently kill snoopers, Brady."

"I know."

"Please," said Charlie. "For once, just back off, will you?"

"Of course," I said. "You think I'm stupid?"

THIRTY-ONE

❯❯————————————————————❮❮

I realized that my stomach was growling. I glanced outside. Darkness was seeping into the yard. I dialed Susannah's number, figuring I'd head over there, maybe bring a pizza for her and Alex.

After three rings, the machine clicked on. "You got Noah Hollingsworth here," came the recording. "Leave a message if you want." It was way spooky, as Paris LeClair would say, hearing the voice of a man who'd been alive twenty-four hours earlier, but now was dead.

After the beep, I said, "It's Brady, wondering what you ladies are up to and thinking you might like me to bring over something to eat. Give me a call."

I disconnected and took the portable phone out onto the deck. I didn't bother turning on the floodlights. The light was fading from the sky, and the hills off to the west were turning purple. I sat there with the phone on my lap watching the bats and swallows swoop after insects, trying to put the pieces together—Charlotte and now Noah, swastikas and threatening phone messages, SynGen and Charlie, a poisoned dog, Susannah's eager mouth under mine . . .

I must have dozed off, because when the phone rang in my lap, it startled me. When I blinked my eyes open, I saw that darkness had spilled into the yard.

I fumbled for the phone and mumbled, "H'lo?"

"Were you sleeping?" It was Alex.

"Guess I dozed off. What's going on?"

"We've already eaten, to answer your question. We've been out on the deck, eating and talking. Susannah's been getting a million phone calls. She's letting the machine take them, because she really doesn't want to talk with anybody. That's why I didn't get back to you sooner."

"How's she doing?"

"As you'd expect, I guess. She cries a lot, and we laugh, sometimes, too. She tells stories about Noah and when she was a little girl, when her mother was alive. She keeps saying, 'Now I'm an orphan.' It's pretty sad, Brady."

"Are you coming home?"

"I'm going to stay with her tonight. Is that okay?"

"Sure. I guess so."

"You understand, don't you?"

"Susannah needs you. I guess she needs a woman with her, huh?"

Alex gave a little laugh. "Well, Paul was here for a while. He was full of sympathy and understanding and caring. It's obvious he's totally enchanted with her, but Susannah just got all tense and bitchy. Poor Paul. He hung around for a couple of hours, and finally he sort of shrugged and left, looking bewildered."

"She doesn't love him," I said.

"No." Alex sighed. "I don't think she even likes him, to tell you the truth. Anyway, she came right out and said she dreaded spending the night alone in Noah's house, so I offered to stay with her."

"Yes," I said. "That's fine. She shouldn't be alone." I hesitated. "Be careful, okay?"

"Oh, we talked about it. My phone calls, then what happened to Noah. Susannah's got Noah's shotgun. She says she knows how to use it and wouldn't at all mind a crack at whoever killed her father. We'll lock the place up tight, keep a phone handy. I've got the feeling we might be up all night anyway. She's pretty wound up, and we've been drinking coffee all day. We'll be okay."

"If you want—"

"We'll be safe, Brady," she said. "I'll see you tomorrow." She hesitated. "You take care, too, okay?"

"Don't worry about me," I said.

Around eleven that evening, I found a navy-blue sweatshirt in the closet and pulled it on. I figured that in my dark jeans and sweatshirt I could skulk through the night woods in perfect camouflage.

Then I went out to my Wrangler, started it up, and headed for Cutter's Run.

When I got to the dirt road that led to Charlotte Gillespie's long driveway, I pulled to the side, turned off my headlights, and lit a cigarette. By the time I'd smoked it down to the filter, my eyes had adjusted to the night light, and I figured I could see well enough to navigate the back roads without headlights. It was eleven-thirty. If the visitors to the tannery kept to a regular schedule, they'd arrive at midnight. I wanted to know what they were up to. And I didn't want them to know I was there.

I slipped the Wrangler into four-wheel drive and crept down the road to Charlotte's No Trespassing sign with its red swastika. I turned into her rutted driveway and followed it all the way to the dry streambed. I parked there and walked up the slope to the meadow on the hilltop where Charlotte's cabin crouched against the edge of the woods.

I realized I'd been half expecting to see a candle flickering inside and a herd of cats lounging outside and a curl of smoke wafting up from the chimney. But Charlotte's cabin was dark and still inside and out.

I sat on a rock beside the cabin and gazed down toward the beaver pond and the old tannery. I couldn't actually see them, of course. The moon and stars washed the meadow in pale light, but the woods down in the valley were dark and impenetrable.

I hugged myself against the evening chill. September had just arrived, and the night air carried a bite.

I waited, hugging myself in my bulky sweatshirt and glancing frequently at the luminous face of my wristwatch. Its hands seemed to have slowed down. They took about an hour to move from eleven forty-five to eleven-fifty, and by the time they reached twelve it felt as if I'd been sitting there all night.

After huddling there for another hour—although my watch insisted only five minutes had passed—I figured it was just one more in a lifetime of wild goose chases. I decided to wait another half hour.

A couple of minutes later I heard it. The low rumbling of an engine in low gear came from off to the right, about where the old tote road joined the dirt road. It sounded like a truck growling along in four-wheel drive. After a few minutes, the pitch changed. It was idling, stopped in neutral, I guessed, while they unlocked the chain that barred the way.

The pitch of the engine shifted again, and a moment later I caught the flash of headlights flickering and jiggling through the trees, and I was able to follow the truck's slow progress across the valley from where I was sitting.

It stopped about where the concrete remains of the tannery were scattered beside the beaver pond. The headlights went out and the engine stopped, and for a moment all was silence and darkness.

Then I heard two doors slam and saw fainter lights bobbing down there, and I could hear deep growly voices, although they were too muffled and far away to identify or to understand what they were saying.

Okay. This was why I had come here.

I took a deep breath, stood up, arched my back against the stiffness that had set in, and worked my way down the sloping meadow where I had kissed Susannah, heading toward the beaver pond where I had fished.

When I got to the woods at the foot of the meadow, I could distinguish the voices more clearly. They were low and conspiratorial, as if they didn't want to be overheard. There was tense anger in those voices, too. They were arguing, but I couldn't make out what they were saying.

I slipped into the thick woods, holding my forearm in front of my face to fend off branches and briars, and worked my slow way along the mud-caked rim of the beaver pond to the dam. The damp night air carried the faint but distinct odor of rot and decay.

When I stepped on a dead stick, the crack in the quiet woods sounded like a gunshot. I stood absolutely still, but there was no indication from the voices that they'd heard me.

The bright night sky showed shadows and shapes, and its reflection on the pond guided me downstream to where Cutter's Run spilled over the dam and continued along its way. I stepped in below the dam and started to wade across. The cold water of the stream came to my knees. It sent a chill all the way to my groin. I moved slowly, feeling for each step before shifting my weight to my forward foot. The streambed was paved with round, slick, moss-covered rocks, and a couple of times I slipped and nearly went in.

When I got to the other side, my feet and legs were drenched and numb. I crept on hands and knees up the steep slope on the other side of the stream. The voices were a little clearer now. They sounded familiar, although I couldn't identify them. I caught a few disconnected words—"beavers" and "damned dog" and "another load"—but I still couldn't make out what they were saying.

I knew I was quite close to them. I moved cautiously, feeling the soft ground under its layer of damp leaves with my hands, hitching myself forward and dragging my knees along behind me. It wouldn't do to snap another twig.

A few minutes later I was crouching behind a screen of hemlocks on top of a little knoll looking down into a clearing. Two men were standing beside a silver-colored delivery van no more than fifteen yards from my hiding place. They both held flashlights pointed at the ground. They were talking softly, but I heard tension in their voices. Now and then the flashlights waved around, illuminating a face.

Leon Staples, in his overalls and work boots, was leaning against the truck. Paul Forten was the other one. He was wearing khaki-colored pants and a dark windbreaker.

Paul was shaking his head. "We've got to find someplace else," he was saying. "First the beavers died. Then her dog. It's starting to stink here. Eventually someone's going to figure it out. Got any bright ideas?"

"All you gotta do is blow the fuckin' dam," said Leon. The van,

I realized, was his. It was usually parked in front of his store. Its rear doors were swung open, and it was backed up to a square slab of plywood which covered a fifteen-foot-square fieldstone foundation that rose a foot above the ground. "Them beavers flooded it," Leon was saying, "and that's how your crud got into the pond."

"How the hell do you expect to blow the dam without the noise bringing someone in to check it out?" said Paul.

Leon shrugged. "I kin do it."

Suddenly Paul held up his hand. "Shh!" he said. He pointed into the woods.

He wasn't pointing in my direction, but I flattened myself on the ground anyway.

The two of them stood there with their heads jutting forward, peering into the darkness off to my right, listening intently and sweeping their eyes around.

I lay there motionless. Surely they'd hear my breathing and my heart hammering in my chest.

Leon reached into the front of his van and pulled out a shotgun. It was an autoloader, the kind that held five shells in the magazine and another in the chamber and would fire as rapidly as you could pull the trigger. He held it in one hand like a pistol, aiming at the sky. His elbow braced the stock against his hip, and his finger was hooked in the trigger guard.

The two of them stood motionless for a minute, listening and looking intently. Then Leon lowered the shotgun to his side and pointed it into the bushes. He jabbed Paul with his elbow and jerked his chin toward where his gun was aiming.

Paul flashed his light into the bushes. Then Leon yelled, "Git on out here or I'll blow holes in you."

Leon moved quickly toward the bushes. I heard the rustle of brush, a cracking stick, a muffled "Shit!" and the sound of someone crashing through the woods.

As I watched, Leon stopped, lifted his shotgun to his shoulder, aimed up into the trees, and fired.

The muzzle flash was a quick explosion of brilliant flame in the darkness. The report echoed through the trees. When it died, I heard a new voice, high-pitched and childlike and frightened. "Okay, okay," it wailed. "Jesus. Don't shoot me."

"That was stupid," growled Forten. "You want every cop in Maine here?"

"What, you wanted 'im to get away?" said Leon. "You," he called. "Git on out here. Come on, now, before old Leon blows yer head off."

There was a moment of silence. Then I heard the sounds of someone shuffling through the woods off to my right. Then a figure entered the clearing.

Paul shone his flashlight on him.

He was holding his hands up in the air. His hair was long and yellow.

It was Paris LeClair.

THIRTY-TWO

⋙————————————⋘

Leon grinned at Paris. "Well, well," he chuckled. "Lookee what we got here. A pretty little yellow-haired girl. Awful late at night for a little girl to be out alone in the woods, ain't it?"

"I know what you guys're doin'," said Paris. "He looked at Leon. "Weezie told me about them swastikas, and I guess I know what you done to Miz Gillespie, and—"

With a motion too quick for my eyes to follow, Leon swung his shotgun, smashing the barrel against the side of Paris's face.

Paris collapsed on the ground. I could see blood trickling down his cheek. He pushed himself up on his elbow. "You guys killed old Noah, too, didn't you? What're you dumpin' in the water, anyway?"

This time Leon swung the heavy butt of his shotgun. Paris managed to block it with his forearm. The crack of the impact and Paris's sudden scream left no doubt that a bone had been snapped.

"Hang on," said Paul to Leon. "Lay off for a minute. I want to talk to this boy." He ambled over to where Paris was lying on the ground and looked down at him. "What's your name?"

"Fuck off," mumbled Paris.

"This here is young Paris LeClair," said Leon. "A dumb little local kid with a knocked-up girlfriend." He nudged Paris in the

251

ribs with the toe of his boot, then turned to Paul. "What're we gonna do with this pitiful little critter?"

"We've got no choice," said Paul. His hand slipped inside his windbreaker and came out holding an automatic handgun. He pointed the gun down at Paris's face. "Now you listen to me, boy," he said.

Paris started to sit up. He was cradling his broken arm with his other hand. "Up yours," he said, and he lifted his chin and spat at Paul.

Paul kicked his shattered arm. Paris screamed and fell back onto the ground.

"You ready to talk to me?" Paul said softly.

Paris's eyes flickered open. He nodded.

"Does anybody know you came here?"

"Someone knows, all right," Paris said. "He's gonna come looking, too."

"Really?" said Paul. "And who would that be?"

"Ain't telling you, asshole."

"It's too late to lie, I'm afraid. Not that it would've made any difference." He aimed his automatic at Paris's face. "You should've stayed home with Mommy and Daddy. Too bad . . ."

Paris squeezed his eyes shut and turned his head away. He looked like a frightened little boy. Which, of course, he was.

This was the kid who thought he'd knocked up his girlfriend and was proud of his manhood. The kid who was so affected by watching *Schindler's List* that he couldn't breathe. The kid who said my boys were lucky to have a father like me.

And the man who I figured had killed Charlotte Gillespie and Noah Hollingsworth was aiming a gun at his face.

I couldn't hide in the bushes and watch Paul Forten murder Paris LeClair, too.

I took a deep breath, got my feet under me, sprang forward through the hemlocks, and charged down the little slope directly at them, howling like an enraged bull elephant. I was vaguely aware of Paul's head jerking around to look at me. His eyes were wide and his mouth was open. He brought up the gun and started to

252

swing it around at me. I plowed into him, knocking him backward, and we both sprawled on the ground. One of his fingers gouged at my eyes, and I twisted away from his knee as he tried to ram it into my groin. I grappled for the gun with both hands. I got hold of one of his fingers, gritted my teeth, and bent it as hard as I could. I felt it snap. Paul screamed in my ear.

An arm hooked around my neck and hauled me off him, and then something heavy and hard smashed into my kidneys.

I lay curled on my side, swallowing hard against the terrible shafts of fire burning in my back.

"You shoulda minded your own business, Mr. Coyne," said Leon conversationally. "This ain't got nothin' to do with you." He was standing over me. His shotgun was aimed at my chest.

Paul came over. He was holding his right hand against his chest, gripping his wrist in his other hand. He peered down at me. "Brady?" he said. "What the hell are you doing here?"

"What's in the van?" I said.

Paul shook his head. "That's none of your business."

"You've been dumping something poisonous in these old holding tanks," I said. "And when the water from the beaver pond backed up, it started leaching into the stream. It must be nasty stuff. Charlotte Gillespie's dog drank it and died. So did the beavers, probably, and it killed all the trout in the pond. What happened? Did Charlotte figure it out? Is that why you murdered her?"

Paul looked over at Leon. "Come on. Drag him to the tank." He gritted his teeth. "My fucking finger's killing me. Son of a bitch broke my finger."

Leon leaned his shotgun against his truck, reached down, and grabbed me under the arms. He dragged me over to the fieldstone tank with the plywood top and let me fall to the ground.

My knee was throbbing. I pushed myself up onto my hands and knees, and a sudden wave of dizziness swept over me. Then I felt my stomach clutch and heave. I bent forward and vomited on the ground.

"Hell," said Leon. "I didn't hit you that hard."

"Get the top off the tank," said Paul to Leon.

253

Leon pushed and shoved at the plywood covering and managed to slide it off onto the ground.

I tried to shake the dizziness out of my head. I was aware of a tingly numbness in my tongue. It felt swollen and hard. The ground seemed to be tipping under me, and I puked again.

When I looked up, Paul was standing over me. He was holding his automatic in his left hand. I was looking straight up into the bore. "Sorry you're not feeling well," he said. "It'll go away in a minute, I promise you. Come on, now. Stand up."

"Fuck you," I mumbled.

"Give me a hand here," he said to Leon.

Leon grabbed me under the arms and tried to lift me to my feet. I slumped there, too weak and sick to resist, as he wrestled me up onto the edge of the tank so that my head was hanging over the top.

The odor that rose from it was more rank and rotten than anything I'd ever smelled in any outhouse. I gagged and retched again. I turned my head and aimed for Leon's pants, but it just dribbled down the front of my sweatshirt. He muttered, "Jesus," and dropped me onto the ground.

Then Paul was there again, his automatic only inches from my face. I felt so sick that I almost welcomed the relief that was coming, and I couldn't do anything except close my eyes and wait for the big white light to flash and then expire in my brain.

The explosion made my ears ring, and it took me a moment to realize that it was not Paul's gun that had fired, and that I was not the one who was screaming.

Paul was writhing on the ground beside me, holding his thigh with both hands. Blood was oozing out from between his fingers.

Paris was holding Leon's shotgun in his good hand. It was braced on his broken forearm and pointing steadily at Leon. "Sit down there beside him, Mr. Staples," said Paris. "Do it now or I swear to God I'll shoot you, too."

Leon shrugged and sat down beside Paul, who was lying on his side, moaning softly. A big puddle of dark blood had formed on the leaves under him. His eyes were closed and his face looked pale.

Without taking his eyes off Leon, Paris said, "Mr. Coyne, you okay?"

"I'm awful sick," I muttered.

"You strong enough to hold a gun on these guys?"

I closed my eyes against another wave of dizziness. "I don't know."

Paris came over and handed the shotgun to me. "Just for a minute," he said. "Come on. Hang in there. You can do it."

I braced my back against the side of the tank and held the shotgun in my lap, pointing it at Leon, who was sitting on the ground beside Paul about ten feet from me.

I took deep breaths. I didn't want to puke again.

Paris reached down, picked up Paul's automatic handgun, and tossed it into the vile-smelling tank. He was holding his broken arm against his stomach, and I could see the pain on his face.

"I gotta go get help," he said to me. "Can you keep the gun on them?"

"I don't know how long I can hang on," I said. "I never felt so sick. . . ."

Leon was grinning. "So now what're you gonna do, boy?" he said to Paris. "We gonna sit here lookin' at each other until poor Mr. Coyne dies? Or you gonna let me go?"

Paris looked at me. Then he shook his head. "Neither," he said. He reached down, took the shotgun from my hands, turned, and shot Leon in the right foot.

Leon screamed and grabbed at his foot. His boot was half gone, and it was a shapeless lump of oozing blood and raw flesh and splintered white bone.

Paris tossed the shotgun aside and came over to me. "You gotta do this," he said. "I only got one arm. Come on. Stand up."

He put his good arm around my back and helped me stagger to my feet. I leaned heavily on him while the woods swirled around me. I swallowed hard and took deep breaths, then managed to whisper, "I'm okay."

Paris half dragged me to the van and helped me into the passenger seat. Then he went around and climbed in behind the wheel.

I slumped there in the front seat of Leon's van, breathing rapidly. Suddenly, bile rose in my throat and spilled onto my lap. "I'm sorry," I managed to say. "It was the water. I waded in it. Cutter's Run . . ."

Then I felt myself tipping and spiraling, and blackness closed in around me.

THIRTY-THREE

⟫————————————⟪

The image appeared through gray swirling mists, blurry and distant but vaguely familiar, and as I looked at it, the fog gradually dissolved, and the image came into focus.

It was Jesus, up there on his cross.

No, I thought. Couldn't be. I'd never believed in any of that.

Sometime later I heard a soft voice calling me.

I felt a hand on my arm. I turned my head and blinked.

Alex's face hovered above me. I tried to smile.

"Hey," she said.

"Hey yourself," I grunted. My head hurt with the effort to speak.

"How do you feel?"

"I thought I was dead. I saw Jesus."

She bent and kissed my cheek. "You're not dead," she said.

"He was up there on his cross. I figured that was it. I'd passed over."

"You've been sleeping for quite a while," she said. "It was a dream."

When I looked past her, I saw that Jesus was still there. I closed my eyes. I didn't want Alex to be dead, too.

The next time I dared to look, it was dark and shadowy and both Jesus and Alex were gone.

A large man with a bald head and a close-cropped gray beard was bending close to me shining a light into my eyes. "How're you feeling, Mr. Coyne?" he said.

"Disoriented," I said. "Fuzz-brained."

"Understandable," he said. "You've been asleep for nearly thirty-six hours."

"I saw Jesus."

He flicked out his light. "Huh?"

"I saw Jesus on the cross. I figured I'd died and had gone to judgment. Thing is, I'm not a believer."

He chuckled. It rumbled from deep in his chest. "You're in Mercy Hospital in Portland, Mr. Coyne. Look."

He straightened up and pointed. On the white-painted wall at the foot of my bed hung a crucifix.

"This is a Catholic hospital?"

"Right." He smiled. "I'm Dr. Epstein. So either way, you're in good shape. A Catholic hospital and a Jewish doctor. The best of both worlds, huh?"

"What happened to me?"

"They brought you in early Thursday morning. Your system was in toxic shock. Liver and kidneys on the verge of shutdown. You were semicomatose, dangerously dehydrated, vomiting uncontrollably. Fortunately the young man with you helped us identify the problem and we were able to treat it."

"What was the problem?"

"You were poisoned," he said.

"I don't remember drinking anything . . ."

"You didn't," said Dr. Epstein. "This was something different. This you absorbed through your skin." He straightened up. "You're out of danger now. Looks like you'll be none the worse for wear. In the future, be careful where you go swimming, huh?"

He gave my shoulder a squeeze and disappeared. A moment later Alex came in. Behind her glasses, her eyes looked red and smudged.

"How do you feel?" she said.

"Thirsty."

She put an arm around my neck to prop me up and held a glass for me. I sucked in some room-temperature ginger ale through a straw. It tingled pleasantly on the way down, but it gave my stomach a little jolt when it arrived. I realized that I had an IV sticking into the back of my left hand, and beside my bed a machine was ticking and blinking.

"I saw that Jesus hanging there," I told Alex, "and I thought I'd died."

"You came close," she said. "Paris LeClair saved your life. He drove you here and told them what was wrong."

"I need another drink," I said. "Help me sit up, will you?"

Alex cranked up my bed and bunched a pillow behind me. Then she handed me the glass. I held it and sipped tentatively through the straw. My stomach made a fist. I handed her the glass.

"I still don't feel so hot," I said.

"You were awfully sick."

"What time is it? I mean, what day is it?"

"It's Friday, a little after noontime. Paris brought you in here Wednesday night—well, Thursday morning, about three o'clock. It was Sheriff Dickman who told me what happened. He's anxious to talk to you."

"I think I can tell him what he wants to know," I said.

"He says you were a hero. He says you saved Paris's life and solved two murders and prevented a disaster from happening downstream from the tannery."

"Paris saved my life, too."

She nodded.

"Wait," I said. "Dickman called me a hero?"

Alex smiled. "No. That's my word. He actually called you a loose cannon. But I think he meant it in the nicest possible way."

Alex stayed with me for an hour or so, and then she said she was going home to change and clean up. She kissed my forehead and said she'd be back.

The nurse took my temperature, listened to my heart and lungs, made notes on a clipboard, asked if I felt like voiding—which I didn't—then helped me into a chair. I made it with just a touch of dizziness. She put fresh sheets on my bed and fussed around the room, and when she was done she asked if I wanted to get back into bed or stay in the chair. I chose the chair.

A few minutes after she left, Sheriff Dickman came in. He was wearing a plaid shirt and chino pants. No sidearm, no badge. It was the first time I'd seen him out of uniform.

"You look like roadkill," he said.

"That's about how I feel," I said. "I bet you want to know what happened."

He pulled up a wooden chair and sat in front of me. "I got a couple versions of it. I'd like to hear yours, if you're up to it."

"The doctor said I was poisoned," I said. "I got it from wading through Cutter's Run below the beaver dam. I didn't drink any of it. It gets you through the skin. The other day after I tried to catch a trout from the pond I felt a little sick. All I did then was dip my hand into the water to see how cold it was. I bet Charlotte Gillespie's dog took a swim in that pond. That's what killed him."

Dickman was nodding. "You're right about the pond. See, here's what—"

"Wait," I said quickly. "Let me see if I got it. That company—SynGen—was dumping some kind of toxic shit into those old cisterns at the tannery. When the beavers dammed up the stream, the water backed up into the tanks and the stuff leached out into the pond. The dog got into it and died, and Charlotte must've figured it out. Her note. She said she wanted to talk to me. That's what she wanted to tell me, I bet. About the poison in the pond. But I was in Boston, and by the time I came back to Garrison, it was too late. They'd killed her." I looked up at Dickman. "How'm I doing so far?"

"Good," he said. "They found the poor woman's body in that cistern by the tannery. She'd apparently been strangled. The dog's body was there, too, and several housecats. They'd dumped lime on them."

260

"Lime," I said. "Like in an outhouse."

The sheriff smiled. "To keep the smell down."

"After the dog died," I said, "someone retrieved it from the vet. To make sure nobody ran tests on it, probably. I know who, too."

"So do I," said the sheriff.

"Paul Forten," I said. "He killed Noah Hollingsworth, too, right? He strangled them both. Noah must've been out pissing off the back of his deck one night and seen the headlights from the truck going in there to dump their stuff. The day before he died, he took out his horse. Bet he went down to the tannery and figured it out. Probably let it slip to Paul Forten. Paul hung out there with Susannah all the time. He knew how Noah got up in the middle of the night. Waited for him and strangled him." I paused. "What happened to him? And Leon? Paris shot them both."

Dickman shrugged. "That he did," he said. "Forten had a big hunk of his leg blown away, not to mention a busted finger, and Leon Staples has got a mangled foot, and young Paris LeClair has a busted arm and a nasty gash on his face. They took Forten and Staples over to Maine Medical." He arched his eyebrows. "Forten's gone."

"Gone?" I said. "What do you mean?"

The sheriff shrugged. "He's gone. He's not here anymore."

"You let him get away? You didn't arrest him? He's a fucking murderer."

"The feds claimed jurisdiction. They took him."

"The feds," I said. "I don't get it."

"We talked to a guy named Arthur Tate at an outfit called SynGen," he said. "Mr. Tate was eager to be helpful. Turns out Forten's the liaison for some federal agency that had a contract with SynGen to run tests on some new chemical they were evidently developing as a weapon. This stuff is a highly concentrated synthetic that works through the skin. In crystal form it's inert. Mix it with water and it's deadly. A piece the size of a grain of salt in a bathtub of water will kill anyone who lies down in it. Dump a scoop into a river and everything downstream that contacts it will die—or at least get damn sick. Supposed to be completely untraceable. SynGen was testing it on animals."

"They were dumping the dead animals at the tannery," I said. "And those animals had this stuff in their systems."

He nodded. "Forten arranged that, and he hired Leon Staples to help him. See, their problem was to find a way to dispose of the waste—those dead laboratory animals—so it couldn't be traced back to SynGen. So they trucked a load up there a couple times a week, dumped it into the tank, and poured lime over it. The chemical's potency dissipates fairly quickly, apparently, so if those dead animals just lay there for a while, they'd pretty soon lose their toxicity. If the beavers hadn't come along, nothing would've happened."

"You're forgetting Charlotte Gillespie," I said. "She knew something was going on. She found a discrepancy when she did the SynGen quarterly audit. There was something she couldn't account for. It was those animals. They were buying large numbers of them, but there was nothing in their records to account for what happened to them. When she refused to fudge her numbers, they had her fired."

"That's why she moved to Hood's cabin," said Dickman. "To check it out."

"Exactly," I said. "Ellen Sanderson told me Charlotte had been having an affair with someone. She thought it might be a client. I bet it was one of the guys from SynGen. Tate, maybe, the CFO, the one she would've worked closely with. Those SynGen guys used Hoodie's place for deer hunting. So Tate took Charlotte up there a couple times, maybe let something slip about that stuff they were making and how they disposed of their dead laboratory animals. It was probably Tate who got her fired. Charlotte wasn't one to shrug and say okay. So she decided to do something about it. She rented Hoodie's cabin and moved there to get the goods on them. When her dog died, she knew she had it."

"Yep," said Dickman. "A woman scorned. Charlotte Gillespie is the real hero here. She refused to knuckle under and change her report. When she got fired for it, she didn't just fade away. She went to Garrison and figured it out."

"She tried to tell me about it." I shook my head. "But I wasn't there for her. By the time I got back, it was too late."

Dickman nodded. "Forten got to her first." He touched my leg. "Not your fault, my friend."

I shrugged and reached for my ginger ale. I took a tentative sip. This time it settled comfortably in my stomach. "So is everybody under arrest, or what?"

Dickman smiled. "It's not that simple. Forten's the main villain here. He masterminded the whole thing, and he's the one who committed the murders. The feds've got him stowed away somewhere. They've shut SynGen down pending an investigation, but it's not clear who has jurisdiction over any criminal prosecution of them, if there ever is one. From what we can get out of Leon, he just trucked those dead animals from Portland to Garrison twice a week and kept his ears open for Forten. He admitted telling Forten about Charlotte's dog and about how you were getting snoopy, and I guess old Noah must've let something slip, too, because Leon was feeling pretty bad about Noah. He swears he didn't kill anybody."

"So who took Charlotte's dog from the hospital and left those messages on Alex's machine? Forten?"

He nodded. "According to Leon."

I shook my head. "Why would a man like Leon get involved with someone like Paul Forten?"

Dickman rubbed his fingers and thumb together. "Money, what else? Forten was paying him a helluva lot of money, by Leon's standards. By the time they were done, Leon would've had enough to leave Garrison. He said all his life he'd been dreaming of dumping that store and dumping that wife of his. Said the store was the chain and Pauline was the ball." Dickman smiled. "You know Pauline. It's kind of hard to blame Leon for that."

I nodded. "So what's going to happen?"

He shook his head. "The feds have taken over. They can't prosecute SynGen without implicating Forten, and that would mean exposing a government scheme to manufacture a chemical weapon. You know how that works." Dickman shrugged. "Big can of worms. Even Leon might get off. So far, no one is showing any inclination to indict anybody for anything. Fish and Game dynamited the beaver dam, and then the EPA sent over a team to incinerate everything in that cistern—including Charlotte Gillespie's

263

body. And that's that, as far as physical evidence is concerned. On the other hand, before too long you might be able to catch a trout out of Cutter's Run, at least upstream of where the pond was."

"What about downstream?"

"That poison has a pretty short life once it's activated in water." He smiled. "Trout will be able to live downstream, too. Which is what you were worried about."

"Oh, I worry about things like that, all right," I said. "But you're telling me nothing's going to happen?"

He shrugged. "It's in the hands of the feds, Brady."

"And that's it?"

"Guess so."

"Wait a minute," I said. "Two people are dead. They're testing some horrible poison, dumping dead animals into a trout stream—"

Dickman touched my shoulder. "Leave it lay, Brady."

I blew out a quick breath. "Like hell."

He looked at me for a minute, then shook his head. "Don't do anything stupid, my friend."

I smiled at that. It's what Charlie was always saying to me. "Sure," I said. "You're right."

Dickman glanced at his wristwatch, then pushed himself up from his chair. He held out his hand.

I took it. "Thanks for coming by," I said.

He nodded and headed for the door. Then he stopped, turned around, and held up a forefinger. "Oh," he said. "One more thing." He reached into his pocket and pulled out a leather case. He tossed it up and down in his hand.

"Hey," I said. "Is that my badge?"

"Not anymore," he said. "You're fired."

THIRTY-FOUR

$\rightarrow\!\!\!\!-\!\!\!\!\longleftarrow$

After the sheriff left, I dozed in my chair. Sometime later a candy striper burst into my room bearing an aluminum tray. She looked about fourteen, short and chubby and cute, and she flashed a mouthful of braces when she smiled. "Lunchtime, Mr. Coyne," she announced. "You wanna eat there in your chair?"

"I'm not sure I want to eat anywhere," I said.

"Oh, you gotta eat. Look what I brought you." She was grinning. "I got a bowl of hot orange stuff and a square hunk of cold green stuff and a glass of room-temp yellow stuff. Mmm."

"You make it sound so appetizing, how can I resist?"

"That's the spirit."

She put the tray on my lap, said, *"Bon appétit,"* and breezed out, leaving the faint scent of bath soap in her wake.

Tomato soup—Campbell's directly from the can, with a glob of sour cream drowning in the middle, just the way my mother used to make it—and rubbery lime Jell-O with a dab of whipped cream, also one of Mom's specialties, with a glass of apple juice for a chaser. I started tentatively on the soup, paying close attention to the reception my stomach gave it. Two spoonfuls assured me that I was ravenous, and I wolfed everything down.

The effort exhausted me. I dozed again.

Alex showed up sometime in the middle of the afternoon. She

had brought some clothes for me and insisted I get dressed and take a walk. So I held on to her arm and we prowled the corridors of Mercy Hospital. I peeked into rooms. They were full of people who looked sicker than I was, and I noticed that each room was decorated with its own Jesus on the cross.

By the time we'd circled the floor and arrived back at my room, I'd begun to feel positively frisky and didn't need to lean on Alex.

I plopped into my chair. Alex sat on my bed. "I've got to get the hell out of here," I said.

"They want to keep you one more night," she said. "If all goes well, I'll bring you home tomorrow morning."

"What could go wrong?"

"They don't know much about that poison. They just want to keep an eye on you."

"I feel great. Tip-top. I am ready to leap tall buildings with a single bound. If not tall buildings, I am at least ready to jump all over your bones."

She gave me a little enigmatic smile. "Not today, Superman," she said.

Dr. Epstein came by Saturday morning while I was eating my dropped egg on toast. He told me I should be ashamed, a healthy guy like me taking up a valuable hospital bed that some sick person could use.

Alex fetched me around ten, and by noontime I was sitting on her deck with my heels up on the railing, rocking and sipping coffee and casting threatening glances at my woodpile. I wanted to get it all split and stacked before Thanksgiving. I thought maybe I'd take a few whacks at it later in the afternoon.

Alex brought out tuna sandwiches, pickles, and potato chips. She sat beside me, then reached over and dropped a computer disk into my lap.

"What's this?" I said.

"I don't know. It was in my e-mail. It's from Skip Churchill. Figured it must be important, so I copied it all onto this disk for you."

"Excellent," I said. "Charlie McDevitt might need this."

After we finished eating, I went inside and called Charlie at home. He told me no one had come around asking questions, and his computer access had been restored on Thursday. "No thanks to you," he said, "it looks like I'm not in trouble after all."

I told him I'd buy him the lunch I owed him at Marie's on Tuesday. "I want to talk to you about what we should do."

"Do? What the hell are you talking about, Coyne?"

"I heard they might not even prosecute Paul Forten," I said. "Jesus, Charlie. We've got to tell the papers. I've got the information on a couple of computer disks, and I know a guy at the *Globe*—Alex's old editor. He'll eat up this story."

I heard Charlie chuckling. "You want to cost me my job?" he said.

"Of course not, but—"

"Brady, listen to me. The latest story going around is about some midlevel operative—I don't know, CIA, probably, though it's not clear—they found this morning in a Holiday Inn outside of Baltimore. The top of his head was blown off. He was holding a thirty-eight Police Special with the serial numbers filed off. Guy named Paul Forten."

"Jesus," I said. "I bet they're calling it suicide, huh?"

"Oh, sure. Case closed."

"Yeah," I said, "and that's not the only case that's closed."

"Put those disks someplace safe," said Charlie. "Then—I'm begging you now, Brady—forget this thing. Okay?"

I sighed. "Okay."

"Listen to me for once, will you?"

"I hear you," I said. "Tuesday at Marie's, then, right?"

"See you then," he said. "We gotta plan a fishing trip before the snow flies."

In the middle of the afternoon, while Alex and I were lazing out on the deck, Susannah Hollingsworth called. Alex talked to her while I rocked and gazed out toward New Hampshire, trying not to listen. When Alex arched her eyebrows at me and pointed at the phone, I shook my head. "Say hello to her for me," I said.

After she disconnected, Alex slouched back in her chair and closed her eyes.

I reached over and touched her hand. "What'd she want?"

"She wanted to know how you were feeling."

"That's it?"

She nodded.

"How's she doing?"

Alex shrugged. "Okay, I guess." She turned to me. Her eyes were solemn behind her glasses. "Brady . . ."

I turned to her. "What?"

She shook her head. "Nothing. It doesn't matter." She smiled quickly. "I'm glad you're feeling better."

I looked into her eyes. She stared back at me, then nodded quickly and turned away.

"How'd you know?" I said after a minute.

"She told me."

"When?"

"The other day. The day Noah died."

"She told you we—I kissed her?"

"Yes."

"What did she tell you exactly?"

"That she tried to seduce you." She shrugged. "That you kissed her, and—and touched her, but that you didn't . . ."

"She didn't try to seduce me," I said. "It was my fault."

"It doesn't matter, Brady."

"I want to explain."

"No, I mean it," she said. "It doesn't matter. It really doesn't."

"You've known all this time."

She nodded. "It was my secret from you. It made us even."

"That doesn't come close to making us even," I said.

"I guess it doesn't."

"I felt awful. I wanted to tell you. I had a whole speech planned out."

She nodded.

"But I didn't want to hurt you."

"I know," she said. "I don't want to talk about it."

I dozed out there on the deck, and when I woke up, the sun was quite a bit lower in the sky. I pushed myself to my feet and went inside. Alex was in her office, working on her computer.

I went upstairs and took a shower, and when I was finished, I lay down on the bed. I was hoping Alex might come up and flop down beside me, but she didn't. After a while, I fell asleep again.

We had clam chowder from a can for supper. It was about all my stomach would tolerate. Afterward we went out onto the deck to watch the bats fly around the yard.

"I've been thinking about Paris LeClair," Alex said.

"What about him?"

"Well, he saved your life, for one thing."

"Yes. I guess he did."

"You saved his, too."

I nodded.

"He's going to marry his girlfriend, huh?"

"He feels that he has to, I guess."

"She's pregnant," said Alex. "But didn't you say that Paris isn't the real father?"

"That's what Leon told me," I said. "I don't know if you can believe Leon. He said it's Arnold Hood's baby. But Paris thinks it's his, and he seems quite proud of it."

"But they're just children," Alex said.

I shrugged.

"This is bad," she said. "Tragic. For both of them. Three, counting the baby."

"I can't argue with you," I said. "It looks like Paris will be driving a pickup truck around Garrison, Maine, for the rest of his life. Live in a double-wide with an unhappy wife and too many kids, who'll marry their pregnant girlfriends when they're seventeen and live in double-wides . . ."

"I want to talk to them," said Alex. "Let's have them over for a cookout tomorrow."

I argued that I had to head back to Boston on Monday, and that I'd been looking forward to a glorious Sunday of leisurely togetherness, sleeping late, reading the *Globe* in bed, eating a big slow breakfast, going for a walk in the woods, taking an afternoon nap . . .

But Alex narrowed her eyes and set her mouth and insisted that I call Paris immediately.

So I did, and he accepted.

They showed up around five on Sunday afternoon. Weezie Palmer had close-cropped dark hair, big flashing brown eyes, and a tentative smile. She wore a loose-fitting cotton dress that didn't quite hide the swell of her belly.

Paris's left arm was in a sling, and he sported a big bandage on his left cheek. Weezie held on to his good arm. It was unclear who was supporting whom.

Paris introduced Weezie to us, and she mumbled "Hi" without lifting her eyes quite up to our faces.

"Come on," I said to Paris. "Help me get the charcoal going."

He followed me out onto the deck, while Alex detained Weezie in the kitchen on the pretext of assembling the ingredients for our cookout.

I got the grill lit while Paris perched on the rail. "So how're you doing?" he said. "You okay now?"

I nodded.

"You were some sick, man. I gotta tell you, I thought you were dead there."

"You saved my life," I said. "Thank you."

"Hey," he said, with a backhanded wave of his good hand. "You saved mine, too."

When I went inside a few minutes later to fetch Cokes for us, I heard the murmuring of voices from Alex's office.

I handed a Coke to Paris. "So you're going to marry Weezie, huh?" I said.

He gave me a shrug and an embarrassed smile. "I guess so."

"You don't sound very enthusiastic."

"It doesn't matter, does it? It's my responsibility."

"Are you sure?"

He frowned at me. "What do you mean?"

"I think you'd better ask her," I said.

Paris stared at me through narrowed eyes for a minute, then nodded. "Yeah," he said. "You're probably right."

Alex and Weezie came out a few minutes later. Weezie's eyes were red and she was hugging herself. She went up to Paris, rested her forehead on his shoulder, and mumbled, "We gotta talk."

He nodded. "Right. We do."

He took her hand and led her down off the deck and around to the side of the house.

Alex dropped into a rocking chair and let out a long breath. "Arnold Hood started fooling around with her almost three years ago," she said. "She won't be seventeen for another two months."

"Jesus," I said. "Somebody oughta—"

Alex put her hand on my leg. "She's not very bright, Brady. But she's shrewd. When Hood found out she was pregnant, he dumped her. So she seduced Paris, then told him the baby was his."

I nodded. "That's about how I figured it."

"She's the one who made those swastikas."

I nodded. "Why'd she do that?"

"Leon." Alex shook her head. "He knew Hoodie had been fooling around with her, figured it was Hoodie's baby. Threatened to tell Paris it wasn't his if she refused. Made her promise not to tell anyone she did it. It was no big deal to her one way or the other. The symbolism of a swastika's a bit complicated for her simple brain. I tried to explain it to her, but she just looked at me as if I was speaking Sanskirt."

I nodded. "The first swastika was to try to scare Charlotte away," I said. "It didn't work. Charlotte would not be scared away. The second one—the one on the outhouse—that was to misdirect somebody like me. Leon probably knew about Hoodie's flirtation with the Klan and figured that sooner or later somebody would make the connection."

Alex shrugged. "Weezie certainly didn't know any of that. But it makes sense."

"So what'd you say to her?" I said. "About the baby, I mean."

She looked up at me. "I asked her if she loved Paris, and she kind of shrugged, like she had no idea what I was talking about. I asked her if she thought he loved her, and she said no, she really didn't think so. 'He's a good kid' is what she said, meaning that he'd marry her because he felt responsible. So I told her she had to tell Paris the baby wasn't his. I told her if she didn't, I would. And if he still said he wanted to marry her, she should tell him she didn't love him. By this time she's crying a little, like maybe there's a little place in her that's starting to understand. Then I mentioned a home I know of outside of Augusta where a pregnant woman can receive free medical attention, room and board, and tutoring for the duration. Afterward, they arrange for adoption."

"And?"

"She said it was up to Paris."

I arched my eyebrows.

Alex smiled. "I told her, like hell it was up to Paris," she said. "I told her it was her body and her baby and her life, and it wasn't even Paris's child. She really started to cry then, but I told her I'd talk to her mother if she wanted, and she said she'd appreciate it."

I smiled at her. "You're pretty awesome, lady," I said.

"I know," she said.

We were having coffee on the deck the next morning. It was Labor Day, the first Monday of September, but already there was a hint of frost in the air. A flock of blackbirds had gathered in the trees out back, eating everything in sight and making a racket as they prepared for their migration. The New Hampshire hills off to the west showed blurry patches of gold and orange and crimson through the early-morning fog.

Alex had pulled a sweatshirt over her customary T-shirt, and she wore sweatpants. I wore a flannel shirt.

272

"Well," I yawned, "gotta head back to the city tonight."

Alex kept staring off toward the hills.

I turned to her. "So what shall we do with this beautiful day?"

"I guess I'll work on my book," she said.

"What?"

"You know," she said quietly. "What I do every day. I write. That's my life right now."

"But—"

"If I were you, I'd head back this morning," she said quickly. "Beat the traffic. It'll be horrendous this afternoon."

"Is that what you want?" I said.

She turned to me. "Yes."

I nodded. "Susannah, huh?"

She gave her head a little sad shake. "I told my landlord I wanted to buy this place," she said softly. "We shook hands on a deal. I'm going to live up here, Brady. This is going to be my home. I'm not going back to Boston. I'm going to write books and tend my gardens and be friends with Susannah and all the other nice folks around here. I'll go to bean suppers on Saturday night and I'll join the Congregational church. In the winter I'll get snowed in, and in the spring I'll get stuck in the mud. And I'll miss you. But I know you'll never live here with me. Maybe it took Susannah—what happened with her and you—to help me figure it out. But no, Brady. It's not Susannah. It's not that simple."

I leaned back in my rocker. "I don't know what to say."

She reached over and patted my arm. "Don't say anything. Please."

So I didn't. I sat there thinking about it, and after a few minutes, I got up and went inside. I packed my stuff, took it out to my new BMW, threw it into the trunk, and slammed it shut.

Alex came around from the back of the house. She was smiling at me. "I still want to talk to you sometimes," she said.

"Friends?" I said.

"Yes," she said. "We're friends. We'll always be friends."

I hugged her familiar body against mine.

"Do me a favor," she mumbled against my chest.

"Sure," I said. "Anything."

"Call Charlie or Doc Adams or J. W. Jackson. Go fishing for a weekend, before the season's over. Be sure you go in your spiffy new car. Drive fast with that sunroof down, and play that ZZ Top CD you like real loud. Okay? Will you do that for me?"

I held her close. "Sure, babe," I said. "I'll do it for you."